WHAT BLOOD REMEMBERS

C. William Phillips

ISBN-13: 979-8-9993559-0-4

Cover design by: Joshua Adams

For Tana.

PART ONE

VIOLENT SEEDS

CHAPTER 1

His Chance

Viggo's fingers curled around the steering wheel in a sweaty grip, squeezing the battered leather like he was looking for a confession. He was parked out back of what must have been the dingiest strip club in the city, waiting for its owner, Joe, to hand him the duffle bag that would make his career. After this job, he would move up, he was sure of it. He would go from driving the cash and coke from one end of the city to the other and squeezing the baker on Fifth Street to lounging in The Cabana and fucking the most beautiful girls in the western hemisphere. He just needed that duffle.

The door to the club opened with a bang, causing Viggo to reach for the pistol in the passenger seat. Upon seeing Joe's pudgy body waddle through the door, he exhaled and placed the gun back on the seat, his hand still resting nearby.

"Hey, Viggo!" Joe flashed him a smile and spread his arms wide, approaching the car. "Got your package, buddy." He shook the duffle for emphasis.

Viggo swallowed the urge to put a bullet in his chest and gave him a smile and nod. "Thanks, Joe. Is it all there?"

Joe feigned offense. "Is it all there? Is it all there? Whaddya take me for, Viggo? A putz? You think I'm a putz?" A moment of silence passed before Joe returned to himself, laughing. "Of course it's all there, you skeptical motherfucker. You know, you need to work on that pessimism, man. It'll send you to an early grave."

Viggo sighed and pulled a cigarette from the pack in his shirt pocket, pointedly flicking open his lighter. He took a draw and exhaled, blowing smoke all through the car's interior. Gripping the cigarette in his lips, he reached through the window and took the duffle bag. Once it was safely in the car, he waved to Joe and drove off before he had time to say goodbye. When he was at the end of the street, he unzipped the bag and looked inside. It was all there — three quarters of a million dollars in cold, hard cash. He needed to go trade the cash for the coke, then make his delivery to the front business. Then it would be done. He would really be a part of the family after today.

He smiled to himself and accelerated.

He arrived exactly on time. It was a narrow place, an alleyway quarantined on either side by brick three-stories which once might have been places of business, but now were abandoned and left to gather dust like the pieces of machinery which no doubt rested inside. The entire thing dead-ended a little more than a hundred feet in. The dealer was sitting in the other car, a blue Oldsmobile. Viggo flashed his lights. The dealer returned the signal. The two men exited their cars and walked toward each other. Viggo had the duffle over his shoulder and a black Colt .45 in his belt, in clear view. He could see the dealer was also packing.

When they were about fifteen paces apart, the dealer stopped.

"That's far enough, man," he said. "Toss the bag on the ground and turn around."

Viggo stopped cold, alert. "What are you doing, man?" he asked.

"Business." He drew his gun and trained it on Viggo.

"Business? Are you serious? This isn't good business. This is fucking suicide. Do you really want to cross the Scolessas? Think about that for a second." Viggo spoke quickly, trying to calm his raging stomach and mask the panic in his voice. Even still, the cold metal of the gun in his belt called to him, making his hand itch.

"Just shut the fuck up. Toss the bag." Viggo didn't move. The dealer smiled and nodded. "Alright, so it's like that. Fine with us."

Us? Viggo thought. As if in response, a figure rose to their feet on a rooftop to Viggo's right. A large man, dressed all in black, a ski mask pulled down over his face and a rifle in his hand. Viggo couldn't tell much, but it looked to be a hunting rifle, a scope affixed to its top.

"Now throw the bag over here," the dealer said again.

Viggo said nothing, looking from side to side, trying to find an exit. He could try to get back to the car, but the sniper would make that difficult. Of course, the dealer right in front of him had a gun, too. That was the immediate problem.

Viggo took one step toward him then threw the bag as hard as could into his face. The dealer was stunned for a split second, allowing Viggo to dive to the ground and roll to the right. The rifle fired, the bullet slicing through the air above him, through what would have been his torso. He heard the bolt slide back, ejecting the cartridge; the weapon was single fire.

Viggo rolled to his knees, his own weapon drawn and trained on the dealer. He fired three shots, catching him in the torso with two and sending the third careening off-target, where it shattered a window. The dealer managed to return fire as he fell, though, forcing Viggo to scramble to his feet and run in a crouch for a dumpster at the end of the alley. A crack split the air as another sniper shot missed, barely, and shattered bricks on the wall as Viggo ran past.

This time, Viggo was ready. As the sniper slid his bolt back, Viggo unleashed a torrent of bullets toward him. He couldn't tell how many times he struck the man, but he staggered, then tumbled over the side of the roof, crashing to the ground headfirst. He didn't move again, blood slowly pooling under his body.

The dealer was struggling to one knee, his breaths coming in ragged rasps now. Viggo approached carefully, but the man didn't even have a gun now, having dropped it when he fell initially.

"Who made the call?" he asked. The dealer coughed, spraying bloody spittle on Viggo's shoes. He shoved the man over with his foot, then pressed his gun to the dealer's forehead. "Only asking one more time: who made the call to double cross the Scolessas?"

A bloody grin split the dealer's face. "Fuck. You. Piece of sh-" Viggo cut him off with a pull of the trigger and an echoing gunshot. He left him in a growing pool of his own blood, sirens blaring in the distance.

Viggo's foot barely left the accelerator until he had gotten to the safe house. Squealing into the driveway, he flung open the driver's side, kicking it when it bounced back toward him. He grabbed the duffle bag and sprinted to the house's front door, slamming it behind him.

He wasn't alone. A man sat in one of the living room chairs, drawing on a cigarette and swirling a glass of scotch in hands adorned with four gold rings apiece. Viggo looked him up and down. He was tall, with hawkish features and slicked-back black hair graying around the temples. He wore a loose white dress shirt, the sleeves lazily rolled halfway up his forearms, exposing a large, faded tattoo of the Virgin Mary. His legs, crossed haphazardly, one on top of the other, wore sleek black dress pants that came to an end in a pair of black loafers, bobbing along to a jazz song crooning from the radio sitting next to him.

"Mal?" Viggo asked. "What are you doing here?"

Mal extinguished his cigarette before speaking. "Waiting on you, Viggo. Why else would I be here?" He downed the remainder of his drink in one gulp, then stood and crossed the room to where Viggo was looking between the blinds at the street. "Viggo?" Viggo felt rough hands grab his shoulders and turn him to look at the taller man. "Viggo, talk to me. What happened?" A quick glance down told Viggo he'd noticed the duffle bag, still crushed to his body in a white-knuckle grip.

Viggo nodded and inhaled deeply. Mal also nodded and gestured to one of the chairs in the room. He took the other chair himself, then poured them both a glass of scotch before lighting another cigarette and taking a deep draw. He pulled two more from the pack, handing one to Viggo. Smoke rolled from the two men's nostrils. Viggo finally managed to slow his beating heart.

"Now," said Mal. "Tell me what happened."

Viggo told Mal the entire story of the botched deal. By the time he was done, Mal had smoked three more cigarettes and finished his glass of scotch. He lit and poured another of each. "So where's the coke?" he finally asked. Viggo knew the question would eventually be asked by someone; better for it to be Mal.

"I don't think it was even there."

"Did you check?" He drew on the cigarette, then expelled the smoke from his nostrils and mouth. He clearly already knew the answer.

"No, Mal, I didn't fuckin' check. For Chrissakes, I almost died. I nearly get capped and you're askin' about the fuckin' coke. No, I didn't check. I got the fuck out, Mal, that's what I did. And you would have, too." Viggo was on the verge of yelling. He had nearly died, had committed double homicide and on top of all that, his promotion was all but impossible. Moving up would be hard now that he had fucked up the deal. Hell, staying alive will be hard.

If the Scolessas wanted him, there wasn't much Viggo could do. And for all any of them knew, he'd been the one to orchestrate the double-cross. The thoughts in his head weren't pretty; he saw himself going into a meat grinder, strapped into a car being compacted, or hanging from a meat hook in the back of an ice truck with two holes in his chest. They had feelers through the whole city, and if Mal wanted a bonus, all he had to do was turn in the 'traitor.'

"Calm down, Viggo. Calm down." Mal chuckled and offered him another cigarette. Viggo ignored the peace offering and turned his head away. He stood and walked to the window, again parting the blinds and glimpsing outside. "You know, Viggo, you're like a brother to me. You know that, right?"

Viggo stopped, his hand resting on the wall by the window. A thought crossed his mind – how had Mal known to come to this safe house? So far as Viggo knew, he wasn't part of the deal. This was supposed to be his big moment, with no assistance. No one would have called Mal unless...

Unless something went wrong.

A chair creaked as Mal stood. Like lightning, Viggo ripped his pistol from underneath his jacket and whirled toward his assassin. Mal slapped the gun to the left and Viggo's would-be kill shot landed in the wall. He delivered a thunderous right punch to Viggo's ribs, then brought his left fist to Viggo's jaw.

Viggo staggered from the second blow and dropped the gun. Mal retrieved it and brought it to bear, aimed directly at Viggo's chest. Viggo had just enough awareness left in him to dive to the right, crashing over an end table and breaking the phone as he did. In the split-second it took Mal to adjust his aim, Viggo grabbed the broken phone, now ripped free from the wall jack, and hurled it at him. It wasn't enough to kill, or even really injure him, but it did give Viggo the moment he needed to lunge toward his enemy.

The two men crashed through the large plate-glass window and tumbled into the yard amongst shards of broken glass and wood paneling. The gun landed somewhere in the street. Viggo rolled on top of Mal and straddled him, grabbing his neck with both hands and attempting to choke the life out of him. Mal placed his hands on Viggo's right arm, at the elbow and the wrist, then hooked his left leg around Viggo's right. Using the leverage, he brought his right knee up into Viggo's back with enough force to cause Viggo to lose balance and pitch forward, releasing Mal's neck and bracing himself against the ground. Mal used the moment to throw his momentum to the left and roll Viggo. Now reversed, Mal placed his hands around Viggo's throat and, with an eerie calm, began to crush his windpipe.

Viggo's eyes were going wide, and blood was rushing to his brain. He pawed the ground around him in desperation. There has to be something. He wasn't going to die now, not this way.

His hand landed on a shard of broken glass. Viggo would have smiled, if he hadn't been in the middle of being murdered. He wrapped his fingers around the shard and brought it up, slamming it into the side of Mal's neck, then ripped it across his throat. Blood sprayed from the wound, covering Viggo and the ground in gore. Mal released him, clutching at the maw of his newly-opened neck. Blood poured from the ragged hole, running down his arm and chest. His eyes rolled to Viggo, wide with stunned fury before he sputtered out one last breath, flopped over, and died on the lawn.

Viggo stood and breathed in heaves. He bent over and placed his hands on his knees. Mucus ran out of his nose in the chilly air and he wiped it away, slinging it into the cold, half-dead grass. He spit a wad of saliva out onto the ground, then stood and stretched his back, feeling his spine crack and pop as he did so. Groaning, he walked to the street and picked up the gun, wondering why he bothered, even as he shoved the gun into his waistband. One pistol wouldn't be enough, with the Scolessas coming for him. When they found out Mal had failed, they would send someone else. And if Viggo survived that, there would be another. The cycle would never end.

He had to run; get as far away as possible. He pulled his shirt and jacket down, covering the gun, and walked back to his car. As he closed the door and turned the key, he looked to the house and remembered the duffle, laying harmlessly in the entranceway. Viggo sighed and opened the door.

He walked to the house and retrieved the duffle, slinging it over his shoulder and walking back to the car. As he tossed it into the back seat, he shook his head and put the car into reverse.

CHAPTER 2

The Storm

The car rumbled along the highway at a speed of 56 miles per hour. Any more might draw the attention of the police, and Viggo couldn't exactly talk his way out of it when there was a duffle bag in the back seat filled with $750,000 of dirty money. Explaining the bruise on his face and the bit of Mal's blood that had sprayed across his jacket wouldn't be easy either. And the gun, serial number filed off and eleven shots spent, didn't look good.

Viggo rubbed his brow. He was still wondering how his day had gone so horribly off track. He was supposed to be made after today. He was supposed to have arrived. If his day had gone even a little bit to plan, he would be sitting in the back room of The Cabana right now, a beautiful woman bouncing up and down on his naked thighs.

Instead, he was covered in blood and dirt, running from a pile of bodies in a '98 Corolla with $750,000 of the Scolessas' money in the back seat. He didn't even know where he was going, not for certain. He'd thought of Canada initially, considering how much closer it was, but then he remembered that the Scolessas had connections in Canada, connections that he had worked with. They knew his face; it would've been suicide.

So he had tentatively decided to head for Mexico. It was a long drive, though, and he had barely started.

A *ding* interrupted his thoughts.

Out of gas.

Viggo slammed his hand down on the steering wheel. "Motherfucker!" he yelled, an accusatory tone to his voice, as though this was all the car's fault. He breathed, calming himself. He had learned long ago that a level head was needed to be successful in his chosen career. He would soon have two forces after him: the cops and the Scolessas. And God knows who else would get involved. Mercenaries? The FBI? CIA? Federales? KGB? Taliban? The Mounties? The SS?

Viggo nearly slapped himself. He was spiraling, and he knew it. The Scolessas would be enough of a problem, not even considering the police. And truthfully, Viggo had his suspicions about Luke Scolessa's ties to the cops. He figured the big man could buy himself some time to "handle the matter internally" before law enforcement got involved.

Ding Ding Ding

Viggo sighed and rubbed his tired eyes. When he looked

back to the road, he was passing a sign:

Traeger Gas and Grocery—Next Right!

He nodded to himself, then flipped on the turn signal and took the exit.

Viggo pulled up to the gas pump, still upset, but calming himself. He turned off the key and got out. He began to slide his credit card into the pump when he thought better of it and decided to use cash. *They're probably tracking my card by now. Time to go old school, I guess.* He pumped his tank full, tossed his bloodstained jacket into the backseat, then turned on his heel and walked to the store, checking his wallet as he went: A single hundred-dollar bill. That was all he had to make it to Mexico. He couldn't risk using the stolen money until he was across the border and had a chance to launder it, in case the Scolessas had a way of tracking the serial numbers.

Doing the math in his head, he realized that a hundred dollars wouldn't be anywhere close to enough. He would need at least two more tanks of gas, possibly three. Not to mention food. He could sleep in the car. He would need at least two-hundred more. He tried to hide his anxiety as he walked into the gas station-grocery store hybrid. The man behind the counter was of medium build, dark blonde hair swept to the side in a comb over he'd clearly been wearing for years. Dark stubble dotted his face and a bright smile spread in its midst. He was slightly taller than Viggo, making him probably six-foot one or six-foot two. A red nametag was pinned to his denim shirt:

Cole Traeger

Here to help

Traeger noticed him looking at it. "In case I forget who I am," he said. Then he laughed heartily. Viggo chuckled. "That'll be forty-six twenty-three."

Viggo briefly considered waiting for him to look away and taking off. Instead, he pulled the wallet from his hip pocket and handed Traeger the hundred-dollar bill. Traeger returned the change correctly and gave Viggo a friendly smile and nod. Viggo returned the nod and headed out the door, a bell chiming over his head as he went.

As he settled back into the driver's seat of the car, Viggo glanced at his wallet, now much emptier. His eyes rolled up to the gas station's front window, through which he could still see Cole Traeger counting money. After writing something down, he hurriedly folded up a stack of bills and shoved them in his pocket, then greeted another customer.

A thought blossomed in Viggo's mind. Hitting a gas station in the middle of the day would be too public to aid him in making it to Mexico. But everyone sleeps somewhere, right? As he watched, Cole left the store in the care of some teenaged employee, exiting through the front door, climbing into a gray SUV and taking off for some errand or another. Grinning despite himself, Viggo started the car and pulled slowly out onto the road. After a couple of minutes, he doubled back and settled into a parking spot out of the way of the front door, where he could wait until closing time. After checking he was sufficiently guarded from prying eyes, he allowed himself to close his eyes and drift off to sleep. He needed rest before the night's work.

SLAM

Viggo woke with a start, grabbing the gun in the passenger seat. After a moment, he remembered where he was: Traeger Gas and Grocery, waiting on his meal ticket. The SUV's driver door had shut loudly enough to shake him from his sleep and as he looked, he realized Traeger had gotten in. The headlights flared to life and Viggo dove across the seat, not eager for Traeger to discover him. The lights swung over top of him and out toward the road as the vehicle rumbled past, crunching gravel as it went.

Once he pulled onto the road, Viggo started his car and went after him. He followed slowly, keeping his distance. It was vitally important that Traeger not discover him until the moment was right. Viggo's nerves were tingling and his heart was racing. It happened every time, leading up to a job.

People had called him a psychopath before, but Viggo thought that was inaccurate. He was simply good at the wrong things, and accepted the hand life had dealt him. He took no pleasure in killing, but it didn't keep him up at night. It was simply part of the job.

He drove on.

Traeger eventually turned onto a gravel road that extended into a densely wooded darkness, the kind that Viggo used to see on those campy 80's horror flicks. Viggo drove on past the turnoff so as to not spook Traeger's instincts. The road looked more like a private driveway, no doubt with more than a few no trespassing signs standing guard along the way. Viggo resolved to wait for a couple of hours until he figured Traeger would be asleep. With any luck, Viggo would be able to get in and get out with enough cash and valuables to make it to Mexico.

The minutes ticked by at an agonizing pace. Viggo tried leaning the seat back and sleeping, but it was a fruitless attempt at rest. He was wired. The day had not been kind to him, and now was forcing him into a compromising position. If he *did* have to kill Traeger, the cops would no doubt be involved at some point. The man had to have friends. And that grocery store looked older than him, maybe a family business, which meant people would know him. They would most certainly know where he lived and come looking for him.

Viggo checked the clock every couple of minutes. Agonizing though it was, two hours did eventually pass, and the clock struck 11:49. He sighed and turned the car around. He pulled onto the gravel road and flipped his lights to dim. This made seeing anything other than the bit of road directly in front of him impossible, but that was all he really needed. The moon and stars were bright enough for him to find the house.

He drove for almost three minutes before he happened upon it; a large wooden house standing in the middle of a clearing. An open garage stood on the right side of the screened-in porch, Traeger's car, along with a small Camry and a boat sitting underneath the cover. There were no lights on, save a dim shine from the uppermost right corner.

In the yard, two bicycles laid on their sides. One was dark blue, with thick tires, clearly for an older child. The other was smaller, pink, with training wheels and a white basket on the front.

Dammit, thought Viggo. *Kids*.

Part of him screamed to get back in the car, turn around, and get on the road. Maybe there would be a convenient store to rob or something. He groaned as he realized he really *could* have just robbed the gas station. But no, that was too public. He needed to have a nice head start before the Traegers even realized anything was gone.

He put his head in his hand and rubbed his brow. Images flashed in his mind of wood chippers and refrigerated trucks. He shook his head to clear them and exhaled. He had come this far; it was time to go to work. He had to get to Mexico before the Scolessas caught up to him. He grabbed the pistol and shoved it into his waistband. *Just in case,* he thought. Then, he exited the car, being sure to softly close the door, and grabbed the tire iron from the trunk. There were only two shots in the gun, after all, and someone living out of the way like Traeger was almost sure to have a gun in the house. If things *did* go sideways, he wanted to be prepared.

As quietly as he could, he crept toward the front door.

Getting in was fairly easy. He had become relatively proficient at picking locks in his time with the Scolessas and there was no deadbolt on the door. Once the door swung open, though, things became infinitely more complicated.

To Viggo, the house might as well have been made of nothing but rusty old metal hinges. The door squawked loudly as he pushed it open, and he stepped on a child's toy while walking into the house, nearly causing himself to fall. Once he was sure of his balance, he took in his surroundings. He left the door open.

The house was wood through and through. It was clear a lot of work had gone into its construction. A large hearth and fireplace rose from the floor in the living room to his right. An ancient double-barreled shotgun sat above it, surrounded by framed family photos depicting people smiling and holding their arms around one another. A couch, large enough for four, rested in the middle of the room, in front of a bear-skin rug that didn't appear to have been purchased. The walls were dotted with various décor and potpourri, such as ornamental plates and fall-colored arrangements of paper flowers with plastic stems. A set of stairs led up to what he was sure would be the bedrooms.

Viggo had to move quickly. He began looking around for places where there might be cash. Something he could trade directly for services or goods. Valuables were of little use to a man who couldn't stop long enough to sell them. And you never know what's a family heirloom with some identifying mark. "Don't steal the Mona Lisa," was a phrase that Viggo had become very familiar with. If the item was *too* valuable, it would be easier to track down.

He searched the entire ground floor with no luck. There were no hideaways, no loose floorboards, no safes, nothing at all. He stood at the bottom of the stairs for a long while, simply staring into the darkness that loomed at the top, feeling the knot forming in his stomach. *So it comes to this,* he thought. He wielded the tire iron in his left hand and the pistol in his right. Slowly, he began his ascent.

The air became heavier the higher he went. It felt to Viggo as though it were clinging to his skin, clamming up his airways. He felt sick. His stomach was churning like a diesel truck. The house was dark as hell itself and nearly as hot. The sick reality settled over him. He was climbing the stairs of a house he had broken into, with the intention of stealing any money he could find. It was entirely possible he would end up killing someone, maybe more than one person. He had to stay calm, keep his heartbeat steady. He felt like he was going to explode. His head was pounding. *Just leave. Just turn around, go back to your car, and leave. You don't need all this. Not this much.* His feet continued forward despite the advice of his rational mind. Sweat beaded on his forehead as he turned the corner at the top of the stairs, into the room directly on his right.

The parents' room. Traeger was asleep in the bed, shirtless, next to a woman that Viggo figured was his wife. Her hair was auburn, and she wore a grey t-shirt, three sizes too big, that read *Sloppy Sal's Southern Style BBQ: We got the best breasts in town!*

Traeger's wallet sat on his nightstand. Viggo very carefully inched toward it, and took it. Inside, there was just over seventy-five dollars in cash, and a credit card. He took it all. Glancing around, he noticed a walk-in closet on the other side of the room, and headed for it. It was even darker inside the closet than it was on the stairs, and just as hot. There was a vanity directly inside, and Viggo searched it as quietly as he could. Inside, he found a small metal box, and fiddled with the latch, trying to open it.

Locked. Dammit. He would need to take the whole box. He stuffed it inside his coat and moved on.

It was on his way out of the closet that he banged his knee on the door frame. He ducked back inside the closet and tried to hide to the left of the door, hoping to avoid being seen.

"Hello?" Traeger asked, and Viggo's blood ran cold as his stomach dropped.

Don't, Viggo thought. *Please, don't.* Even as he thought the words, though, his hand tightened around the tire iron.

The floor squeaked when Traeger got up, and again on each step he took. When he was just outside the closet, he spoke again. "Hello?" Viggo clutched the tire iron in his left hand. A quick swing would put an end to this. He wanted to hold out, and hoped beyond all hope that Traeger would simply walk away and go back to bed, thinking he was simply hearing things.

No such luck. Traeger continued into the closet and flipped on the lights. Viggo didn't give him a chance to see him coming. Whirling to the right and laying his shoulder into the wall for leverage, he brought the tire iron around with his left hand, slamming it into Traeger's face with a *crunch*. He tumbled back and fell with a loud *thud*, shaking the floor. Viggo came out of the door swinging downward. He caught Traeger in the face again, and again on the side of the head, across the ear. His words of protests were becoming more and more mumbled, as his mouth filled with blood. It wasn't long before he stopped making any noises at all. His wife was up now, screaming.

"Cole! Cole! Oh God, who are you!?" Her voice was shrill, grating against Viggo's eardrums. In a panic, he looked up. She was on the other side of the bed, but was coming around the end, screaming her husband's name all the while. He lifted the pistol in his right hand and pulled the trigger, almost in a single motion. The gunshot exploded through the room, deafening him. The bullet caught her in her right breast, spinning her violently around before crashing in a heap on the floor, going silent.

Viggo wasn't sure how long he just stood there, the gun pointing at the place where the woman had stood moments before. He realized he had forgotten to breathe and exhaled in a rattle, then inhaled just as unsteadily. A couple of deep breaths later, he had managed to collect himself. His heart was still racing, and his ears were still ringing, but he could breathe now.

He turned when he heard a noise in the doorway. He saw a young boy, maybe twelve, in his pajamas. The boy was wide-eyed and his mouth hung open. His brow furrowed when his eyes moved to Viggo, standing in the middle of the floor, gun in one hand, bloody tire iron in the other. The boy looked at his father's crumpled body and let out a scream. He rushed in, past Viggo, sliding to his knees in front of Cole Traeger's diminished form.

Viggo turned to him. "No! Look, don't...just go back out, kid. Okay? Please? You don't need to be in here right now." The boy didn't respond, or offer any evidence he'd even heard him. "C'mon kid. Just go back to your room!" Viggo was screaming now.

The boy stood and turned slowly to face him. His face was streaked with tears and he stared with hate from eyes crisscrossed by red veins. His fists were clenched and his knuckles were white. His face was flush with rage and he was shaking all over. He opened his mouth and let out a scream, shrill in his pre-pubescent voice. He charged at Viggo, fists raised. Two steps away, he leapt at him.

Viggo reacted instinctively and pulled the trigger when the boy was nearly to him. The scream went silent mid-jump and the boy's slack weight hit Viggo in the chest, knocking him off-balance and causing him to fall to the floor. He slid the boy off of him and found his coat slick with blood. He checked and found the boy was still breathing, albeit shallowly. Blood poured from a pulsating wound in his abdomen.

Viggo's mind was racing. *Help him,* said one part of him. *Leave him,* said the other part. *You have to go.* He looked the dying boy in the eyes. There was a look of pleading, but also a tinge of pure, unbridled hate. The life was leaving him. *There's nothing you can do now. Just go.* "I'm so sorry." He was barely able to whisper.

The boy moaned a bit, but it was only moments before his final breath rattled out of his body and his head lolled to the side. His eyes remained open, only a bit. Just two small slits. Viggo turned away and walked into the hallway. He leaned against the wall and breathed deep. He hadn't realized previously how much he had been sweating. He wiped the moisture from his forehead and ran a hand through his hair. He was again reminded of how much blood he had been soaked with and removed his jacket, leaving it in the hallway.

He walked down the hall a bit and managed to stagger into a bathroom, outfitted in pink and green decor. His fumbling fingers found a light switch, and he nearly blinded himself by flipping it on. Through the violent haze of new light, Viggo managed to turn on the sink and wash the blood from his hands. Then he ran water through his hair and cleaned his face. He didn't look in the mirror and turned the water off, turning and heading back toward the bedroom to see what else there was to grab.

I've come this far, he thought. *I can't let it all be in vain now.* But as he rounded the corner to the bedroom, he was stopped in his tracks by what he saw there.

A little girl knelt over Cole Traeger's body. She wasn't crying or screaming. She just sat there on her knees, her arms hanging limp at her side. A stuffed purple armadillo was in her right hand. It smiled with what were once bright white teeth, now tarnished from dirt and mud and countless playtimes. The girl didn't see Viggo, so he ducked back to the bathroom and retrieved his clothes. When he was redressed, he returned to the bedroom, half expecting the girl to not be there, to have been a product of a mind overcome by stress and exhaustion. However, to his dismay, she *was* still there, exactly as she had been before. Completely still. When Viggo approached her, he moved slowly at first. As he passed the boy's body he stopped. She hadn't seen him. He could just leave. He could sneak back out the way he came in. He doubted she would have heard him, or cared either way.

Could he leave her like this? Sitting in an empty house by the corpses of her entire family, just waiting for someone to find her? Thoughts of his own childhood entered his mind unbidden.

Or, Viggo thought, *I could take her with me.* It was a crazy thought. He was going on the run, she'd be dead weight. But maybe he could find a life for her out there. He felt responsibility for her now, and he knew he *should* see to her in some way.

Of course, there was another option. He shuddered as he thought of it. But it had to be considered.

Careful not to be heard, he exited the room and walked back down the stairs to the living room. The shotgun still rested above the hearth, surrounded by the family photos, which Viggo found much more unnerving now than he had a few minutes ago. He took the antique gun from the mantle and opened the barrel; it wasn't loaded. There was a box of shells sitting behind one of the pictures, though, so he grabbed it. He slid two shells into the gun and then snapped the barrel closed. The rest of the box, he gripped in his right hand.

He noticed a backpack laying in the entryway, emblazoned with a New York Yankees logo. Probably belonged to the brother. Viggo unzipped it and turned it upside down, shaking it. Books, papers, binders, and pencils all came tumbling onto the floor. A few more shakes ensured it was totally empty. He stuffed the box of shells down into the bag, along with the money he had gotten from the house, and some of Traeger's wife's jewelry.

After loading his spoils into the bag, Viggo slung it over his shoulder and went back upstairs. He finally knew what to do with the girl, and how he would go about it. At the doorway to the bedroom, he stopped. She was still there, just as she had been. The purple armadillo, the pajamas, the three corpses; everything was exactly as it had been. He pondered her for a minute, and again considered walking away. In the end, however, he simply dropped the bag of stolen goods where he was and proceeded into the room, shotgun in hand.

CHAPTER 3

The Sound of Rain

Marcus held his hand out, shaking the tin cup. A few pieces of loose change rattled about inside it. A man and woman walked by, laughing before they reached him but inevitably twisting their faces into mixtures of pity and disgust and quickening their pace as they drew closer. Once they passed, Marcus sighed and put the cup down next to his crossed legs. Another fruitless effort. The city wasn't in a giving mood today.

He had seen it before. Nothing to panic about. Next week, he could bring home a hundred and fifty dollars a day. Maybe he needed a new spot, somewhere a little less... *nice*. A little dirtier, and the people might be able to commiserate a little better. They might understand a little more than the folk that threw him furtive glances as they cover their children's eyes and hurry past. Occasionally, they would throw him a couple of coins. It was a worthless gesture, though. He could see their discomfort as easily as if they had been waving their arms and yelling, "This is a dirty homeless man, but I'm an upstanding citizen. Look at how upstanding I am."

Marcus chuckled to himself. He tended to do that, he knew. It *did* help lend credibility to the whole "crazy homeless guy" routine. If people genuinely thought he was crazy, they were much more likely to toss a few coins his way, and the cops tended to leave him alone once they got used to him and knew he wasn't going to hurt anyone. He never had to take the act too far. Most people simply steered clear once they made their donation.

Marcus stood and brushed himself off a little. He dumped the cup's contents into his hand and then thrust that hand into his jacket pocket. The cup was placed on a loop on his belt and dangled there the entire way back to his car, parked two blocks down the street. Once there, he dug the keys out from his pant pocket and opened the door. Flopping into the seat, he turned the ignition on and drove away.

The apartment where he ended up had served him for the last 8 months. It was small, but had enough room for him to work. The kitchen was nearly spotless, since Marcus tended to live off microwaved food on paper plates. There was one bookshelf, filled to bursting and nearly covered by stacks of books around it. One thing Marcus loved about his "job," there was plenty of time to read.

He tossed his keys into the basket on the table to his right as he walked in the door and slid his shoes off without untying them, then dumped his coat to the floor. Within moments, the heavy pants and multiple layers of shirts and sweaters had been shed and Marcus was walking through the apartment completely naked. He headed straight for the shower.

After he had cleansed his body, he slid a paper plate with four microwaveable chicken fillets into the sauce-caked microwave and pressed the number 4. The little machine fired up and the chicken started turning on the safe plate.

Marcus sat down at the kitchen table and pulled the leather binder sitting there close to him. It was getting thick now; he could feel it as he gripped the leather. A year's worth of work had led him to this and he was nearly done now. He slipped off the string-tie lock and opened the front cover. He ran his fingers over the dried ink on the front page and then gingerly flipped to the second and third pages, repeating the ritual over and over. He became immersed in it and just as he was about to reach for his pen, the microwave began *beeping* to tell him that his chicken was done.

The soft, breaded strips of chicken were plain, but for Marcus, food was simply a means to stay alive long enough to finish the book. He immediately returned to the table after retrieving some Mexico Bill's Habanero Hot Sauce. A large plastic cup of water was his refreshment for the evening, as he settled in and put pen to paper.

The first words came with difficulty, as they always did. Once he hammered the first sentence out, though, they began to flow.

Stephen stood above the city, looking down on it as he had so many times before.

There we go, thought Marcus. For the next six hours, he wrote almost constantly. He had been thinking all day about the story's direction, and finally had a heading. He was on the final chapter now, and it had to be perfect. 670 pages in and he suddenly required perfection of himself.

And yet, he couldn't think of a title. That aspect, more than any other, seemed to elude him. The story was nearly done now and he still couldn't come up with a title for the damned thing.

Without warning, he stopped. There was just no more. The story had simply ended in his mind, but he knew that this wouldn't do. There was no ending here, no conclusion. The important things weren't resolved yet, and he couldn't simply leave it here. No, he would need to stop for the night and try again tomorrow. Perhaps he would dream up an ending overnight, this would all be done tomorrow, and he could start calling agents.

When he rose to make his way to bed, Marcus did so like the dead from the grave: slowly and with much effort. His muscles protested the sudden movement after so much time idle. He dragged himself to bed and fell into the recesses of the covers, completely exhausted.

Initially, Marcus thought the rain had woken him. Thunder clapped loudly and he found himself wrested from his dreams and thrust back into the world of the waking. In a groggy half-sleep, he thought he heard a beating on the door.

"Oh, come *on*." He considered just rolling over and ignoring the sound until it went away, but another *bang bang bang!* echoed down the hall, killing those thoughts. "Who the *hell*?" Again it came. "Oh, fine! Dammit, I'm coming!" He rose, angry now, and pounded down the hall toward the door. When he reached it, he nearly pulled the door open, but thought again as his eyes rolled down to the Louisville Slugger sitting by the door. He grabbed it, flicked open the deadlock, and wrenched the door open. "What the hell do you-" He stopped.

"Marcus Traeger?" One of the men said.

Marcus nodded weakly, now suddenly completely awake.

"I'm Detective Jonathan Faraday." He gestured toward the other man, slightly shorter, balding, but seemingly very

stout. "This is my partner, Detective Mance Kirkpatrick."
He produced a badge from inside the tan trench coat that he
was wearing. Kirkpatrick did the same. "We need to speak
to you, regarding your father, a Mr. Cole Traeger. Do you
mind if we come in?" The detective craned his neck, looking
past Marcus, into the apartment.

"Uh-no. No, come in." Marcus turned and walked back
into the living room and began clearing space from the
couch. The two detectives took their seats, Marcus took his
in a chair across from them, and for a little while, they all
just sat and stared at each other. "Can I get you some coffee
or something?"

Faraday held a hand up. "No, thank you." Kirkpatrick
shook his head politely.

"OK. You said something about my dad?" Marcus's
heart was pounding and sweat was beading on his forehead.
He hadn't seen his father in almost a year and they had
never had the best of relationships, but still, his breath was
suddenly coming short.

"Yes, I'm afraid that's right." Faraday looked to
Kirkpatrick, who nodded in approval. "I'm sorry, there's no
easy way to say this. Your family was the victim of a home
invasion."

Initially, Marcus felt relief. So there had been a break
in, what was so important about that, that they had to come

knocking on his door in the middle of the night? Then he saw that there was more.

Faraday was visibly unsettled. He looked at the floor and twisted his fingers together, resting his arms on his knees. "It seems your father caught the intruder. There was a fight and..." He swallowed hard and Marcus could suddenly hear nothing aside from the blood pumping in his ears. "Your mother and little brother were killed. Your little sister is missing and presumed dead. And your father is at Mercy General, barely hanging on." Faraday's eyes met Marcus's for the first time since he had begun speaking. "You need to come down to the hospital. They don't know if he's going to wake up or not. You'll want to be there, whatever happens."

Marcus didn't speak. He wasn't even sure what he would say. He managed a weak nod, then left with the detectives. He barely remembered to dress, but he slid on some sandals and walked out with them, nonetheless. The car they took was nicer than most police cruisers and didn't smell as bad. Marcus was glad for that, not that he would've noticed the smell anyway, but it was something to distract him from the moment, even if fleeting.

At a red light maybe a mile from his apartment, Faraday turned to look at Marcus over his shoulder. "There's one more thing, Mr. Traeger." Faraday was again visibly uncomfortable. "You'll be needed to identify the bodies."

The bodies. Not "your parents," or "your family" or "the little brother you taught to shoot a basketball." No, just "the bodies."

They're not even people anymore, Marcus thought, a chorus of panic rising in his chest, simmering bile coating his throat. He vomited in the floor of the seat beside him. Aside from a barely audible groan, the detectives said nothing.

The morgue was stark and sterile. No smell. No odor of any sort. On a metal table about waist-high laid two figures, covered in white sheets. As Marcus breathed deep and nodded, the medical examiner pulled back a sheet to reveal his younger brother Bryce. Well, it looked like Bryce, but it clearly wasn't him. The skin was white and waxy, and no playful smile adorned his face. His messy blonde hair was matted with blood and his lips were a pale purple. Marcus simply nodded, trying to look away. The sheet was replaced with a clearly-practiced speed and efficiency.

When he thought himself ready, he walked to the other table, facing the other, larger sheet-covered lump. This time, when the sheet was pulled away, Marcus lost all composure. His mother, clear as day, unmoving, not breathing. She had been asleep. He could tell from the way that her hair was pulled up in that bun that his father always made fun of. "Trashy bedtime bun," he had called it. Marcus turned away as the tears flowed in full. The detectives must have taken his breakdown as confirmation of his mother's identity, because no sooner had he turned around did he hear Faraday issuing thanks to the examiner and ushering him back to the car.

When they arrived at the hospital, Marcus barely registered the walk in. The detectives spoke with a stocky older woman at the front desk and confirmed the room number. Then he was moving, his feet claiming their independence from his conscious mind and carrying him forward without his consent. Doorways and hallways popped into and out of existence around him, each fluorescent bulb overhead another *tick tick tick* on the clock counting down to yet another body. His father was alive, he'd been told, but barely. Was he still?

Did I miss yet another chance to make this right?

Faraday and Kirkpatrick walked a couple feet ahead as the group snaked its way through the various corridors and hallways, past waiting rooms, all full of anxious and waiting people who would soon have to face news, either good or bad. Marcus found himself apathetic to their moments, their sadness.

When they reached his father's door Marcus didn't wait for the nurse to inform him of his condition. He simply brushed past her and into the room. He briefly registered Faraday issuing hurried and hushed apologies as the two detectives followed.

Cole Traeger lay on the hospital bed, whiter than the sheets that were stretched across the mattress beneath him. His face was beaten and broken open, his eyes and cheeks a blotted mass of purple, yellow, and brown. He scarcely looked like the man that Marcus had remembered; strong, with an unbreakable will, always wearing that stupid comb-over and his stubble beard.

Marcus inched toward the bed, fearing it would open up and swallow him whole. As he drew closer, he could hear his father's breath, coming as wet rasps. With each sharp intake of air, the machine next to him beeped. *Oxygen tube. Life support.* It was then that it dawned on Marcus that they were all convinced his father would die. As he looked around the room for the first time, he registered the faces of the two doctors and three nurses. They looked at him with expressions of pity. One doctor closed his eyes and shook his head before turning back to the chart in his hand.

Marcus shut them out. He walked to his father's bedside and grasped his limp hand. For a moment, he would've sworn his father reacted, but deep inside he knew there was nothing. He waited there for an amount of time he took no care to measure. He simply *was*. He thought about the times before he'd left home, playing with his father, and little Katie, and Bryce. His thoughts drifted around a bit in his high school years and he thought about the times that he had let his father down, like when he had stumbled in at sunrise, drunk off his ass and smelling like perfume, just to find his father sitting at the kitchen table. That was a bad day.

But most of all, he thought about his last night at home. The words that were thrown around, the names, the curses. He had never heard his dad use words like that before. It hadn't mattered. Marcus had marched right out, leaving Cole standing in the doorway, midsentence, another *"Fucking disappointment"* hanging on his lips. He had still been there the last time Marcus looked in the rearview mirror.

And now, he was here. In a hospital bed, bruised and broken and dying, and there was nothing Marcus could do but sit and wait. His mother and brother and sister were dead, his father was dying, and all he could do was *wait*.

"Mr. Traeger?" The voice coming from the other corner of the room shook Marcus from his thoughts. "Mr. Traeger?"

"What?" The word came out sharper than he'd intended, but he didn't care.

"I'm sorry, but we need to ask you some questions."

Marcus sighed heavily and rubbed his eyes as he nodded. He knew this time would come eventually. Better to get it over with.

"Right." Faraday flipped open his notebook and clicked open his pen. "So...when was the last time you spoke to your father?"

"Um...about a year ago. It was...not pleasant. We had an argument, and I stormed out." He buried his face in his hands, and then ran his fingers through his hair. "We hadn't been in contact since."

"Okay..." Faraday scribbled away furiously in his pad. "And what about your mother and your siblings? When did you last speak to them?" He raised his eyes and peered out from under thin gray brows to meet Marcus's stare.

This was the one he had wanted to avoid. The thoughts of his mother and siblings hadn't occupied him as much as his father to this point. When he had stormed out, his mother had tried so hard to get him to come home and make amends and he had refused her every time. She had even come to his apartment after Thanksgiving and eaten with him because he had refused to go to the family dinner. His father hadn't even called. Bryce and little Katie had wanted to see him. He knew, because his mother had told him, that Bryce missed him deeply. Marcus had told her she could bring them, but she had refused.

"No," she had said. "No, until you come and talk to your father, you won't lay eyes on them."

"There's no talking to him!" Marcus had nearly screamed his reply. He stood and walked around his living room, like a child throwing a tantrum. "He's a maniac! Do you really think that we can just *work things out*?!" He had looked at her like she was an idiot, like she had no idea, no understanding of his plight. He had seen her reaction and felt her pain almost immediately. If words were knives, Marcus could've been a butcher that night. She had issued no reply other than to stand and walk away, brushing tears from her eyes. As she walked out, Marcus rushed to the door. "Mom!" he called after her as she hurried down the hall. "Mom! I'm...I'm sorry. Just...I'm sorry." She had paused ever so briefly, and then kept walking.

Later that night, he called her and apologized. He even promised to talk to his father. That was a week ago. It was also the last time he had spoken to anyone in his family. Marcus buried his face in his hands and groaned. *How did it come to this?* He thought.

"Mr. Traeger? Marcus?" Faraday was saying his name.

"Oh. Right. What did you ask, again?" He knew that he sounded groggy and distant, but he didn't care because he *was* groggy and distant. The detectives would want to talk to him again later, he assumed, to try for some better answers.

Faraday sighed and rubbed his brow with his thumb and index finger. "When was the last time you spoke to your mother or your siblings?"

"Um...I talked to Mom about a week ago. I haven't talked to Bryce or Katie for...about a year. The same time as my dad, I guess." *How could I leave them like that? God, I'm stupid.* There was a stinging in Marcus's nostrils as he realized that his nose was bleeding. Faraday moved to offer him a handkerchief, but Marcus waved him off and grabbed one of the tissues on the bedside table.

"Are you alright?" asked Faraday.

Marcus turned and fixed him with a stare he hoped was sufficiently icy. "Really?"

Faraday dipped his head. "Right." He stood and flipped his notepad closed. "I apologize. Mr. Traeger, we'll talk again tomorrow." He and Kirkpatrick moved toward the door. As he was walking out, Faraday caught the door-frame, drumming his fingers lightly for a moment. "And don't leave town."

Marcus sank into the chair by his father's head and buried his face in his hands. He kept expecting tears to come. The weight in his chest told him he should cry, break down, rage, whatever. But it never happened. His soul was too crushed, his body too tired for that tonight. He pulled his knees to his chest and made himself as small as he could. Watching his father's chest steadily rise and fall, he eventually slipped under the cover of a fitful sleep.

CHAPTER 4

Fratello

Luke Scolessa examined the man standing in front of him: skinny, shaking, and scratching at the inside of his track-marked arms. His skin was a motley conglomeration of brown, black, purple, and blue. He looked to be about sixty, but Luke knew better. He placed him at roughly forty, fifty at a stretch. A scraggly white beard adorned his gaunt cheeks and dark black circles surrounded eyes that were yellowed from what Luke expected to be hepatitis. Maybe cirrhosis.

All in all, the man disgusted him. Luke had certain expectations of people, though, and he knew what to expect from a strung-out addict who brought him information when he needed a fix. The piece of trash shaking in front of him tended to bring reliable information, at least. If that was considered a redeeming feature, then he at least *tried,* which was more than could be said for most of the informants that Luke's men dragged in front of him.

"All right. Go over it again, from the beginning." Luke's

voice was deep, with only a tinge of a Brooklyn accent. He tried to hide it, but it always bled through a little. He swirled the glass of scotch that he held in his left hand and took a draw on the cigarette that rested between the index and middle fingers on his right hand. The smoke filled his lungs and he held it there for a moment before blowing it out through his nostrils, where it thinned and eventually dissipated into the air.

The man stirred a bit and moved his arms as though he were shielding himself from some invisible man's attacks. Luke thought maybe he did see someone, a shadow or reflection of his broken mind. When he spoke, his voice warbled, giving it a shaky feel. "I saw the guys get out of their cars, then your guy got spooked, and the other guy, he tried to take the bag and pop your guy, but your guy, he killed 'em and took off." He spoke without taking a breath and when he finished, inhaled deeply. He started to speak again, but Chris, one of Luke's men, cut him off.

"From what we could tell, Viggo went back to the safe-house after the busted deal. That's where he killed Mal. I checked the cameras. Mal made the first move. If Viggo thought he was under our orders, it could explain why he took off."

Luke downed the rest of his scotch. "So, Viggo didn't know Mal was pissed about his promotion. If he'd known..."

He rubbed his brow with his left hand, then took another draw of the cigarette before putting it out in his glass. "So what now? Do we know where he is?"

Chris spoke again, shaking his head. "We think he headed south, but we lost him last night."

"Well, then. Get him." A thought occurred to Luke. "What if we sent Leon?"

Chris whistled. "I'm not sure you want to let that one out of your sight."

Luke nodded. "Besides, Viggo would probably see him coming from three states away in that stupid plaid suit." Both men chuckled.

Chris cleared his throat. "We can find him the old-fashioned way. What do you want us to do with him once we catch him?"

Luke sighed. "He's in the wind with $750,000 of our money. If he got collared, he would give us up in a second. He thinks we betrayed him and tried to have him killed. Who knows what stupid-ass thing he'll do. You catch him, you kill him." It was regrettable, but it was the only way. He would never really trust them again, and Luke couldn't have anyone who didn't trust him in his employ. He was dangerous, so he had to go.

"What about the money?" Chris was speaking again.

Luke retrieved another glass and poured some more

scotch. After taking a drink of it, he spoke. "It's still green, isn't it? Get back whatever you can." Chris nodded and then exited, dragging the addict with him, pleading for his fix. Luke briefly registered Chris producing some syringes from inside his jacket and handing them to the man.

Once he was alone, Luke lit another cigarette. He found the smoke helped him relax, helped him focus on the task at hand. God knows, if he ever needed to focus, it was now. Viggo was missing with $750,000 of the family's money, headed to God-knows-where, and he had more information than he would ever need to cripple their organization. It was a grade-A cluster-fuck.

Luke downed his glass of scotch and poured another as he took a draw on his cigarette. He noticed it had burned almost halfway down, and was the last one in the pack. This sent him rummaging through the drawers of his desk to try and locate another pack. He finally happened upon a pack of unfiltered Lucky Strikes he had been hanging onto for a 'special occasion.' *If ever there was a special occasion, it's now,* he thought. As he lit one of the white, unassuming cigarettes, he felt a brief tinge of sadness, like watching an old friend go on a long trip. Once he took the first drag though, that feeling melted away as the strong, rich taste of tobacco filled his mouth. He almost didn't want to exhale.

It took a moment, but his mind eventually returned to

the business at hand, this time with renewed vigor. As he leaned back in his chair and examined the situation, he could still find no way around Viggo's death. Maybe if he was relocated somewhere? No, too risky. He could always come and cash in on anything he wanted with them, he had too much information. Besides, he would never work for them again, after he thought they tried to kill him. He drew from the cigarette again and downed the rest of his glass of scotch.

As the smoke swirled around him, Luke thought for a moment he could see a pattern in it, a message, speaking to him. It looked like a ship, sailing off into an endless horizon, its sails filled. An invisible ocean tossed it with gentle waves, cold froth sliding over the deck. Luke shook himself, thinking the alcohol must be getting to him. He opened a drawer on his desk, placed a stopper in the bottle of scotch, and stored it. He extinguished the cigarette in his glass after another draw and, his mind heavy with thought, leaned back in his chair and closed his eyes.

He awoke three hours later to his office door swinging open and banging hard on the wall. Chris rushed in, screaming. "Boss! Boss, wake up!" Luke took a moment to stir. Chris yelled again. "Luke! Wake the fuck up!" A gunshot split the air somewhere outside.

"What..." Luke's head was pounding and his throat was dry and cracked. "What's going on?" His mind was cloudy and his eyes blurred until he blinked them a few times.

Chris was watching the door; gun in hand, while Luke gathered himself. "It's an all-out assault. Tommy and Jim are dead already, and I've gotta get you out of here. So come on!" He was glancing around frantically, from Luke to the door and back again.

"Who is it?" Luke's mind was clearing, but his head still pounded, and his voice was hoarse and cracked with pain when he spoke. *Too much damn smoke,* he thought, knowing he would laugh at himself as soon as he could light up. If they managed to make it out of this alive.

"You know that coke dealer Viggo killed? His people have decided it's time for blood. They've declared war on us."

"What about my brother?" A polarizing clarity cut through the fog. He needed to know his brother was safe. When Chris failed to answer, he grabbed him by the shoulder. "What about Marc, Chris? Where is he?"

Chris turned to Luke, meeting his gaze. "I don't know. And we'll never find out if we don't get out of here. Now come on." Luke nodded, shaking himself and retrieving the loaded nine-millimeter from his desk drawer as he stood. Chris grabbed Luke by the shoulder. "Stay low and stay behind me. Help me watch the corners." As they moved out of the room, Chris swung around the doorframe, checking each direction with the pistol. Luke was struck by the fluidity and ease of his movements. He knew Chris had spent time in the Army, but not much about the specifics.

I guess some things never leave you, Luke thought.

Once Chris had determined they were clear, he motioned Luke on. The two of them moved into the hallway, then hurried down the stairs. On the stairs, one of the men from the rival gang appeared around a corner, brandishing a shotgun. He noticed the pair just as Chris put two bullets in his chest. After he fell, Chris retrieved the shotgun and handed it to Luke. "Let's get out of here. You know how to use this, right?"

Luke barked a laugh that held no levity as he hefted the gun. "Not my first time. Let's go." The pair progressed down the stairs and into the kitchen, toward the house's back door. As they approached the door to the kitchen, voices from the other side stopped them in their tracks. Chris motioned Luke to the side, and the pair pressed themselves against the wall.

Luke tried to listen to the conversation on the other side of the door, but could only make out the occasional word. He was sure of only one thing: they were not his men.

Silently, Chris put up three fingers. Then he lowered one, counting down. When all three fingers were lowered, Chris spun, faced the door, and kicked it in. It burst open, slamming into the wall with a sound that was overtaken by the immediate chorus of gunfire as Chris took aim. He dropped one of the intruders immediately with three shots to the torso. The other one was quicker to react, raising his gun, a submachine gun that could almost assuredly cut Chris in half with its payload.

Luke was faster. He turned the shotgun on the man and squeezed the trigger, feeling the impact in his shoulder as the gun bucked. From this range, he couldn't miss if he'd tried. The attacker's hand dissolved in a red spray of buckshot, leaving the gun to fall to the floor as he cried out and fell against the wall. Luke pumped the slide, sending a shell bouncing along the kitchen counter, and fired again, opening the man's chest and silencing his screams in a red mist.

Chris didn't slow down, stepping over the bodies and toward the back door. Luke exhaled a breath he hadn't realized he was holding, then wiped sweat from his forehead.

Been a minute since I had to do that, he thought. Then he pumped the shotgun again and followed after Chris.

When they were out of the back door, they saw another

man guarding the exit from the yard, but his back was turned to them. Chris began to talk, but Luke ignored him and walked up to the man. He wielded his shotgun like a club, gripping the barrel. Swinging it low, he took out the man's legs, then stomped on the hand in which he held another of the SMGs. Luke felt a satisfying *crunch* as the bones in the man's hand shattered. With another swing of the shotgun-club, he broke the man's jaw, which blacked him out. Luke retrieved the man's gun, and then returned to Chris.

With a nod that looked like approval, Chris took the gun, stuffing his pistol into his belt. The pair moved out of the yard, into an alleyway behind the house, toward the car that was always parked at the end, in case of an emergency like this. They flopped into the seats, their guns resting on their laps. Chris turned the key and the car hummed to life.

"Where to?" said Chris, once they were on the road. His eyes still darted about like a scared rabbit, but his brow had relaxed and he generally looked less on-edge.

Luke sighed. "Marc's house. We have to make sure he's okay."

"Right. No problem."

A moment passed. Luke looked around the car, and then asked, "You got any smokes?"

The car rolled up to the curb at Marc Scolessa's house roughly fifteen minutes later. There were no other cars nearby, but there were two people standing outside the house. As soon as Luke opened the car door and showed his face, one of the men standing outside reached around to the back of his waistband. Luke didn't give him the opportunity; he raised his shotgun and squeezed the trigger, blasting a hole into the man's chest cavity. His comrade turned to come to his aid and Luke put a shot into his abdomen, throwing him onto his back. Once he was sure there were no more of them, Luke lowered the shotgun to his side and took a draw from the lit cigarette that still hung off his lip.

"Well," he said. "Looks like they beat us here." He dropped the cigarette to the sidewalk and ground it to ashes with his toe. "We have to get in there."

Chris looked around, as was his way. "All right. And we gotta move fast. Your..." He gestured to the two men Luke had killed, their blood still pooling on the sidewalk. "... handiwork is going to attract some attention. The cops will definitely be here soon. We've got maybe five minutes." He readied the stolen SMG. "So let's move." The two of them moved toward the front door of Marc's house. Once they were at the door, Chris looked at Luke, who nodded. Then he took a step back and kicked the door in. The wood around the lock splintered and broke, while the rest of the door flew inward and banged against the wall. There was no one in the entry way. The two of them moved on into the house. Once they were inside, Chris whispered, "How much ammo you got left?"

Luke checked his shotgun. "I got three left. You?"

"I'm full. Let's take it slow. Which way is your brother's office?"

"Upstairs."

"Okay, then. Here we go. I'll lead." As they moved toward the stairs on the left of the entrance, Luke noticed a dead man lying in the kitchen, a butcher knife protruding from his chest. He recognized the man as one of Marc's. He couldn't help but notice the house was eerily silent. They couldn't even hear footsteps or voices coming from upstairs.

Luke's mind was racing, and the worst possibilities were the most prevalent. He thought about what would happen if the other gang had kidnapped Marc, taken him alive. They could be interrogating him about the organization's finances, their forces, anything. Or, they could have killed him and his family and been done with it. Luke knew that it was entirely possible that they were rushing in to save a ghost.

Once they were at the top of the stairs, they progressed down the second-floor hallway, careful of each room. There was nothing aside from the silence that seemed to pervade the entire house. At the door to Marc's office, they waited. Luke's heart was racing, but he tried to calm himself. Chris drew his breath in and kicked the door in. As they stepped inside, they saw the damage. The office was in shambles, books were strewn around the room, the end table was turned over, and the desk was stripped of the decorations that usually covered it. There was no one to be found, though. Luke let his shotgun rest over his shoulder as he walked through the office.

"Well, shit." He finally said.

Chris lowered his gun and lightly nudged some of the debris from the desk, now cast haphazard into the floor. "Gotta think he's a prisoner now," he said after a moment. "They probably had the same planned for you. Take you both hostage, then force you to work for them."

Luke nodded. "It's more money in their pockets if they can keep our operation intact." He pointed at Chris. "Go check the rest of the house. We need to know if his wife and son are still here." Chris left the office without a word. Luke sat at his brother's chair and put the shotgun on the desk. He reached into the bottom drawer and began rummaging through it. Eventually, his hand landed on it, and he recognized the familiar feeling of cellophane packaging. Pulling his hand from the drawer, he saw the Lucky Strike packaging and smiled. He produced a cigarette from the package and slipped into his mouth. His Zippo lighter came aflame with one strike and, when he lit it, the cigarette produced the wonderfully powerful taste of unfiltered tobacco.

As he blew smoke into the room, he thought about Marc. *Don't worry, little brother,* he thought. *Stay strong, and I'll be there soon. Just like I always am.*

CHAPTER 5

Lost in the Dawn

Cole Traeger opened his eyes to the pressing darkness of the pre-dawn hours. A film covered his eyes, forcing him to blink several times in an effort to make his vision correct itself. As he finally gained some focus in this newfound darkness, he took in the surreal and strange place in which he'd found himself.

He noticed the starlit sky above him, though he realized that the stars, too, were fading. It appeared to Cole as though the time was roughly an hour before dawn. The air had an odd milky quality to it, making it difficult for him to see, though he recognized the shapes of trees, maybe a mountain off in the distance. As he got to his feet, he realized there was no breeze, no wind to speak of. The air hung still and heavy, making his shirt cling to his skin. Though he realized this, he was not uncomfortable. He simply *was*.

He took a step and realized he was barefoot. For the first time, Cole turned his examinations to himself and noticed he was wearing a light black t-shirt, flannel plaid pajamas, and no shoes. He remembered putting these clothes on, but he had no idea why he was still wearing them, or how he had ended up here.

He had awoken on a grassy knoll that sat above a long, low, flat plain. A lake was barely visible in the distance, as was what appeared to be a forest roughly a mile in the distance. The mountain Cole had noticed earlier was probably five miles away. It didn't appear overly large, but instead looked almost flat, like a children's pop-up book. Cole couldn't help but laugh a bit at the absurdity of it all.

His face hurt, but it was an odd sort of pain, like it was pushed deep beneath the surface of his skin, numbed by powerful medicine. As he took a step, he realized his abdomen also ached but, like his face, was numbed.

The sky was dark, but tints of purple, blue, and a fading starry yellow blended overhead in swirling patterns, like a canvas smeared with finger paint. There was an ever so faint line of orange on the horizon, heralding an impending sunrise. Cole took a few more tentative steps toward the breakage of the knoll. When he reached the edge, however, he was greeted by a drop that was much farther down and much steeper than Cole thought ought to be possible. Yet here he was, standing on the edge, looking over this impossible knoll to the plain that stretched out at its bottom and he couldn't help but think it all made sense somehow, in a way that he didn't care to understand. With a sure foot, he stepped off the edge of the knoll.

He didn't remember falling, but he supposed that he must've, since he was lying on his back at the base of the knoll when he regained consciousness. Nothing hurt that hadn't hurt before, so he supposed he must be all right. Cole's abdomen panged as he pushed himself to his feet, and his muscles cried out in protest from the strain.

Suddenly, his mind exploded with clarity, as though the pain had purified him somehow. He knew where he must go. The lake seemed to call out to him with a sound that rang through his mind like one of his own thoughts. He set out with a newfound resolve toward the lake, still barely visible in the pre-dawn twilight.

Cole took a step toward the lake. He guessed it was roughly a half-mile journey, and he wanted to make it before the sun rose.

As he arrived at the shore, Cole noticed that the water gave off an odd purple sheen. Waves lapped upon the shore with an oddly silent report. Cole registered a slight breeze that grew stronger the closer he got to the lake. By the time he stood on the rocky shore, the wind had mussed his hair and was tugging at his shirt.

Cole took a deep breath, taking in the place's strange,

too-strong smells, then blew it back out. Since he had awakened, he had been lost. He had no idea how he had arrived at this odd place. That thought should have scared him, he knew, but for some reason, his heart was still. Calm, even, in a way Cole found almost wrong.

At this point, Cole noticed the lake house, off to his right. It hadn't been there before, he was sure of it. It didn't matter; he knew at once that it was his destination. The rocks on the shore of the lake stabbed his feet as he walked but, like the rest of his body, the pain was far away. By the time he reached the door of the lake house, blood dripped from cuts an inch deep into the soft flesh of his feet.

Cole wrapped his hand around the cold metal of the doorknob and for the first time since he woke up, his heart leapt into his throat and he felt fear. *Real* fear. Something gripped at his chest and his jaw tightened and as if he might explode from all the pent-up emotion. He hesitated and almost didn't open the door. In the end, however, he knew there was no other choice for him. It was either risk opening the door or leave and see if there was any way home. He still had absolutely no idea where he was and the only direction he had was the clear, bright-as-day ringing in his head that told him to open that door. He took a deep breath.

With a turn of his wrist, the door gave way.

Once he crossed the threshold, Cole didn't find himself

standing in a lake house, but instead lying in his own bed, in his own bedroom, next to his sleeping wife. He felt as though he had just come to, but he knew he had been awake for a long time. He could still remember the grassy knoll, and the steep drop, and the long walk, and the clear ringing in his mind, bringing him to the lake, but it all seemed somehow different. As if, instead of actually having happened, it was simply a very vivid dream, from which he had now woken up.

It all made sense. He had simply been dreaming. Cole exhaled, feeling better. Turning to his left, he wrapped his arms around Lillian in an attempt to drift back off to sleep, hopefully to more pleasant dreams. It was only a couple of minutes later when he heard the door to the bedroom creak open.

Cole fought the urge to sit up and look. At first he thought it was one of the kids, but that didn't make sense. They usually knocked. Light footsteps moved across the floor, making it creak ever so slightly. At this point, he became sure that the intruder wasn't one of his children. Whoever it was began taking items from Lillian's jewelry box and stuffing them into a bag. After a moment or two, the person moved to the closet. Cole took this opportunity to risk a glance toward the closet. He saw a man, roughly his height, heading inside. Cole got out of bed as quietly as possible and began moving toward the closet. The man clearly heard him because he ducked inside where he couldn't be seen. Cole pressed on.

It proved to be a mistake. As he placed his hand on the doorframe, the man blitzed him with a tire iron. The first swing caught him across the face and knocked him onto his back in the floor of his bedroom. His vision blurred and flashed yellow as his nose broke under the pressure of the blow. Before he could gather himself, the man pounced on him and swung the tire iron down onto his head again, catching him on the right side of his face. His vision went completely black. Another blow came almost immediately and he blacked out as it smashed into him.

Cole was standing outside, his hand once again gripping the cold metal doorknob. His head no longer hurt. The dark sky sat above him again, and the purple water lapped against the rocky shore. He looked around, his eyes wild. His mind was racing, and he struggled to make sense of the thoughts he was having. He knew only one thing to do.

The knob slid round easily as he turned his wrist.

Again he was in his bed, Lillian beside him. Cole felt again as though he was waking up, but there was an odd sense of déjà vu, a feeling of familiarity with this place and time. He decided he wouldn't attempt to confront the man in the closet this time, but instead would meet him at the door.

He rose from the bed and crossed the bedroom to the door. As soon as it creaked open and the man stepped inside, Cole delivered a punch to his face and sent him reeling back against the wall. As Cole stepped forward to deliver another blow, the man stepped to the right and sent Cole's fist into the drywall. Before he could free his hand, the intruder elbowed him in the ribs and threw a right-hook to his jaw.

Cole swung backward, wrenching his fist free. He tried to raise his guard, but the other man was too quick, and he fought like a man with experience. A punch to the abdomen knocked the breath from his lungs. The other man delivered an uppercut with his right elbow and put Cole on his back. As Cole tried to gather his strength, the intruder stepped forward, retrieving something that he had dropped during the fight. Cole thought it looked somewhat like a tire iron. Before he had time to gather himself, the man brought the weapon down on his face with a grunt and sent Cole wheeling off into blackness.

Cole once again found himself standing outside in the cold pre-dawn darkness with his hand wrapped around the metal doorknob. He stumbled back from the door, falling onto the cold, wet grass. He sat there, propped up on his arms. He was breathing heavily, his heart was racing, and sweat stood on his brow.

A chill crept over Cole's body, into his bones, as if something had infiltrated his soul and was touching his innermost being. Closing his eyes, he rubbed his jaw and tried to slow his breathing. After a moment, he had calmed himself down, so he stood and walked back to the door. Taking a deep breath, he wrapped his fingers once again around the cold doorknob, and prepared to enter into the lake house.

As he turned the knob, it squeaked ever so slightly.

As he found himself once again lying in his bed next to his wife, he wondered, for the first time, if he was dead. It made sense. He had survived both of the previous ventures into this place when he shouldn't have, and he continued to relive the same events, over and over. If he were dead, perhaps he was reliving the moments of his own death over and over again. Maybe this was hell.

His thoughts were interrupted as the door once again squeaked open and the man once again crept through the room. After he entered the closet, Cole started to get up, but decided to instead stay in bed. As he lay there, he opened his eyes, just enough to see the man's outline as he exited the closet, crept back across the bedroom, and out the door. Cole lost his footsteps as they descended the stairs.

Lying there, he realized that he had finally figured it

out. This was the only way he made it through the night. He simply had to lie there and do nothing and everything was okay. Cole was amazed by his own stupidity. His own bravado was what had cost him his life.

He dropped his head against the pillow, exhaling. Lillian stirred beside him slightly and Cole slid his arm around her. His mind strayed to thoughts of his wife and children, and how they couldn't be real. Not here, not now. If he was dead, then she surely wasn't with him.

Cole felt hot tears stinging his eyes. Freeing his arm from the empty visage of his wife, he rolled over to the edge of the bed. A flash of light crossed his eyes and he found himself standing outside again. This time, the air was not cold and the sky was not dark and the lake house was not in front of him. He gasped as his eyes took a moment to adjust to the sudden change in light.

He found himself standing on a high hill, overlooking the ocean. The ground sloped off in front of him before breaking off into cliffs that descended an interminable distance to the ocean that crashed against them. The wind was blowing into Cole's face, pushing his hair back and ruffling his shirt and pajamas. The most noticeable change, however, was the horizon. Where there had been a thin line of sunlight, providing only enough illumination to be visible, there was now a brilliant sunrise, an exploding dawn bursting through the darkness and cutting the chains which had held Cole in this strange place. Suddenly, things began to fall into place. As awareness overtook him, the world around him began to fragment and shatter into pieces. Cracks of great light appeared in the strange scenery that surrounded him and, all at once, with a sound like thunder and the voice of God, the brilliant light overpowered everything and Cole was suddenly falling wildly into nothingness.

Cole Traeger's eyes fluttered open slowly, to a painfully bright light and a lightly mustached face looming over him. He spoke, his dry throat howling in painful protest.

"There was nothing I could do." The light stung his eyes and the pain in his throat was intense, but he said it again. "There was nothing I could do."

CHAPTER 6

Blood and Water

Marcus had never seen his father cry before, but he cried now. He cried constantly. When Marcus had broken the news to him about what had happened, he had sobbed for hours. Now, the slightest inconvenience could set him back to it.

If he was being honest with himself, Marcus got some sick pleasure out of watching his father cry. In his darker moments, he even enjoyed it, and that caused him to hate himself. For all they had been through, Cole was still his father, and that meant he needed to try and be there for him, especially now that they were all that the other had left.

The doctors had said Cole's injuries would take at least a couple of weeks of recovery, during which time he needed to remain in the hospital. This meant that Marcus had to make daily trips to and from his apartment, which drained his already meager funds to almost nothing. Normally he would've gone to one of the more giving streets in town and plopped himself down on the sidewalk for a week. When it was done, he would've had enough to sustain him for a couple of weeks, until he started the process over. As it was, however, he couldn't simply stop going to the hospital. Cole was still in a precarious state, and he needed to be there in case anything happened. If it came to it, Marcus knew he had ways to get some quick money, but he knew those deals came with a price, often much more than the simple dollar amount.

It was late one night when Cole first cried out to him. It had been about two days since he'd woken up, and Marcus had scarcely slept in that time. He was finally about to drift off in the soft silence of the early morning hours when he heard his father stir. There was an odd moaning that became more discernible as he repeated himself.

"Marcus." He rolled over and looked at his father. There were tears in his eyes, but that was nothing new. It was what he said that took Marcus aback. "I never wanted this." Marcus swallowed.

"Just go back to sleep, Dad."

Cole shook his head as much as he could as more tears came streaming out of his eyes. "I never...wanted you to leave. You know that, right? You know that I never wanted you to leave, right? Please tell me that."

Marcus fought back tears, but inside he felt rage

bubbling to the surface. "I know. I know, Dad. Just...just, go back to sleep."

"No. Marcus, just...please...tell me that you know that this wasn't my fault. Please."

Marcus closed his eyes, blinking away tears. "I know it's not your fault, Dad. I know it's not your fault. Now...please, go back to sleep." Cole managed to stay awake for almost another hour, eventually slipping off to sleep, fresh tears still wetting his pillow. Marcus was unable to sleep the rest of the night, so he got up and went to the gas station next door, bought some cigarettes, and sat on a bench outside the hospital. He sat there and smoked until the first tendrils of light showed on the horizon. Marcus thought it was the most beautiful sunrise he had ever seen.

It was a week later when Cole finally stopped crying. The silence was so pervasive that Marcus found it actually bothered him. They still hadn't spoken much, but neither seemed to be complaining very much about it. Cole seemed pleased enough to have his eldest son by his side, and Marcus was certainly happy to have his father still breathing

But, of course, a brutal crime doesn't fix everything.

What Marcus found the most frustrating was his own anger. Of course, he was angry about the murders. Beyond angry, really. But he was still angry with his father, too.

After all they'd been through, after all the shit Cole had said, *he* had been the one to fail them. He had been the one to *lose* them. And now Marcus was here, trying to put *him* back together.

Marcus had to shake himself to stop the anger bubbling in his stomach. It didn't matter. He'd decided to see his father through this, to help in whatever way he could. After that...

Well, he'd cross that bridge when he came to it.

Detectives Faraday and Kirkpatrick had been back to the hospital regularly in the five weeks that had followed Marcus's first meeting with them. They had tried once to question Cole, but at the time, he wasn't coherent enough to give them any leads. They came back a week later, when Cole's weeping had ceased, and tried again. Marcus had just come back from the hospital cafeteria when he found them standing over his father's bed.

He stopped in the doorway. "Detectives." They both looked at him. Faraday regarded him coolly, as usual. Kirkpatrick simply looked at him in a manner that suggested he didn't see him at all, instead staring through him to the hallway outside.

"Mr. Traeger. How are you doing?" asked Faraday.

"My father isn't ready for questioning." he said matter-of-factly, leaning against the doorframe.

"I can speak for myself, son." Marcus whipped his head around to find his father sitting up in bed, reading glasses folded and sitting on top of a newspaper in his lap. He nodded to the detectives. "We were just getting started."

Faraday looked to Kirkpatrick, who nodded, then pulled up a chair at Cole's bedside. Marcus sat down on the couch and waited. The questioning took nearly two hours, most of which was spent trying to calm his father down during the more difficult questions. At the end, they still had next to nothing, with no description of the killer, no timeline, and no idea what had happened to Katie. None of her blood was at the house, but her nightgown was there, laying on the floor of her bedroom. The detectives had no leads on her whereabouts, though, and only speculation as to why the killer might've taken her.

Marcus groaned internally as his thoughts turned to his little sister again. He'd spent much of the last five weeks in a state of panic over her. He just couldn't reconcile the innocent, pudgy-faced little girl whose hand he'd held as she took her first steps with the face looking back at him from the missing child posters.

"It's possible he felt guilty for the murders he had already committed, and thought taking Katie was a way to make up for it." said Faraday, flipping his notebook closed. "All evidence we have suggests a burglary gone wrong. It's possible he didn't intend to kill anyone."

Like it fucking matters, Marcus thought.

The detectives stood and Faraday buttoned his jacket, placing his notepad and recorder in an inside pocket. "We'll get out of your way," Faraday said. "Thank you for the information, it's been a big help." The two detectives shook Marcus's and Cole's hands and took their leave.

Once they sat alone in the room, Marcus spoke. "So, what do you think?"

Cole stirred a bit in the bed and rubbed his eyes. "I don't know how these things work, Marcus. I just want them to find the son of a bitch and bring Katie back."

Marcus looked at the floor, not willing to say that they might never find her, or she might already be dead. She'd been gone for over a month already. "Me, too." he eventually said. For a long while, they simply sat in silence. There was nothing left to be said. "I'm going to go for a walk. You need anything?" Cole shook his head. Marcus nodded silently and made for the door.

He found himself standing in the beer cave of the gas station next door to the hospital. The hole in his chest had grown steadily during the conversation with the detectives, and it threatened to swallow him whole. He could feel himself standing on the edge of a pit, staring into an abyss, desperately wishing he could throw himself in. His hand wrapped around the twelve-pack of beer, and he made his way back to the register. He bought the beer and two packs of cigarettes and trekked back to a bench outside the hospital. He sat there for at least a couple hours, until he'd polished off the beer and most of the cigarettes. Of course, he got an occasional odd look from someone coming or going, but he knew these benches were regular beds to more than one homeless person. And he was so used to blending into that world, he'd pass for a vagrant at a glance. Then he made his way back inside the hospital and stumbled back to his father's room, where he passed out on the couch. Just before he slipped off, he remembered his wallet, which he had left on the bench outside of the hospital.

Tomorrow, he thought. *I'll just get it in the morning.*

Marcus awoke groggily the next morning. His head was pounding and his mouth was dry and tasted of tobacco and alcohol. "God*damn* it." He massaged his brow and buried his face in his hands.

Cole was already awake and propped up in the hospital bed, reading a newspaper. A different paper, Marcus realized dumbly, than he'd had the previous day. "You know," Cole said. "I don't think you've ever smelled any worse than you do right now. It's impressive, really." The paper snapped back straight as he shook it.

Marcus sat up straight, with some difficulty, and spoke.

"Don't start. I'm not in the mood." The light from the window caught his eye, paining his retina and causing him to close his eyes in a grimace.

"I'm not starting anything. You're a – what was it, again? Oh, right. You're a 'grown goddamned man,' if I remember correctly." He looked at Marcus and put the paper on his lap, sighing. "I'm sorry. We've both been through a lot lately. I shouldn't give you shit over the way you deal with it. Just don't let last night become *every* night, okay?"

Marcus nodded, his eyes still closed. "Okay."

"Now, for Chrissakes, go get cleaned up. You smell like shit." Cole returned to his paper.

"Right. Okay." Marcus grabbed his keys and coat and headed for the hospital exit.

He was nearly home when he got pulled over.

The blue lights caught his attention almost immediately. "Damn it." He said to himself as he pulled to the side of the freeway. His stomach tied itself into knots as the officer approached the window and knocked on it, signaling Marcus to roll it down.

"Can I help you, officer?"

The blue-clad police officer looped his thumbs into his belt and leaned forward slightly, peering into the car. "Are you aware of how fast you were going, sir?"

Marcus sighed. "No, sir."

"65 in a 55 mile-an-hour zone."

"I didn't realize."

The officer removed his ticket pad from his pocket and flipped it open. "License and registration, please." Marcus retrieved the registration from the glove box and went for his wallet. His heart jumped into his throat when he realized that it wasn't there. Rapidly, he began to reexamine the events of the past day. Vaguely, he remembered leaving the wallet on the bench and deciding, in his drunken stupor, to get it later. The officer's voice broke his concentration. "Is there a problem, sir?"

Marcus turned to face him, then handed over the registration. "I...I don't have my license on me."

The officer sighed and began scribbling away in his ticket pad. "So, speeding, driving without a license..."

"Hey, no, wait a minute. I *have* a license, just not with me." Marcus rolled his window down further.

"Okay, where is it? We'll go right now and get it, if you can tell me where it is." The officer looked him in the eye.

"I left my wallet on the bench outside the hospital. It might still be there."

"Uh-huh. This was when, exactly?"

"Last night. I'm telling you-"

"Right. So, you expect a wallet that you left outside,

overnight, in the middle of the city, to still be there at ten o'clock the next morning?"

Marcus sighed. "No, not really."

"That's what I thought. *So*, like I was saying before: driving without a license." Marcus leaned back against the headrest. "Sir, could you step out of the car for a moment?"

Marcus looked back to him. "What for?"

"Just step out of the car, please."

"Oh you've got to be kidding."

"No, sir. Please step out of the car."

Marcus flung open the door and stepped out. "Okay. And now?"

The officer produced a breathalyzer from his belt. "Come here, please."

Shit. Marcus was sure the alcohol would still be on his breath. It was inevitable. Hopefully, he wasn't over the legal limit. He stepped forward and placed his mouth on the breathalyzer. It was with heart-pounding anxiety that he blew into it. The seconds ticked by like an eternity, it seemed. Finally, it let out a long *beep*.

"0.4." The officer said. "You're lucky it had enough time to wear off."

Marcus breathed a sigh of relief. "What do you mean?"

"It's ten in the morning. I know you haven't been drinking that much already."

"How?"

"Because you'd still be drinking." He tore the ticket from the pad and handed it to Marcus. "Pay this ticket. The court will get you help if you want it, alright?" The officer looked at Marcus with something like a half-smile.

Marcus felt heat rising through his body. He tried to contain himself, but wasn't sure of his own resolve. His face was turning red, he knew. "I don't have a problem." He finally said, his teeth grating against each other.

The officer sighed. "Just pay the ticket, okay?"

Marcus managed to nod silently. Then he stood there while the officer walked back to his cruiser and drove off. After he was out of sight, Marcus looked at the ticket for the first time. Hopelessness overcame him. There was no way he had the money to pay for it. For a moment, he simply stood there and stared at the little slip of paper. Before long, though, he returned to his car and drove off, thinking all the while of how he was going to get enough money to keep him upright until the world made sense again.

Marcus arrived at his apartment at close to eleven o'clock. He took a shower, brushed his teeth, and made a cup of coffee. It wasn't until he sat down at the kitchen table that he remembered the book. It was still open to the last page, which was blank.

Marcus sat the cup of coffee down and picked up his

pen, which was still lying in the crease of the pages. Just as he touched it to the paper, his heart began pounding. He realized how much his hand was shaking and dropped the pen. Tears rolled from his eyes. With a howl, he swept the table clean, throwing its contents to the floor. The coffee cup smashed into a hundred pieces and the hot beverage splashed over the floor and cabinets and other items.

Marcus found himself sitting in the floor, against the cabinets, knees to his chest, sobbing wildly. Over a month since the murders and this is the first he'd cried.

"I'm sorry," was all he could squeak out between sobs. "Oh God, I'm so sorry."

After everything he had been through with his father, after the murders of his mother and brother, after his sister had been kidnapped, now that he was out of money, unable to pay the rent, he was still a poor writer, and no one else seemed to care that his life had fallen in around him. He would probably lose the apartment and he had nowhere to put his things, so he'd lose all of them, too.

He wiped his eyes on the sleeve of his shirt, then caught sight of a business card lying on the floor, soaking up the spilled coffee.

Mick

555-920-0459

He gingerly picked the sodden card off the floor and

laid it out flat on the tabletop. Memory flooded his mind – an old man, hobbling past him where he sat on the sidewalk. A hand dropping a $100 bill into his can, then giving him a wink when he looked up.

"You're not bad," he'd said, a smile in his voice. "But you could do better. Give me a call sometime, if you're interested in learning how to really work this." And he'd dropped the business card, with only a first name and a phone number, after the money. The gold rings on his aged hands, the fine suit he wore, and the beautiful polished walking stick he carried all pointed to a life spent in different circles.

He'd seen Mick regularly over the next few months, as he made his way in the world after leaving home. The old man had helped him back on his feet, taught him how to panhandle like a real pro, and bought him more than a few meals. When he'd finally gotten an apartment, Mick had paid the first month's rent and told Marcus to call if he needed anything. Of course Mick's past and present connections were an open secret, but he'd never put pressure on Marcus to take part. Not yet, anyway.

Marcus swallowed hard. Then, slowly, as if it would explode if he went too fast, he took out his cell phone and dialed the number.

CHAPTER 7

Toasted

Luke massaged his brow without patience. "What do you mean, you can't meet their demands? It's my brother, you jackass!"

Owen, Chris's underling, stammered about. "But, I-"

"Make it work." Luke lit the cigarette that he held on his lip. "Before I put an end to your...*career.*"

The man started to speak again, but decided better of it and nodded before making a quick exit. Luke shook his head as he drew in on the cigarette. Chris spoke from where he stood, near the door. "We'll find him."

Luke blew smoke from his nostrils. "You'd damn well better. What's so difficult about meeting these demands, anyway?"

Chris took a seat across from him. "They want compensation. They want Viggo."

Luke raised his hand to his brow. "Goddamn it."

"So, you see the difficulty now?" Chris took a cigarette from the open pack lying on the desk and lit it. "If we can catch up with Viggo, maybe we can make the trade. I'm not holding out hope, though. Everything we've found is pointing to Viggo having already made it to Mexico."

"You're not offering me solutions, Chris. Give me solutions."

Chris pulled in on the cigarette. "We could try and get one of their men."

Luke shook his head. "We'll just get him killed. Is there no chance we can track Viggo down?"

"I don't think so. I've got someone on it, regardless. Who knows? Maybe we'll get lucky." Smoke rolled from his mouth. The doorbell rang downstairs, causing both men to jump slightly. Chris's hand moved to the gun that hung at his waist. They could hear a brief exchange between one of their men and the person at the door. Then, the door closed and there were pounding footsteps coming up the stairs. Owen emerged in the doorway, holding a bundled package.

Chris relaxed his hand and Luke sat back in his chair, again drawing on the cigarette.

Owen looked at the two of them for a moment, then shook his head and approached Luke, the package extended toward him. "It's for you, boss."

Chris stood and grabbed the package from his hand. Owen looked surprised, but nodded and made a quick exit. Once the door had closed behind him, Chris laid the package on the desk and extinguished his cigarette in the ashtray. Luke did the same, then picked up the package and looked it over. He weighed it in his hands and listened to it. It was light, so there were probably no significant components inside. An easy shake of the box didn't betray much, other than it sounded like whatever was inside was padded. Once he was satisfied that it was not a bomb or some otherwise deadly object, he pulled the string that tied it together.

The package fell open all at once when the bundling was undone. It was a manila envelope, but something was obviously inside. Luke and Chris exchanged nervous glances. All at once, with a deep breath, Luke dumped the package's contents onto the desk. Chris groaned and placed his hand over his mouth. Luke stood, pushing himself back from the desk. He let out a curse and placed his hands on his hips. The nicotine stain on the fingernail was an identifying mark, but it was the ruby-embossed silver ring that differentiated the finger now lying on the desk as Marc's.

"Damn it!" Luke screamed. "God*damn* it!"

Chris moved to the door and yelled down the stairs. "Owen! Get the fuck up here! Now!" There was the sound of feet pounding up the stairs and Owen appeared in the doorway. His eyes widened at the sight of the finger on the desk. "Who delivered that package?"

"A mailman." Owen's eyes never left the finger.

"A mailman? Well, go find him and bring him back here." Owen nodded, but made no move to leave. His eyes were still transfixed on the finger. Chris grabbed his jaw and forced him to look in his eyes. "Do you understand?" Owen nodded and made a quick exit, his steps again pounding down the stairs. Chris returned to the desk and sat. He pulled the finger closer and examined it.

Luke sat again, opposite him. "Well?"

Chris put the severed digit down. "I can't tell for sure if it's Marc's. My guess is yes, though, going by the ring."

Luke rubbed his brow. "We don't *have him*," he groaned. "I can't give them what I don't have."

Chris shrugged and shook his head.

Luke looked into the distance for a moment, considering his options, weighing the consequences. Suddenly, an idea struck him like a bullet in his chest. "Give them me."

Chris scoffed, and then became serious when he realized Luke was not joking. "You can't be serious."

Luke nodded.

"It's moronic. They'll kill you, and for what?"

Luke shook his head. "They won't kill me. I won't be alone."

Chris looked intrigued. "What are you thinking?"

"Remind me what you did in the Army?"

Chris's brow furrowed. "Marksman. Why?"

Luke nodded, the plan coming into focus. "I'll go in alone, but you'll have a vantage point nearby with a rifle. Once I'm in the door, drop any of them that you see. I'll get one of their guns and try to make my way to Marc. They still may kill him, but they *definitely* will if we wait any longer." Upon seeing Chris still wasn't satisfied, he said, "I'm going to do it whether you help me or not. I would prefer to have some help, though."

Chris massaged his brow. "I don't like it."

Luke scoffed. "No shit, I don't like it either. I don't see another way, though. That is, unless you can track down Viggo. Can you track down Viggo?" He leered at Chris.

The other man fidgeted in his seat before conceding. "I wouldn't count on it."

"Alright, then. Make the call, tell them that they can have me. I gotta be worth something, right?" Luke smiled wryly at Chris and clapped his hands together. "Let's get to work."

CHAPTER 8

A Deal with the Devil

Marcus was standing on the porch of the old house, shifting his weight from one foot to the other almost constantly. It had been difficult for him to make the call that led him here and even harder to actually come.

Until now, Marcus hadn't needed a thing since Mick had set him on his way. Now, though, things were different. Now, he needed money. Thankfully, Mick had agreed to meet with him. So, here he was, standing on the old man's porch. His thoughts were interrupted by the door swinging inward and a kind-looking middle-aged woman appearing in its place.

"Can I help you?" she asked, her voice slightly on-edge.

Marcus stammered, looking for his words. "Um...yes, I..." He gathered himself and took a deep breath. "I'm looking for Mr. Schael."

The woman nodded. "Alright, come on in." And just like that, she disappeared into the house. Marcus followed. The inside of the house was mostly barren, save the pieces of dusty furniture that were sitting around the living room. The entrance room smelled like the inside of an old closet. The air was thick with dust particles that floated in the light that streamed in from the window.

Marcus felt as though he were walking through an old curtain as he made his way through the living room, the kitchen, and into the bedroom. The bedroom smelled much like the rest of the house, with a dash of body odor thrown into the dust mote cocktail. On the bed there was the emaciated figure of a human being, drawn tightly in his old age. The man was gaunt, and thin, white whiskers clung to his cheeks and chin. The hair at the top of his head was nearly gone, but still held on in thin, wiry clumps at his crown. The man's breath came in gasps and wheezes, his skeleton chest rising and falling with each of the few breaths he had left.

Marcus was taken aback. There was no way that this could be the same man that had taken him in and helped him get on his feet. It didn't make sense. Just six months ago, he had seen him. He had been as strong as ever. "Is this...this is Mick?" The words rolled from his mouth like a dog whose tongue was too dry.

The lady nodded. She could see that Marcus was unsatisfied, stuck in a state of disbelief, so she offered further explanation. "Lung cancer. It was inevitable, really, much as he smoked. Always had one o' those cancer sticks on his lip. It's a miracle he made it this far, if you ask me."

Marcus nodded. It was true; Mick always had a cigarette on his lip. "Can I...have a moment alone with him? Just for a minute." The woman looked skeptical, so he added quickly, "I promise, I'll be quick." After a moment's consideration, she nodded.

"You've got five minutes."

When she had gone and the door was closed, Marcus sat on the bed. He placed his hand on Mick's shoulder and gently shook the old, dying man. Mick's eyes fluttered open like the wings of a moth and searched the room. As the withered, cataracted orbs rolled around, seeing what little they could, the decrepit man's breathing became more haggard, as though being awake somehow made the air heavier. As he laid his eyes upon Marcus, he began to smile, toothlessly.

"Marcus." The word came out as a wheeze, devoid of almost all life, yet somehow still managing to sound happy. "I'm glad to see you." With that, Mick fell into a coughing fit. As he recovered, he grabbed Marcus's elbow with one bony, ghostly hand. "Tell me, how are you?"

Marcus forced a smile. "I'm good. How about you?"

Mick laughed hoarsely. "I'm in the best shape of my

life!" He laughed again, and again fell into a coughing fit. When it subsided, he said, "What do you need, Marcus?"

Marcus fidgeted a bit. "My mother and my brother were..." His voice trailed off as he spoke. Tears were gathering in the wings now, and his voice was becoming shaky. "They were..." Again, he was unable to finish the thought. In lieu of words, he simply looked into Mick's eyes. The two men met stares, and understanding crossed between them. Mick blinked, and grasped Marcus's hand tightly.

"Ah, kid, I'm sorry." His voice was low and grainy, like a heavy boot in loose gravel. "Is there anything I can do?"

Marcus swallowed hard before continuing. "My dad got beat up pretty bad. We almost lost him. But he woke up, and he's getting better. But I can't...I can't afford to keep living like this. I need some money to tide me over until he's better and I can work again." He had spoken without taking a breath and when he finished, he sucked air in through his teeth.

Mick blinked and coughed again. He rubbed his jaw. "Son, I can't give you anything. I don't *have* anything." He gestured at the IV pumping drugs into his veins. "The treatment has me pretty tapped out."

Marcus put his hand up. "No, I didn't mean...I just want to know if you can put me in contact with someone who can help me. I know you mentioned before that you used to run with some people in that...business." His eyes pleaded in a way that words could never express.

Mick frowned. "Kid...are you sure this is something you want? These people I know, they can get you some money, but they'll want it back some day. And when they come to collect..." His voice trailed off, but his eyes spoke volumes.

Marcus knew the risks. Or rather, he thought he did. Of course, there was no way to be sure. As far as he could tell, though, there were no other options. "I need this, Mick. I wouldn't ask you if there was any other way."

Mick closed his eyes. "I know, kid. I know. Alright, give me the phone. Then leave. I'll call you later with the details, okay?" Marcus nodded, and handed him the phone. "Good. Now, write down your phone number and give it to Tasha. I'll call you later." As Marcus stood to leave, Mick grabbed him by the arm. "Marcus," he said. "Be careful."

Marcus closed his eyes, and nodded.

Once he was back outside, his feet firmly planted on the sidewalk, the noise of the city bombarding his eardrums, Marcus found himself with a pit in his stomach. He knew what he'd asked had been necessary, but part of him still thought he shouldn't have done it.

Marcus began his plodding course back to the bus stop two blocks away. He took the walk slow; it gave him time to think. When the call came, he would need to make a decision as to whether or not he would follow through. If he took the money, he would eventually have to pay it back, and he didn't have a clue when he would be able to do that. He could see no other option, though. It was either that, or go bankrupt waiting on his father to recover.

Of course, some part of him knew there was another way. But he couldn't do it. He had considered asking his father for money before now, but it was simply not an option. He had spent a year making his own life, and he wasn't going to break down now. He remembered his mother's words.

"You're just like him," she'd said when she came to visit his apartment after he'd moved in. "That's the problem. You're too alike."

Marcus banished the thought and quickened his pace to the bus stop, shoving his hands into his pockets. He no longer wanted to think. Things had been mulled over enough.

CHAPTER 9

Mick

30 Years Ago

The cigarette was half-smoked, smoldering in the bronze ashtray that sat on the old mahogany desk. Ashes decorated the various papers and folders that rested on the knotted old desktop. The office smelled of smoke, the result of God-knows-how-many cigarettes burning into the air. The windows were caked with a thick yellowish substance that stank of old nicotine and the single greasy light in the center of the room gave luminescence to the otherwise dingy office.

The man who sat in the chair normally reserved for guests to the office was large, but not particularly intimidating. He was more of the "long and lanky" type. His voice was deep enough, though, so he could possibly be intimidating over the phone. But not in person. No, definitely not in person.

"Luke's gonna be here any minute." he was saying. Smoke rolled from his mouth, but it was not from a cigarette. No, rather, he was cupping a wooden pipe in his right hand. The pipe's odor was more pleasant, but the taste needed to be acquired. Cigarettes could be smoked by nearly anybody. Pipes took some work.

"And?" The man who owned the office retrieved his cigarette. Before taking a drag, he spoke again. "I'm not scared of Luke Scolessa, Jack. He's a kid, not a gangster." He drew on the cigarette. As always, the taste calmed him.

Jack spoke. "You know, they're saying he's the next big thing. They're saying he's gonna be the next *Basilio*." He puffed on the pipe.

The man behind the desk laughed. It was a deep laugh, and it rolled through the office with a sort of vigor that seemed to linger, even after the laugh had faded. "Right, and I'm the next Mickey Mouse. Look, Jack. It's all gonna work out fine. Luke's gonna come here, we're gonna give him the coke, he's gonna give us the money, and then he's gonna leave." He took another drag off the cigarette, which was burned about three-fourths of the way down. "So stop worrying."

Jack clenched the pipe in his teeth and snorted a chuckle. "You know, Mick, sometimes I think you *want* us to get popped."

Mick smiled as he expelled smoke from his mouth. "That's it, Jack. You've figured me out. I'm undercover." There was a moment of silence before the two men burst out in uproarious laughter. Mick extinguished his cigarette and rolled another. As he did so, he registered a car flying past on the street below his window. Out of instinct, he reached for the revolver that was strapped to the underside of his desk. But it roared off into nothing, and he moved his hand away from the gun, silently admonishing himself for being reactionary.

"Actually, you know what?" Mick returned to the gun, pulling it free from its holster and setting it on the desk. "This might be a nice conversation piece to show our new friend."

The polished black barrel and chamber shone in the light that swung over the desk. The grip was deep brown Maplewood, shaped and worn to perfection. It was heavy, almost a club in its own right. The chamber contained nine .38 caliber shells, all Grim Reaper's scythes waiting to be swung.

The knock on the door caused Jack to start, but Mick remained calm. He placed his cigarette in the ashtray before standing and buttoning his jacket. "Come in," he said. Jack remained in the chair, lounging with one leg swung over the other, his foot bobbing to some unreal tune. The doorknob turned, squeaking ever so slightly as it did. As it swung open, Mick got his first glimpse of the Syndicate's golden boy. Luke Scolessa stood roughly five and a half feet tall.

His head was covered in a thick mop of black hair, haphazardly combed into something that resembled a style. Spotty stubble decorated his cheeks and chin. In general, he was a thin, gangly teenage boy, not yet comfortable in his own skin.

He stepped into the office and stood in front of the door after he had closed it. He spread his legs to shoulder width and stood straight up, his arms descending in a 'V' to clenched hands at his waist. When he spoke, it was clear that he was trying to hide a Brooklyn accent, but it was too thick. "I'm here for the product."

Mick chuckled a bit and sat down, offering a seat to the boy. "Sit, please." He retrieved his cigarette and made an offertory gesture toward Luke. "You want one?" he said.

Luke swung his head from side to side in a silent 'no.' He sat down, still looking awkward, though less so now. His eyes caught the revolver as he sat, and widened a bit at the sight of the beautiful gun. Mick knew that it would be an effective method of keeping the boy in check. He threw the gangly boy a sly smile. Luke responded to this smile with unmasked contempt.

"Lighten up." Mick said after a moment or two. "We're all friends here."

"It's not my job to be your *friend*." Luke's voice dripped with hatred. "It's my job to get the product and get back to the front business."

"No, *that's* where you're *wrong*, Luke!" Mick slammed his hand down on the desk, causing Luke to give a start. Jack simply sat and puffed on his pipe. "Your *job* is to do what you're told!" He was screaming now.

Luke was eyeing the gun. His muscles were tense, his knuckles white in his grip on the chair. Mick's eyes flicked down to the pistol just as Luke's hand lashed out for it, a small scream bursting from his mouth. Jack stood, grabbing Luke by the elbow and slamming his shoulder into the desk. Standing over him, pipe in his mouth, Jack was in complete control. Mick picked up the gun and pressed the barrel into the kid's forehead, from which veins were now popping, red and bulging.

Spittle flew from Luke's mouth as his eyes struggled to get a good look at his captors. Mick leaned down to look in the boy's eyes. "Listen, Luke." Mick drew on his cigarette, expelling smoke from his nostrils. "The Syndicate knows me. They know me well. But *I'm* the one who's in the business of information. The sign on the door when you walked in said 'Schael and Wilson: *Private Detectives.*' Now, 'Private Detectives' insinuates a certain type of business. I don't make a living if I'm no good. And I make a *very* good living." Luke's eyes were still darting from side to side, feverishly. Mick smiled as he continued. He was whispering now, deathly quiet. "I know *everything* about you, Luke. You, and your boss, and his boss, and that guy's boss, all the way up to the damn *Basilio*. So, Jack here lets you up and I take this gun off of you, I need your assurance that you're gonna be calm, and we're gonna do business like grown men. Okay?" No response. "*I said*, okay?" Luke nodded, begrudgingly.

Mick nodded to Jack, who released Luke and again let his hand take hold of his pipe. The boy stood and brushed off his sleeves, adjusting his collar and tie. His nostrils flared and his mouth clenched. His fists were held in tight balls, white with pressure. The muscles in his arms were knotted and corded, pulsing with every breath, each of which was clearly audible in the small office. Jack chuckled lightly and slapped him on the back before sitting back down. Luke remained standing.

"Now, Luke. Back to the issue at hand." said Mick, taking a drag on his cigarette before extinguishing it and breathing the smoke from his mouth. "You say you want the product. Is that right?"

Luke nodded slowly, still standing.

"Well, that's fine and dandy. But I need something, too. I need money. And I see that you don't have a bag with you and, well..." Mick looked Luke up and down. "There's no way you have that much in your pockets." He chuckled, rolling another smoke. "So, you can see that we're at an impasse here." He lit his cigarette and drew in. He made a shrugging motion. "Any ideas as to how we can resolve this situation?" In his free hand, Mick held the revolver in a ready grip, his finger laying loosely alongside the trigger.

Luke adjusted his collar again and slid his hand over his hair, attempting to style it, but it was a futile attempt. He looked around the office, toward the door. "It's in the car."

Mick laughed. "Right, right. And what, you want us to follow you out there? Then two of your guys are gonna jump out of the car and unload on us?" He examined Luke. The boy wouldn't hold eye contact and seemed fidgety. "No...no, this is personal, isn't it?" Suddenly, it seemed to fall into place. "*You! You* were supposed to do it!" He laughed again, heartily. "We're your initiation! Your ticket into the family! Wow, I must say, it is *quite* an honor, isn't it Jack?" Jack laughed as well.

Luke appeared to grow even angrier, if that were possible. "The money's in the goddamned car." He looked incredulously at Jack and Mick. "You assholes. What the hell is wrong with you two?" He turned and headed for the door, stomping all the way. He looked back once before slamming the door behind him.

Jack waited a beat before speaking. "That went well, don't you think?"

Mick frowned slightly. "He's a pissy little kid who doesn't know to fold when he's got no hand. He'll learn, though." He took a drag on the cigarette and knocked the ash off into the ashtray.

A wordless minute passed. Jack opened his mouth to speak, but was interrupted by the door to the office slamming open again. It banged against the wall loudly. Jack stood, his pipe dropping to the floor as he ripped a snub-nose .38 revolver from the holster hooked into the back of his waistband. In the doorframe stood a thick-chested man, broad in the shoulders, dressed in a white dress shirt and black suit coat. He held a nine millimeter pistol in his right hand. As he stepped into the office, he began to bring the pistol to bear, but Jack was faster. The revolver was already pointed at the man.

Mick raised his gun and leveled it at the man in the doorway.

"Now, just hold it right there." A moment passed between the three men.

The man in the doorway's eyes darted from Jack to Mick and back again. When he spoke, his voice was grizzled and low. A thick accent covered his words, but Mick was unable to discern its origin. "This is the way it has to be." He turned to Mick. "You of all people should know that."

"Fuck you." Mick's voice took on a vinegary tone. "I

know how this works. I *also* know that your guy has to earn his spot." They glared at each other furiously. "So let *him* earn it."

The man lowered his gun after a moment of hesitation and stepped to the side. Luke stepped into sight. He took the gun from the man and looked at it. The gun looked unnatural in his hand, as though it were too large for him. Wordlessly, he lifted the weapon and pointed it at Jack. His breathing became rapid and haggard. After three heartbeats, he breathed deep, readying himself. Jack didn't give him the chance.

The snubnose sounded like a cannon in the small office. Jack's shot caught Luke in the shoulder, causing him to fire wildly in response. Jack stumbled back against the wall, firing again, but this one went wide and thudded into the wall in a puff of plaster.

Mick aimed down the barrel of his gun at the grizzled man who had kicked in his door. The gun kicked like a horse and the gunshot deafened him as the man crumpled to the floor in a heap. Luke managed to catch himself on the door frame, bringing his gun to bear on Mick. As he fired, Mick dropped behind the desk, the bullet whizzing over his head and shattering the large window behind him. The glass fell to the street in a cacophony.

Jack was nearly behind the desk by now, crawling

slowly. The bullet had caught him in top of his right leg, and it was bleeding badly. Luke pulled the trigger three times in rapid succession. Each bullet collided with the thick mahogany desk and stuck there, failing penetration. After the third shot, Mick heard the kid take off running, his footsteps echoing down the hall. A minute later, a black car screamed past underneath the now empty window.

Mick was breathing heavily. He glanced to Jack, who threw him a painful smile that more resembled a grimace. The large revolver felt heavy in his hand, so he placed it back on the desk. He helped Jack into a chair and then took his own seat. His cigarette still sat smoldering in the ashtray, so he retrieved it and breathed deep.

"How's the leg?" He asked after a moment.

Jack grimaced as he spoke, gingerly laying his hand on the bleeding wound. "Been better. Been worse, too."

"You need a doctor."

Jack laughed humorlessly. "You know of one that works for coke?"

Mick smiled. "I know of one that doesn't ask questions."

After a couple of seconds' deliberation, Jack nodded. "Let's go." As they were heading out the door, Jack hanging on Mick's neck, hopping along on his one good leg, he spoke again. "What do you think is gonna happen with the boy?"

Mick stopped for a moment and wheezed out a few

breaths. "I think he'll redeem himself and we'll do a lot of business in the future. A little more peacefully, I hope." Both men laughed.

Jack regarded the body of the unknown man who had kicked in the door. "What about him?"

"I'll deal with him after I drop you off with the doc."

"Mick, be careful. You never know, they may go for us again."

"You're the one who should be worried. *You* were the target." More wheezing as they made for the single flight of stairs that led to the door.

Jack grunted in pain as they took the first step. "I'll be fine. You're a bigger prize. And I can handle myself."

Mick laughed slightly as they hopped down the second step. "I can tell by the way you took that bullet."

"Fuck you." They both laughed.

Mick was alone in the office. Jack was with the doctor, and the doctor would do his work silently, as always. The body was easily enough disposed of; as it was with everything else, there was a guy for that sort of thing. The window would cost a shit-ton to fix, but that's how things go sometimes.

The wind blew through the window and rustled his hair. It was late, and the city was sleeping.

Now

Mick groaned and coughed up bloody spittle as he adjusted himself on the bed. When he had his breath back, he tried to lay still and avoid any sudden movements or exertions that might cause him to fall into another fit.

"Goddammit," he cursed. "What a mess."

He rubbed his eyes with aging hands and wondered, not for the first time, if he'd done the right thing. Luke would get his message, but at what cost? Marcus was so promising, but this might get him killed. Or worse yet, it may force him into a life he never wanted.

Mick sighed, coughed again, cursed again.

Nothing to be done about it now, he thought. *He's gonna get what he asked for.*

CHAPTER 10

Coalescence

Darkness was encapsulating as Luke lay awake in his bed. Sleep was difficult on the eve of his attempt at rescuing Marc. His mind was racing, flashing thoughts of what the next day could entail. Part of him was sure that he would never return to this house. Another part of him, though, was positive that not only would he return; he would return as a hero, his brother by his side.

But that was for tomorrow. Now, he needed to sleep.

Daylight came too quickly. Luke woke with the sun, at 6:30 in the morning. There was no gradual waking. Instead, he was immediately awake. He swung his feet out over the side of the bed and stood, rubbing the back of his neck.

As he opened the curtains, the sun flooded the room, outlining floating dust particles in the air. The light was blinding, and caused Luke to squint his eyes. It seemed fitting in some way, for the sun to be so bright on this morning, of all mornings. Perhaps it had always been this bright, and he simply hadn't noticed it. The air felt heavy, despite the room's constant temperature of 68 degrees, and Luke found that he was sweating.

He picked up the pack of cigarettes from the bedside table and placed one on his lip. Lighting it, he instinctively took in a draw of hot smoke. The end of the cigarette flared, and then faded as he expelled the smoke into the air. Luke tossed the lighter back onto the table, along with the cigarette pack and sat on the edge of the bed, massaging his eyelids. It was mornings like this that he felt older than he was. In truth, the two packs a day for the last twenty five years probably didn't help. But he felt so *tired* now.

There was a knock at the door, rousing him from his thoughts.

"Yeah?" said Luke sleepily.

Chris spoke on the other side of the door. "Just making sure you're up. Still good to leave in an hour?"

Luke sighed and rubbed his eyes. This was it. "Alright. I'll meet you downstairs." Chris's steps echoed away from the door and down the steps, once again leaving Luke alone with his thoughts. This was what he had truly dreaded. The silence. When everyone else left, it was always just going to be him, alone, in a room. And that's what it would be today, too. He would walk into that house alone, and he would either walk out with Marc, or he wouldn't walk out at all.

Luke stood and dressed himself. He wore a black button down shirt, tucked into a pair of black slacks, polished black shoes, and a black suit-coat. He slicked his hair back with pomade, and shaved the stubble that had been growing over the past couple of days on his cheeks and chin. The whole process seemed to Luke to be eerily similar to the way that a mortician would prepare a body for viewing.

Luke came down the stairs in forty-five minutes, dressed to kill or be killed. Chris was standing at the door, impatiently tapping his foot. The room fell deadly silent when Luke came down the stairs. They could see a look in his eyes unlike what they had seen before. He was on a mission today, and had no time for the typical banter that took place between his men.

Chris was the first one to speak. "Here." He extended a hand, holding a black semi-automatic pistol. "Take this."

Luke shook his head. "I don't want it. They'll just make me give it up."

"Take it. You might get lucky. You just need to get in the door, anyway." He shook the weapon.

Luke sighed. "Fine. If you insist." He took the gun and checked the magazine, which was full. Then he shoved it in the back of his waistband and looked at Chris. "Satisfied?"

Chris scoffed and turned to his men. "You park four blocks away and stay out of sight. You don't say anything.

Radio silence, people. You don't follow us. You find your own way there. If they think something's up, we're fucked. This is, as much as I hate to admit it, our best chance to get Marc back. We do it now, or we die trying." He looked his people over. "So, let's make it happen." He turned to Luke. "Ready?"

Luke inhaled deeply. "As I'll ever be." As they headed out the door and toward the cars, his mind began to run wild. It was time now to do the act and, like it was his first job, he was hesitating. His heart was pounding, and his breath was coming in weak, shallow wheezes. He lit a cigarette and drew deep. It calmed his shaking hands, and steadied his rapid heart. His drag was so hard that it burned his tongue. It didn't matter; it was the only thing that would calm him.

The ride was hell. With every bump of the road, Luke jumped as if he had been shot. It was odd to him, being alone in the car. It had been so long. Now, it was always full of two or three bodyguards, not to mention whoever had business with him, if in fact anyone did. The silence now, though, was pervasive. It resonated, shaking him to his core.

He moved to massage his brow and found that his hand was shaking. "No, not now," he said to himself. "Gotta stay steady. Gotta bring Marc home."

On some level, Luke had always been able to count on his hands being steady enough to get him out of a sticky situation. Now, though, when he needed them more than ever, he couldn't seem to calm himself. He lit another cigarette. It helped, but he knew deep down that nothing would focus him like the overdose of adrenaline waiting in his veins.

He made the final turn and headed down the street toward the house. He knew Chris had taken a back way and was perched on a building across the street, like they had planned when they'd come and scouted the place out the day before. The plan was solid. Risky, but solid. Their execution needed to be flawless.

And the house was in sight now. Luke pulled the car to the curb and put it in park. He pulled the emergency brake, mostly so he didn't have to get out just yet. A quick glance in Chris's direction. Of course, he couldn't see his right-hand man, perched atop the adjacent building, sniper rifle carefully aimed in his direction. That was the point, after all.

As soon as Luke opened the door, he was accosted by two men, one dark-skinned, one white as fresh snow.

"Come on," said the larger of the two, a behemoth of a man, tribal and prison tattoos spiraling down his rippling arms, and long, thick dreadlocks hanging from his boulder of a head. His accent sounded African.

Luke lifted his arms without protest, and the smaller of the men, still large in his own right, but dwarfed by his companion, began to frisk him. He laid his hand on the pistol that was stuffed into Luke's waistband and pulled it out. He laughed slightly.

"Oh, so this is how it is, huh? You wanna take advantage of our goodwill by bringing a gun to our home?" He pistol-whipped Luke across the face, sending him to the sidewalk. A split-second later, he was being hauled back up, and the man was inches from his face. His breath stank, and his teeth were rotten – from methamphetamine abuse, Luke assumed. "Listen here. I can rip your fucking head off if I want to. So don't test me. Do you understand?"

Luke managed a weak nod and a grunt.

The man smiled his rotten smile. "Good." He almost crooned. "Now, let's go see your brother." The larger man came and took Luke by one arm, dragging him into the house.

This is it, Luke thought. He was waiting for Chris to begin shooting. It was time now to be a hero. It was time to mount the rescue.

No shots came.

Luke's heart began pounding, which caused his head to ache. Something had happened. There was a reason that

Chris hadn't fired. Whatever it was, Luke was going to need to improvise. He looked at the huge man that was dragging him along. The man had shoved his pistol back into his waistband. The smaller man had both Luke's pistol and his own.

Alright, then, he thought. *Time to call an audible.*

He began slapping the enormous man's arm with his free hand. After a couple of seconds, he stopped walking and looked at Luke.

"What is it?" his accent was thicker than Luke had initially thought.

"I...I..." Luke was putting on a show about his head wound. "...bathroom. Bathroom..." He gripped his stomach and gagged a little.

The large man looked at the smaller one. "What do you want to do?"

The little one grimaced. "Yeah, take him to the bathroom. I don't want him throwing up on the boss's shoes" And he continued on walking. Luke paid careful attention to his direction. At the end of the hall, he took a left, and then it sounded as though he descended some steps to a door, which opened and closed.

The large man went a different direction, dragging Luke with him. Once they were in the bathroom, the man let him go as he pushed him toward the toilet. As soon as he did,

Luke spun and cracked him in the jaw. The punch was solid, knocking the big man off balance for a beat, allowing Luke to go for the gun shoved in his waistband. When it was free, he clocked him in the back of the head with the gun's butt. The big man stumbled forward and hit his head on the toilet. As he fell to the floor, Luke lifted a foot and brought it down on his head. One, two, three, four times. The man's cries of protest were lost in the garble of blood and bone that filled his mouth. As soon as he stopped fighting and fell still, Luke collapsed against the wall, partially from exhaustion, partially from the vertigo caused by his head wound. The man was twitching slightly.

Luke wiped his shoe on the man's shirt and moved toward the door. He opened it as quietly as possible, then stepped out and proceeded down the hallway, the direction the smaller man had gone before. As silently as possible, he began down the steps toward the basement. He felt the sweat beading on his forehead. The salt from his perspiration mixed with the blood from his wound and caused a painful reaction that helped keep him from drifting into delirium from the throbbing in his head.

As he reached the basement door, he stopped. His hand hovered over the doorknob. *This is it,* he thought. *Do or die, Luke. Do or die.*

With a deep breath, he gripped the knob and turned.

The door flung open wildly, and Luke stepped into the room, gun raised. He found himself standing in a dank, unfinished basement, the concrete walls and floor coated with a layer of grime from lack of upkeep. Two concrete support pillars decorated the interior of the room. Beyond that, the room was unfurnished. A single lightbulb in the center of the room provided a greasy yellow light, which was buoyed by two floor lamps pushed back in corners. In that ugly little room, Luke found three men, all armed with pistols that were holstered. The smaller man from earlier leaned against the wall, fiddling with the gun he had taken from Luke. And, in the center of the room, sat the man Luke was looking for. Marc was tied to a chair, but there was too little light in the room by which to see his face.

The men all turned to look at Luke, who was already bringing his gun to bear on one of them. He squeezed the trigger and his target stumbled back, reaching for his own gun. Luke fired another shot, catching him in the stomach. He collapsed, sliding down the wall with a scream as he frantically tried to stop the blood pouring from his belly.

Luke caught movement to his right and spun that direction, firing as he moved. The shot was wide, but it gave him a moment as his new target ducked away behind a concrete support pillar.

By now, the other men had their guns turned on Luke.

He ducked as a shot went over his head, and then took off running toward the room's other support beam. As he slid behind it, he heard a bullet catch the other side, sending a sharp reverberation through the room. From behind cover, Luke could sit safely in the midst of the deafening gunfire. His thoughts turned ever so briefly to Marc, who sat tied to a chair a few feet away. He was vulnerable. Luke gritted his teeth, then spun out from his cover.

He fired wildly as he ran toward the two remaining thugs. They either couldn't hear him approaching or didn't dare risk themselves in the hail of wild gunfire. Luke rounded the corner of the support beam to find one of them looking the wrong way. A quick bullet to the head dropped him.

One left, Luke thought.

A gunshot reverberated through the room as Luke felt something slam into his right arm. He screamed and dropped his gun, looking up in time to see the man who'd searched him upstairs advancing, gun drawn. He was smiling, his mouth of black teeth making Luke's stomach turn.

"You. Fucking. *Asshole,*" he seethed. "I should probably wait on the boss, but..." he trailed off as he looked to where Marc was sitting, still tied to the chair.

Luke realized his brother had sat through that entire

exchange without making so much as a move to help.

Oh, fratello, he thought. *What have they done to you?*

The meth-head was speaking again. "...I think we can make do with just one Scolessa brother." He turned, pistol levelled at Marc, and Luke spied his own gun shoved in the man's waistband. He reached up with his left hand, taking hold of the pistol's grip, and squeezed the trigger without even pulling it out. The thug screamed, dropping his gun as he reached back to grab at Luke's hand.

Luke wrenched the gun from the waistband and fired it point-blank into the thug's back three times, dropping him like a bag of rocks. He was still whimpering as Luke climbed to his feet. Another shot put an end to that.

And that was it. All of them, dead. And somehow, inexplicably, Luke was still alive. There was a muffled noise off to his left that caused Luke to spin and lift his weapon before remembering that it was Marc. He ran over to his hostage brother and dropped to his knees, bringing him to eye level. He quickly removed the bag from the man's head and was taken aback at what he saw.

Marc's face was hardly recognizable. He was bloodied and beaten. His hair hung in clumps from his scalp and his nose appeared to be broken. His lips were busted and swollen from what appeared to be multiple punches to the face. Several of his teeth were knocked out. The most astonishing feature, though, were the empty holes where his eyes had once been. They had been removed, and not gently. There were marks around his eye sockets that seemed reminiscent of the claw on the back of a nail hammer. He had been tortured mercilessly.

Luke cursed himself. *Why did I wait so long?*

"Marc," he spoke softly. "Marc. Marc, can you hear me?" His brother tried to speak, whereupon Luke realized his tongue had been cut out as well. *Motherfucker. This is more than these guys would usually do.* "Marc, it's me. It's Luke. Come on. Let's get you out of here." He picked up a knife that was lying nearby and cut his brother's bindings. "Can you walk?"

Marc whimpered in a manner that sounded like a "no." Luke sighed and shoved his gun into the back of his waistband. He then looped one arm under Marc's legs and another underneath his arms. Marc's cries of protest were getting louder and louder and he was now shaking his head.

"Marc. Marc, what the fuck? What do you need?" Luke plopped his brother back down in the chair.

"He's trying to tell you there's a pressure controlled switch underneath the chair that's going to blow this entire place to kingdom come." The voice coming from behind Luke was far too familiar. Luke tried to reach for his gun, but the man spoke again. "Now, why don't you toss your gun on the ground for me?"

Luke sighed. *Shit.* Begrudgingly, he removed the gun from his waistband and tossed it on the ground about five feet away. It skidded to a stop against a support beam.

"Now, hands on your head and turn around slowly."

Luke complied. As he turned, he saw he'd been correct. And a new anger, burning white-hot, ignited in his chest.

Before him, standing on the stairs, brandishing a shining, chrome pistol, was Chris.

CHAPTER 11

To Find the Beauty of Things

C ole held the newspaper tightly in his hands, his reading glasses down on the bridge of his nose. As per usual, he found none of the news to be good. Especially now, only a week and a half after his awakening to find a world devoid of any beauty, he was not in a mindset which allowed him to take much pleasure in things.

He folded the paper and placed it on his lap, at the same time removing his glasses and laying them on the bedside table. They tended to give him headaches ever since his injury, of which he still had only foggy memories. That was the most frustrating part, he decided. Not only was he unable to protect his family, he couldn't even remember their deaths. The funerals had been held while he was comatose, so he wasn't even able to say goodbye to them. No, when he awoke, the only notification he had was Marcus's attempt to console him.

And then there was *that* mess. Marcus and Cole Traeger had never been particularly close, but now they were forced to be father and son again, and to unite and help each other in the search for their family's killer. Marcus was throwing his life down the drain, and Cole couldn't help but try and dive in after him, no matter how old his son was, be it 19 or 90.

That was what Marcus couldn't seem to grasp. Cole didn't come down on him hard because he was disappointed or angry. He did it because he was worried. Marcus was sure that Cole simply hated him and his way of thinking about things, but that couldn't have been further from the truth. He was an incredibly bright child, and everyone always knew that he had great things ahead of him, but Cole always felt that it was more beneficial to him to keep him grounded, and his head out of the clouds. Not for the first time, he was considering the possibility that he had been wrong in how he went about it.

There was a knock at the door, causing Cole to look up suddenly. This action set his head to spinning. The stranger knocked again, more eagerly this time.

"Mr. Traeger?" came a voice from the other side of the door. "Mr. Traeger, it's Detectives Faraday and Kirkpatrick."

Again? Cole closed his eyes. "Yeah, come in."

The door swung open, and Faraday's tall, gaunt figure stood framed in its absence. After a moment, he proceeded into the room, Kirkpatrick trailing by a couple of feet, as always. He sauntered toward the bed in his typical manner and sat in the chair next to it. Kirkpatrick remained standing.

After a moment, Faraday spoke. "Mr. Traeger. How are you doing?" His voice was smooth, and it was obvious from the way that he spoke that he had news of some sort.

"Detectives." Cole regarded them coolly. Regardless of the news they carried, Cole hated the way Faraday considered himself to be a step above everyone else in the room. He knew, however, that he had to remain on their good side – at least, their amicable side – if he ever wanted Katie to be found, or his family's killer brought to justice. "I'm doing well. How are you?"

"You look like you're recovering nicely." Faraday crossed his legs and leaned back in the chair. "Well, we have some good news for you." He waited for a moment, as if looking for Cole's reaction, or expecting him to beg for the news. Upon receiving nothing but an intrigued smile, he continued. "We think we know who's behind the murder of your wife and son, and the kidnapping of your daughter."

Another pause. "Okay, then." Cole said. "Who is it?"

Faraday held his hand out to Kirkpatrick, who produced

a manila folder and handed it to him. He glanced inside before handing it on to Cole, who took it anxiously. His heart was pounding now, as he thumbed the edges of the folder. Inside, the face of his family's murderer awaited him. He'd finally look on the face that had taken his entire life from him and reduced him to little more than a vegetable for the past five and a half weeks. He took a deep breath and flipped it open. Inside, he looked upon a criminal record and a photo. A young man, hair a mess, about a week's worth of scrabbly beard on his face. His expression was calm, but his eyes betrayed anger, a rage deep inside him. It was clear, staring into those cold agates that this man held little in the way of remorse or compassion.

Suddenly, like a flood ripping through a house, it came back to him. This man had been in the store the day of the murders. He had looked him right in the eye, handed him his change, and flashed him a smile as he went on his way. He could feel his anxiety building, welling up inside of him. He had been within a couple of *feet* of his family's killer, and hadn't even known. Cole let his eyes drift over to the man's name: Viggo Lassiter.

Faraday spoke again, upon seeing Cole's reaction to the file. "What's wrong?"

Cole tried to articulate what was racing through his

mind, but he found it difficult. "I...I...I've seen him. I've seen him!"

Now Faraday was concerned. His former cockiness had vanished and he seemed genuinely interested. Kirkpatrick was making his way back to the bed. "Where? Where did you see him?"

"In the store! In the store! He was in the store the day that...that he..."

Faraday turned to Kirkpatrick. They exchanged excited glances. "Mr. Traeger."

Cole didn't respond.

"Cole!" Faraday placed his arms on Cole's shoulders and forcibly turned him to look in his eyes. "Cole. I need the security tapes from your store."

"Take them," Cole said, biting off the end of the words. He had looked at the devil's face and hadn't even had an inkling of an idea that he was evil. As Faraday was turning to leave, Cole grabbed his arm. "Faraday." The detective turned to look at him. "Bring my daughter home."

Faraday nodded, then ran out the door, Kirkpatrick following close behind, leaving Cole to his thoughts. The implications of what had happened were beginning to sink in. Viggo Lassiter was the man responsible for the death of his wife and son and the kidnapping of his daughter. He had looked him in the eye, and hadn't even thought he seemed 'off.' The memory was fuzzy, possibly due to his head trauma, but Cole remembered that he had seemed anxious to leave. Who knew his reasons? It didn't matter to Cole. He wanted Lassiter in prison, and he wanted to be there when they shoved the needle in his arm, no matter how long it took.

It was then that his thoughts turned to Marcus. Cole reached for the phone on his bedside table and punched out the numbers for Marcus's cell phone. It rang once before his eldest son picked up.

"Hello?" He sounded anxious.

"Hey."

There was a long sigh on the other end of the line. "Hey, Dad. What's going on?"

Cole took a deep breath. "The detectives just left."

Marcus's breath caught in his throat, and his voice was tense when he spoke again. "What did they say?"

"They think they know who did it." Cole closed his eyes and swallowed. The inevitable question was coming.

"Really? Who?" Marcus sounded excited. Cole understood. They finally had someone to go chase, someone to direct their fury at.

"His name is Viggo Lassiter." There was a long pause before Cole spoke again. "Son, I have to tell you something."

"Yeah, okay. What?"

He breathed deep. After a moment, he nearly blurted it out. When he spoke, he spoke quickly. "He was in the store earlier that day. He looked me in the eye. I don't..."

No one spoke for a long time. Finally, Marcus said, "It's not your fault."

Cole was surprised at Marcus's reaction. He had expected him to be angry, to blame him. Instead, he responded with empathy and understanding. "I know, son. Thank you."

"It's alright." There was a *beep* on the other line. "Oh, Dad, I have to take this. I'm going to head back to the hospital soon, okay?" Another *beep*.

"Okay, Son. I'll see you later."

"Seeya." And he was gone. Cole placed the phone back on the receiver and sat back in his bed. For the first time since he had woken up, he felt alive.

CHAPTER 12

With Blind Hope and Dumb Luck

Chris was standing a little taller than normal. A side effect of double-crossing your boss and pointing a gun at him, Luke supposed. He seemed so cocky now, so righteous.

Yeah, go on and bask in the glow, you son of a bitch. I will rip your throat out before we're done here. Luke was standing still, his gun on the floor and out of reach, his maimed brother sitting on top of a bomb behind him, and his right hand man pointing a gun at his head.

Fuck me, this went poorly.

"Luke, why don't I just put a bullet in you right now?" Chris was smiling as he spoke, advancing down the stairs step-by-step.

"Well, if I had to venture a guess, I'd say you're chicken shit." Luke regarded him with pure, unabated hatred.

Chris chuckled. "Well, I suppose you're entitled to that

opinion. It remains to be seen, though."

"Look, shithead, just get on with it. You've won. You've got me where you want me." Luke shook his hands in mock celebration. "You want a parade?"

Chris shook his head. "No, I *want* your organization."

Luke laughed. "I hate to tell you, but there's not much of it left. I haven't exactly been able to conduct a lot of business these last few weeks, as you know."

"Oh, I know. But the Scolessa name still holds *some* weight. If I take over, I could use your reputation to build the organization again. I could get it back to what it was in the glory days of the Syndicate." Chris's voice had a starry tinge to it, like a child who had just met his favorite baseball player.

"Kid, I was around back then, I was *part* of the Syndicate. It wasn't all that people make it out to be. If you had pulled this shit on them, you would've already been dead."

Chris laughed. "Right. Okay, then. It doesn't matter. We all know that you don't exactly have a multitude of options here, *Luca*." The use of his Italian name sent shivers down Luke's spine.

"You little shit."

Chris bowed mockingly. "Thank you, sir."

Luke scoffed. "So, tell me. How did you pull it off?

When did they come to you? What was their offer?"

"Well, after we escaped the first time, I got a phone call. Someone wanted to meet with me. So I went. They offered me your organization, if I could help bring you down. They just wanted revenge on you for what Viggo did. The rest is history, really. You made it pretty easy, if I'm being honest." Chris stepped off the last stair, onto flat ground. He was now at eye level with Luke.

"So, you just waited for me to do what you knew I would always do. You waited for me to get angry, which I did. And then you played along with it." Luke smiled a bit. "Not bad, to tell the truth." He sighed. "But I have to ask. Why? You had a good life, working for me, right?" He tried to keep the hurt from his voice, but he couldn't help it sneaking in, just like his accent always did.

Chris's smile turned to a snarl in an instant. "Because *you*-" He gestured toward Luke with the gun. "-you fucking idiot, you would've been dead ten times over, if not for me. And still you act as though I'm just another hired gun." He calmed himself somewhat, stifling his anger. "I wanted more, Luke. But I'm not a *Scolessa*, so I might as well be dirt under your shoe." He punctuated Luke's last name by pointing again.

Chris was only a couple feet from Luke now, drawn toward the object of his hatred.

"And now you'll get to see me run your organization better than you could've ever hoped." He smiled. Luke smiled, too, turning Chris's into a confused frown. Luke took one step toward his underling, just enough to disrupt his aim. The gun sounded with a *bang* and a flash, but the bullet just grazed Luke's shoulder as he ducked and launched himself, catching Chris around the ribs in a spear tackle that drove the air from his lungs.

As they landed on the hard concrete floor, the gun went careening off into the dark. Luke straddled Chris, punching down hard.

"You-" Punch. "Think-" Punch. "You-" Punch. "can kill *me*?" More punches. Chris put his arms up to guard his face, but Luke still made contact all around his head and neck. Finally, the pain from the bullet he'd taken to the arm earlier forced him to eschew punches. He reached down and wrapped his hands around Chris's throat. The former right-hand man was clawing at Luke's face, so he gave his head two quick slams into the concrete to make him less difficult.

As Luke squeezed, the fight went out of Chris. And when he stopped breathing, his eyes bulging and staring at Luke from a face turned ugly purple and red, the old gangster felt just a pang of sadness. He should've seen it coming. He knew he'd taken advantage of Chris's skills, but that's how it was, being the boss. Still, he had to admit it hurt.

He turned to Marc, and his stomach immediately tied itself into knots. His brother, his little brother sat there, whimpering, unable to see, unable to speak. He approached him.

"Marc? How're you doing, buddy?" Luke's voice sounded far away after the gunshots and brawl earlier. It was hard to hear himself speak.

Marc pathetically whimpered out his reply, which Luke could not interpret.

"I...I know. I-" Luke was cut off by voices upstairs. It sounded as though they had just burst in and discovered the dead man in the bathroom. They would be coming downstairs momentarily. Luke knew that there was no way he could fight his way out in his current condition. He looked around the room, desperately searching for an exit. Eventually, his eyes fell upon a door in the back corner. His only hope.

Then he looked back to Marc. There was no way to take him, too, even if he *could* get him off of the chair. Marc seemed to understand. Something about being brothers, he suspected. They had always known what the other was thinking.

"Marc," he said. His voice was drenched in sadness, the heaviness of his heart. He felt as though he could throw up, but there was no time now. The adrenaline was still pumping in his veins, and he needed all of his energy and awareness to get out of here alive. "I need your help." Marc nodded. "When these men come in here, I need you to... to..." He sighed. "I can't take you with me. You know that, right?" After a moment, Marc nodded solemnly. "So, you know what I need you to do, right?" Again, he nodded. Before he turned to leave, Luke placed a kiss on Marc's forehead and said a quick prayer for his soul. "Goodbye, *fratello*." And with that, he turned and left.

Luke sprinted for the door, tears stinging his eyes. As he pounded back up the stairs, out of the dank tomb of a basement, he registered shouting and heavy footsteps in the house above. He burst through the door at the top of the steps, rounding the corner and heading for the outside without looking back. Shouting followed him, and then a few stray bullets. Luke kept running.

No looking back, he thought.

He burst outside into the cold gray light of the afternoon. The street was nearly abandoned, save Luke's own car. He ripped the door open and dove inside. In a second, he was tearing away from the house, his tires squealing and the acrid smell of burnt rubber filling his nose. He was no more than fifty feet down the street when the explosion went off. From here, it was a dull *thud* that signified the end of his brother's life, but he knew hellfire had been unleashed down in that basement. A glance in his rearview mirror told Luke the house itself was catching fire now.

With tears pouring down his cheeks, Luke focused his eyes ahead and drove on.

CHAPTER 13

The Mad Whore

Marcus blinked furiously in an attempt to force his eyes to adjust to the sudden darkness as he stepped into the dusty warehouse. As his sight focused, he realized he was not the only one in the room. Roughly fifty feet from him stood three men, two of them with that overly serious look about them that assured Marcus they were security. The man that stood in between them, though, was of a different breed. He stood about six feet tall, and was dressed in a plaid suit, like something out of the 70's. His hair was slicked back smartly and his face was clean shaven. His mouth adorned his face in a wild smile and his eyes sat locked in an emotionless stare that seemed to Marcus as though it were cutting through him.

"Hello there!" The man exclaimed. "I assume that you are Mr. Traeger?"

Marcus swallowed hard at the mention of his name. He had given them a fake name, so how this man had come across his true identity, he had no idea. "That's not my name." His eyes gave away whatever his quaking voice didn't, he knew.

The man frowned in feigned sadness. "Marcus – you don't mind if I call you Marcus, do you?"

"That's not my–"

"No!" The man shouted him down. "Do not lie to me again, Marcus. You have lied to me once, you will not do so again if you wish to walk out of this building on your own legs." The look of anger on the man's face faded back into his manic smile. "Unless, of course, you would prefer to crawl."

Marcus's heart was pounding. Not for the first time, he was questioning his actions. For the first time, however, he felt as though he was dealing with someone that he could not comprehend. "No, no. I think...I'll just walk."

"Good. No more lies, then?"

Marcus shook his head. "No more lies."

"Very nice." The man clapped his hands together and began to walk briskly in Marcus's direction. Every step that he took shook Marcus to his bones. It was as if the world gave way just a little every time that his foot impacted the ground. The air itself seemed to make way for him, as Marcus felt the breath catch itself in his throat every time he tried to inhale. "So, *Marcus*." The man drug out his name, smiling all the while and never breaking eye contact. "What brings you down to our little corner of the city?"

"I...well, I need..." Marcus found the words impossible to verbalize. Try as he might, they wouldn't come out.

The man laughed hauntingly. "*Money*. Man's greatest enemy, and also his best friend. It's an interesting dichotomy, isn't it, Marcus?"

"Uh...yeah. Definitely." Marcus squirmed slightly.

The man dropped his hands to his side and looked inquisitively at Marcus. "Is something wrong, Marcus? Do I make you *uncomfortable?*" He feigned offense as he clasped his hands over his chest. "Oh, that *hurts*, Marcus. That hurts." The man now stood at his full height, just slightly taller than Marcus, as he proceeded toward him. "Let me make something clear to you, friend. I am not someone with whom you should feel uncomfortable. I am someone with whom you should feel *terrified*." He was less than an inch away now. His breath was hot against Marcus's skin and spittle flew from his mouth when he spoke. Marcus wasn't sure whether his heart was pounding or had stopped beating altogether. "I am not the one they let loose when they want a return customer." He licked his lips. "So, Marcus. How much *money* do you want?"

"I..." Marcus looked for some clue in the man's eyes as to what he would do next, but all he found in those cold orbs was bloodlust. This man wanted nothing more than to rip him limb from limb, and he didn't try to hide it. The other men, the crazed man's handlers, Marcus suspected, were fidgeting now, and keeping their hands near to their weapons. He had to steel himself, and prepare for whatever may come. He breathed deep, and then spoke. "Thirty thousand."

The man smiled manically. "Thirty thousand." He chuckled, and then clasped Marcus on the shoulder. "You want thirty thousand dollars. We can do that. We can do that." He turned on his heel and walked back to the other men, one of whom held a briefcase. Snatching it up, he returned to Marcus and popped it open. Inside, Marcus saw hundred dollar bills, rolled into bundles and bound with rubber bands. The man reached in and grabbed three bundles, then tossed them to Marcus. Afterward, he closed the case and returned it to the other man.

"Now," he said, turning back to Marcus. "This is not an interest-free loan, Marcus. In fact, we are very pressed for cash at the moment, and I'm not sure why the boss is feeling so generous, to be honest. Maybe he's feeling sentimental." The man feigned sadness. "His brother passed away just the other day. Very sad. Anywho, this loan is not free. If you don't pay it back in the next month, we *will* come after you. If you don't pay it *then*, well..." He smiled again, as insane as ever. "Then they send *me*. And I don't give a damn if you pay them back or not." He winked then, and it sent shivers down Marcus's spine and pimpled his arms. "See you around, *Marcus*."

The three men then turned and left. Marcus waited until they were gone and then collapsed against a metal support beam. He slid down the pillar, and into a sitting position, breathing hard. He didn't think he had ever been closer to death than just now.

He looked at the money. Thirty thousand dollars of hard cash sat in his hands. It was more than he had ever held, but he didn't feel happy or satisfied. He felt embarrassed and stupid. He felt like a child who couldn't learn when to give up on something.

You should've gone to him. He berated himself mentally. The gravity of what he had done was beginning to weigh on him. He had been so convinced that he had no other avenues that he had done something stupid and dangerous. It was asinine, and he was feeling it now.

A *buzz* came from Marcus's pocket and shook him back to reality. He pulled the phone out and groaned when he saw the caller I.D. His father was calling again. He answered. "Hello?"

"Hey." Came the simple reply on the other end.

"Hey." A moment of silence passed. "What'd you need?"

"I was wondering if you wanted to go out for dinner

tonight."

Marcus was surprised. "Really, Dad? I...are you sure you're..."

"What? *Allowed* to? Yes, Marcus, I'm sure. They told me that I'm doing much better than they expected and that if I was careful, I could go out for a bit. They still want me to come back, because my heart rate's been elevated while I'm asleep, apparently. But, if you don't want to, that's fine."

"No. No, I do. I'm just surprised. Okay, so where do you want to go?"

"Come back to the hospital and pick me up. We'll decide when you get here."

"Okay, Dad. Sounds good." Marcus smiled involuntarily. "Seeya soon."

"Bye."

The sight of Cole Traeger standing in front of the hospital doors was almost enough to bring tears to Marcus's eyes. He was standing, with the help of a cane, and was wearing a simple plaid button-up shirt, dark blue jeans tightened by a black leather belt, and white tennis shoes. His hair was combed, if a bit long, and he had shaved. His eyes were still a little swollen, but the stinging green irises still shone like drops of food coloring in water. Marcus jumped out of the car and jogged around to open the door for his father, but Cole insisted he could do it himself. He managed, with some difficulty and much groaning and cursing, to climb into the car and fasten his seatbelt. Marcus was amazed at not only his tenacity, but also his stubbornness.

As he plopped into the driver's seat and they took off, Cole began to speak. "So," he started off, sounding uneasy. "How have you been?"

Marcus was unsure as to how to respond. "I've been fine, I guess. I mean, recently, you know, it's been tough. But before that I was doing okay." Cole nodded to show he had heard. Marcus decided to brave the next question. "How about you?"

Cole whistled through his teeth. "To be honest, Marcus, it's been rough for a while. Ever since you left, things have been different."

Marcus was surprised at his father's sudden honesty. "Different how?"

"Your mother didn't speak to me for two weeks. It was the first time in our entire marriage I thought she was going to leave me." He sighed and rubbed his eyes. "Now, it all seems so petty, but at the time..." Cole's voice trailed off as he choked back tears. "Anyway," he said after a moment. "Where do you want to eat?"

Marcus sighed. "Well, there's a pretty good little

barbecue joint up here on the left."

"That'll do just fine."

The place was dingy, but it was decent enough. Marcus had eaten here a few times over the last year and it had always been good enough for him. His father seemed less impressed, though, and there was little conversation for most of the meal. Eventually, as they were both picking at their food and delaying paying for the check, Marcus cleared his throat and spoke up.

"You didn't like it?" Marcus gestured at Cole's mostly-full plate.

Cole grunted. "It's fine." He laid his fork down on the plate and rubbed his eyes, then kept them closed.

Marcus shifted nervously. "I thought you liked barbecue."

"It's not the food," Cole said, still not opening his eyes.

Marcus nodded, not sure what to say. Eventually, he decided to push a little. "Dad, what are we doing?"

Cole sighed. "What does that mean?"

"After everything that's happened, I just thought maybe we could be..." He struggled to find the word. "I don't know. Better, I guess."

Cole didn't respond for a long time. Then, quietly, he said, "I don't think I have it in me to be better."

Marcus didn't have a response to that, and the anger

still rising in his chest kept him from any sort of sympathy. So rather than say something he would regret, he simply paid, and the two of them made for the door. As they were crossing the parking lot to their car, Marcus slowing his pace to keep up with Cole's hobble, his phone rang. As he glanced at it, his breath caught in his throat. The screen read: "Incoming Call: Detective Faraday."

He answered, his hands shaking. "Hello?"

"Hi, Marcus." Faraday sounded exhausted, as though he had been up all night. "I wanted to update you on the case."

"Okay. What'd you find out?"

"We've been in correspondence with the U.S. Marshalls since we came across Viggo Lassiter's name. He was most recently seen at a gas station in El Paso, Texas." He sighed again. "He was headed for the border."

Marcus was dumbfounded. "Well, okay. Maybe he hasn't gotten there yet!" His mind was racing. "Just try and head him off at the border!"

"Marcus, that was two days after the murders. He's been in Mexico for over a month."

The impact of what had just been said hit Marcus like a train. "He's...he's gone?"

"I'm afraid so. We're working with the Federales, but I don't hold out much hope. You never know in situations like this, though. He may slip up."

"Well...what about Katie?" Marcus was still numb from the news he had just received, but that didn't change the fact that his baby sister was still gone.

Cole was beginning to catch on now. "What'd he say?" When Marcus didn't respond, he spoke again. "Marcus, what'd he say?" His voice sounded panicked and scared.

Faraday's next words chilled Marcus to the bone. "No sign of her."

Marcus felt the heat rising through his body. "How was there no sign of her? How is that possible?!" He was nearly screaming.

"Marcus, we knew her survival was a slim chance at this point."

"Maybe you knew that, Detective. But I didn't. I held out hope! And you let me!" He was hysterical now. "Fuck you! Fuck you all!" And with that, he hurled his phone across the parking lot and collapsed onto the ground in a heap of tears and anger.

Cole knelt down, too, albeit slowly, and put his arm around his son. For a while, they just sat there, trying to comfort each other. The world was still spinning around them, but for now, even time stood still.

CHAPTER 14

Dream House

Cole leaned on his cane as he stood in the driveway, losing a staring contest with his front door. Marcus stood by him, but he felt utterly alone. He had built much of this home with his own hands. It had been his and his wife's dream to own this home. They had drawn it out when they were first married, and built it some ten years ago. It was a long, hard process, but it had paid off in the end. The house was finally theirs, and that was all that mattered.

Detectives Faraday and Kirkpatrick had driven them out here to the house that morning. It was time for Cole to leave the hospital, as his bills were piling up, and he had nowhere to go, so he figured he would try to go home. He had been standing in the driveway for almost a half-hour at this point. Something seemed to be keeping him from taking another step. It was at this point that Faraday approached him from behind and placed a hand on Cole's shoulder.

"Are you ready?" His voice was lower than normal, more serious. Marcus turned away at his approach. The two hadn't been on the best of terms since the news about Viggo's crossing into Mexico had reached them. Marcus viewed it as a failure on Faraday's part, and Faraday thought Marcus had set impossible standards. They were at an impasse.

Marcus thinks she's dead, Cole thought. He understood it. But he couldn't – *wouldn't* – believe it. Not until he knew for sure. *She's still out there. She has to be.*

Cole looked to his son, then to the detective, and nodded weakly as he began his walk to the door. Each step was more laborious than the last, as his cane made it difficult to walk very far at once. His therapy had gone well to this point. Well enough for him to be out and about, anyway. He was still going to need to attend therapy twice-weekly until his doctor freed him to return to his "everyday routines." The thought of that made Cole chuckle. He wasn't sure what "everyday routines" even were anymore. His entire perception of the world had been altered in the last six weeks. He used to believe that he could keep his family safe, and that people didn't just walk into other people's houses and kill them. He used to think that there was some order to things. Now, he didn't know what to think. There was chaos, his life was in a tailspin, and there was a madman who had taken his daughter. And at the bottom of all of it was the constant thought, raging in the back of his mind, that he was unable to stop it. He had been lying helplessly unconscious on the floor, ten feet away as Viggo Lassiter brutally murdered his wife and son and stole his daughter.

Cole blinked away tears as he tried to push the thought from his mind. It didn't work, but he continued on his trek to the front door of his house, stopping periodically to lean on Marcus's shoulder and rest. When he felt sufficiently rejuvenated, he would continue on. It felt to Cole as though he could only take three or four steps at a time. Regardless, though, he pushed onward. As he reached the steps, he hesitated, then grabbed the railing and pulled himself onto the first landing. Once there, he rested for a few moments. After repeating this process with the next three steps, he found himself standing on the front porch, the door just a few feet away. Cole realized now that he was sweating profusely. He wiped his hands on his shirt, and then leaned on Marcus's shoulder as he prepared himself for the next step.

Faraday spoke again. "Cole, this won't be easy. But it's something you have to do."

Cole choked back tears as best he could. "Are you sure?" His voice was weak.

The detective's hand came to rest on his right shoulder. "I've seen this happen before. You won't be able to move on until you go back in there and face down the monsters."

But what if it doesn't matter? Cole asked himself. *What if I still lose?* He steeled himself. "Okay." And with that, he was moving again. He resigned himself to not stop at the door, but instead to push through it. And so he did. At the door, he simply shoved it open. The detectives had made sure that it was unlocked beforehand.

Cole was surprised; things looked much the same as the last time he had seen it. The gun over the fireplace was gone. Some things had clearly been moved about by the investigators, but they had put everything back well enough. Overall, though, things seemed fairly docile in the front room. Cole hobbled into the kitchen. Here, the investigation was more evident. Dishes had been scattered about on the counters, and a glass had been broken and thrown into the trash.

Cole looked at Faraday. "Looks like your boys were a little rougher than they needed to be."

Faraday sighed and rubbed the back of his head. "It happens sometimes. I'm sorry, Cole."

Cole shrugged. It didn't matter to him, really. He just felt as though he needed to say something. The silence was killing him. He was also trying to stall the inevitable trek up the stairs to the initial scene of the crime, where his entire life had been shattered like that glass that the investigators had dropped.

He felt himself begin to shake slightly and headed for the living room. "I need to sit down for a minute." Marcus nodded and again began helping him along. They reached the couch and he tried to sit slowly, but ended up flopping down unceremoniously and sinking a few inches down into the cushion. He sighed in frustration. "Goddamnit!" he finally said, louder than necessary. "I can't even fucking walk anymore, and the son of a bitch that killed my family is somewhere, God knows where, in Mexico, with my little girl." He hurled his cane across the room angrily, breaking it on the fireplace. Marcus tried to put his hand on Cole's shoulder, but he shrugged it away with a grunt. "Don't touch me. Please." He spoke a little more quietly now. He looked at his son. "Marcus, he's got Katie. He's...oh, Jesus fucking Christ." With that, he buried his face into his hands. Then came the tears. He couldn't help but open the floodgates now.

"Detective, could you give us a minute?" Marcus spoke to Faraday, who then excused himself and stepped outside. Marcus took a seat next to Cole. There were several minutes of silence, save Cole's sobbing. Finally, Marcus spoke. "Dad, I don't know where Viggo is. I don't know where Katie is. I don't know if either of them are even alive now. But I do know that you and I are. We're alive. And, fuck it, Dad, that's all we've got." He turned to face Cole and lowered his voice. "I don't think Mom and Bryce would want us to do this, do you?"

Cole stopped crying and shook his head. He did not look up.

Marcus nodded. "So let's go upstairs." And with that, he stood and extended his hand to his father. Cole looked at him shakily for a moment before breathing deep and grasping his son's hand. After he had struggled to his feet, Marcus made a move to retrieve the broken cane.

"No." Cole said, matter-of-factly. "I'm going to climb these stairs on my own two legs."

Marcus smiled. "Okay, then. I'll be right behind you."

Cole nodded and began to shuffle towards the stairs. Once there, he stared up into the darkness and wondered what he would find there. He took hold of the rails and began to pull himself up. As he took the first step, he felt pain shoot through his body like fire in his veins. It caused his knees to buckle. Desperately, he tightened his grip on the rails. Marcus ran to him.

"Dad! Dad, are you okay?" His voice was panicked, rushed.

"I'm fine!" Cole grunted, out of breath, teeth gritted in

pain as he pulled himself back to his feet. Standing on the steps, his knees shaking beneath him, he felt as weak as ever. With an effort that he did not think possible, he once again pulled himself up, bracing with his arms on the rails. As he topped the next step, he felt his lungs burning with every heaving breath.

The next step came slightly easier, as he was becoming used to the pain that it caused. Marcus was now standing behind him, his hand on Cole's back for extra support. It was like this that they slowly moved up the rest of the stairs and emerged into the hallway at the top. For a long while, they stood at the top of the stairs, heaving from the effort.

It was then that Cole noticed the door that sat directly to his left. His bedroom door was polished, a deep brown, though clearly worn from years of use. It was the door that Viggo had passed through on that night, when he had ended Cole's world. A coldness was creeping through him. His stomach sank, and his heart quickened as he tried to force himself to take one step toward that door. Somewhere within, he knew that life could never return to normal until he confronted the monsters that waited beyond that door.

After a few breathless moments of staring, Marcus made a move to open the door, but Cole grabbed his shoulder.

"No," he said, still a little out of breath. "It needs to be me." Slowly, he hobbled his way over to the door and placed his hand on the knob. It was cold against the sweat that had built on his palm during the climb up the stairs. His heart was racing now. It felt as though it was going to overheat and explode. There was a part of him that wasn't sure if that would be better or worse than the pit that was currently coalescing itself in his gut. His ears were ringing, and the world seemed to be closing in on him from all directions. As he turned the knob, Cole felt almost numb. His surroundings no longer mattered. The tunnel vision had set in, and all that existed lay beyond that door. The deep red of the wood seemed as blood to him as it swung inward. Cole released the knob and let the door swing round, contacting the rubber stopper on the wall and bouncing slightly back in his direction before coming to rest in the open position.

Cole stood there, staring into the room with which he was once so familiar. Now, it seemed like a strange place to him, completely devoid of life. It was an alien planet, the husk of Mars, flying around the sun while he stood motionless, immovable, and inexpressibly small. The life that he had spent so long cultivating, caring for, and fighting to protect had slipped away from him. And no matter where he looked, attempts to bring it back had failed. He had thought that coming here would bring tears to his eyes, but instead, he simply felt what he could only call a "dead feeling" crawl into his stomach. It was as though he finally realized that his wife and son were dead, and now, he suspected, his daughter as well.

It was with a creeping sense of defeat that Cole collapsed on the bed that was no longer his. No, Viggo had taken this from him, as well. He had taken everything from him. The woman he had loved, the children he had raised, and the house that he had built. In one fell swoop, Viggo Lassiter had stolen Cole's entire life. Sitting on the bed, looking around the room, Cole could see the stain left by a large pool of blood by the doorway. There was another, similar stain on what had been his wife's side of the bed and floor. The sights tightened Cole's chest. With that, he laid back on the bed, which had been stripped of sheets and comforters and pillows, and stared at the ceiling. Slowly, he let his eyes trace the stucco on the ceiling down to the other end of the room, to the top of the closet door. He then followed the door frame down to the floor, then sat up on the bed and stared at yet another pool of dried blood. Seeing it sent shivers through Cole's body, and a coldness came together in his stomach.

Suddenly, he felt the undeniable urge to vomit. He rolled over to the edge of the bed, and flung the window open, just in time to project the half-digested contents of his stomach out from the second floor, and onto the woodpile that sat against the back of the house. Briefly, Cole considered the fact that, had things remained normal for his family, that wood would be in the fireplace, completely ablaze.

Marcus came running in from one of the other rooms. "Dad! Are you okay?"

Cole managed to nod as he wiped the sick from his mouth and flung it out the window. "Yeah. I'm fine. It just got to me a little, I guess." He gave the room another glance. "Let's go. I've seen enough of this for today." He climbed off of his knees slowly and began to hobble his way toward the door. Marcus took a step to help him, but Cole held up his hand to stop him. "Not this time. I have to do it for myself." Marcus rolled his eyes and breathed out, but stepped back and let him through. Cole braced himself on the door frame, and moved shuffling toward the stairs.

Marcus spoke from behind him. "Hey, I'm going to spend a little more time up here, okay? I want to see the other rooms."

This stopped Cole mid-shuffle. His son, though he didn't know it, had said the one thing that could keep him in this place any longer. He needed to see the other rooms, the ones that his children had slept in. He needed to feel that closeness to them again, and he knew that it was the one thing this house had left to offer him. This realization struck fear into his soul, and he felt the coldness creeping back into his stomach. Afraid he might wretch again, Cole placed his hand over his mouth and breathed deeply. "Okay." He finally said, when he felt his stomach had calmed enough for him to speak. "I'll come, too."

The trip down the hall was difficult for Cole, not only because walking was still a chore, but also because his body seemed to be attempting to sprint in the opposite direction with every step. He could feel the war raging in his limbs, and knew that there was no solution but to continue onward. So he walked on down the hall, until he reached Bryce's room. Stepping inside was slightly easier this time. He realized that very little had been touched in this room. It was mostly as before, save a few things that had been moved about, and the missing laptop that must have been confiscated. Either that, or Viggo had taken it. He didn't linger in that room. He could feel hot tears rising through him, and turned away before he broke down again. Marcus turned and stared out the hall window, and Cole knew that he did so to avoid letting himself be seen as weak. This made the pit in his stomach grow.

Somewhere deep inside of himself, Cole knew he had caused his son to be this way, so afraid of showing weakness. He had pushed him too hard when he had been young, been more a boss than a father. And try as he might, he couldn't convince himself that he had "done his best," as some might say. No, he knew that he had been wrong more than he had been right when it came to raising Marcus. That's why he had left much of the parenting to Lillian with the other children. He had lost his confidence as a father a long time ago, and that shook him deeply. The feeling of nausea began to resurface as Cole continued to push himself down the hall, step by step.

He passed by Marcus's old room, the door to which was closed, with a scarce glance. He did not feel like tackling the issue of his relationship with his oldest son at this point, not head on, at the very least. Instead, he continued on to Katie's room, which he had most dreaded of them all.

Upon reaching her door, which sat at the end of the hall, he froze. Again, he felt fear rising through his body. Still trying to calm himself, Cole slid his hand around the cold metal knob and turned it. He tried not to hesitate, but that was a futile effort. He was considering giving up altogether and going back downstairs until he felt Marcus's hand on his shoulder.

"I'm right here with you." Although Marcus would never know it, those words meant more than Cole could ever express. With a renewed power of will, he pushed open the door and faced down whatever it was that sat on the other side. What he found did not shock him. It was the same room that he had looked in on hundreds of times. The bed where he had tucked his daughter in so many times before was still messed, from Katie's sleeping in it or from the investigators' prodding, he was unsure.

This room was more tidied than the others. The investigators' presence was more evident here. It was clear that they had taken a lot of evidence and had cleaned up furiously. It looked almost sterile, with the exception of a few toys that remained on shelves or in toy chests about the room. It felt as though Katie were already dead, like the room had been cleaned out to make space for a new tenant. That thought nearly brought Cole to tears again.

Standing in the midst of this horror, surrounded by the ruins of his former life, Cole nearly found it too much to stand. It was as though the world sat squarely on his shoulders, and his already weakened legs were beginning to fail him. He collapsed against the door frame in a heap as the tears began to flow in force.

The evidence of his failures was all around him, and the gravity of his situation was finally beginning to sink in. This house, these rooms, they were all reminders of a world that had ended. The relics of a bygone day. His memories seemed almost unreal to him now, as though they were visions of someone else's life, a television show that he knew would not have a happy ending.

Marcus knelt beside his father. "Come on." He said, helping Cole to his feet. "No use sitting here." There was sympathy and pain in his voice. For all of their differences, Cole knew that he and Marcus were in much the same position. Both had lost nearly their entire family and were now struggling to pick up the pieces. All they had left was each other, and that made it exponentially more difficult, given the state of their relationship. Cole was trying to make things smoother between the two of them, but he knew that it would take years to fix, were it even possible.

Standing there in that doorway, clinging to his son to avoid the failure of his broken legs, Cole was forced to take inventory of his ruined life. His family was gone, killed or kidnapped. His legs wouldn't keep him upright. His only family, his oldest son, whom he had driven away, was the only thing keeping him straight as his world tumbled and cracked and shattered all around him. It was humbling to realize how irreversibly broken he was.

When he was on his feet, he leaned back against the doorframe, sweating. "We can't do this anymore." He said between heaves. "We just can't do this."

Marcus looked perplexed. "What do you mean?"

"Just...spinning. We're just spinning." Cole swung his pointer finger round in circles to illustrate his point. "We're stuck. Gotta break the cycle." He stopped his finger suddenly, in front of his face. Marcus's eyes drifted to it and lingered there confusedly.

"How?" Realization was coming over his face.

Cole dropped his hand to his side and let his eyes slide upward and gaze directly into his son's face. It was then that he realized how alike they looked. It was like looking into a mirror. "We're going to get her."

CHAPTER 15

Down South

The physical therapy clinic was alive with activity. Marcus sat back in the stiff, lightly-padded wooden armchair that was open for guests to use while waiting. He was watching his father walk on a treadmill, but his mind was elsewhere. Ever since their visit to the house three weeks prior, Cole had spoken of little besides his new plan to go to Mexico and rescue Katie.

Marcus had done his best to not indulge his father's ideas. He did find it slightly difficult to not get caught up in the heroics of it all. It felt like a movie, the hero riding off into the sunset, revolver in hand to dole out the justice that the law couldn't. However, at the end of the day, it didn't matter. There would be no trip to Mexico. There would be no gunfights or little girls rescued from the devil. There would be, most likely, nothing. Nothing at all. They would sit at home and hope for the best. And if good news came, they would celebrate. If bad news came, they would mourn. But they would not be going off to rescue anyone.

Marcus hadn't had the heart to tell his father this. He had hoped that this idea would dissipate, but it unfortunately hadn't. Every night's dinner was spent drawing up plans, deciding how much money would be needed, checking to see if the nest egg would be enough, and then doing it all again. There was always someone that they needed to go see, or call, or something of the sort. Of course, little of this was actually carried through, but it kept his father's hopes up, and Marcus hadn't been able to bring himself to tear that down just yet. But it was becoming problematic, and he knew that something needed to be done about it.

Cole's struggling gait was becoming more like a normal man's walk. It was inspiring to Marcus to watch his father fight so hard to regain the abilities that had been lost to him. Even in the face of such adversity, he continued to battle with himself, and force his body back into the work that it strained so hard against.

Marcus sighed and leaned back in the chair, cracking his spine as he did so. Slowly, he let his eyes drift around the clinic. There were all sorts of sad cases here. He saw emaciated men, slowly losing hope of ever urinating on their own again; women who were fighting to lose enough weight to walk of their own volition. Mixed in with these sorts were the more inspirational ones, the ones like Cole, that still had a fire in their eyes.

To Marcus's left was a girl to whom he had spoken a few times on his previous visits to the clinic. Her name was Patricia Browning. She was 22, and a former marine. Marcus had found her story to be truly sad. During her first month in Iraq, her convoy had hit a roadside explosive. The blast took out her Humvee first, and killed everyone else inside. She alone had been spared. However, when the dust cleared, and she tried to stand, she had realized that her entire right leg was gone, along with her right hand. The explosion had left her half a person.

Tears had swollen in her eyes when she told this story to him. She was a pretty girl, with amber eyes, the kind that stared into Marcus's soul. Her face was lightly freckled, and adorned by a large scar that ran along the top of her forehead. She had hidden it, he learned later, by dying her hair black and wearing her bangs down. He only ever noticed it when she was sweating after a session.

Cole had asked several times about Patricia, but Marcus had deflected the questions, albeit honestly.

"We're just friends," he told his father, smiling slightly. It was true. Marcus had no intention of pursuing anything serious at this point. Their lives were in too much flux to be fooling around with anyone, at least in his mind. Aside from this, there was too much he could not share with her. He still had not told her his sad story. She only knew that Cole had suffered an injury during a home invasion, and that was all he could bring himself to tell her.

"Your dad's doing great, Marcus." Frank Little's voice snapped Marcus back to the present.

"Thanks, Frank." Frank was Cole's physical therapist, as well as a friend of theirs. They had known each other for years, though in what capacity, Marcus did not know.

"Yeah, he's got a lot o' fight in him. Tough ol' S.O.B." Frank hailed from just outside of Nashville, and it showed. His accent seemed as thick as ever, even though he had been in the city for a decade.

Marcus laughed a little. "Yeah, that he does." He hesitated a bit before continuing. "Frank, has he mentioned any 'plans' of any sort?"

Frank seemed to consider the question for a moment before responding. "Nah, not that I can think of. Wouldn't surprise me, though. He's gotta do somethin' to get his mind off o' this."

Marcus nodded mutely. "Thanks, Frank. I'm glad you're keeping an eye on him."

Frank smiled largely and nodded his head a bit, in that typical southern gentlemanly way. "Jus' doin' what I can." And with that, the mustachioed southerner took his leave to help another patient that was struggling along on the treadmill.

Marcus turned back to his father. Cole was hobbling over in his direction, leaning on his cane, though less now, it seemed. Marcus let a bit of hope creep up inside of him. *Perhaps,* he thought, *things are going to get back to normal after all.* He knew that this thought was less than realistic, but it still made him feel better, if only slightly. He had learned to take solace in the small victories.

"How was it?" He asked as Cole made his way toward him.

Cole grunted. "Same as ever. Frank talks too much, and I hope to get out of here with a little less shit in my pants than last time." A hollow sort of chuckle escaped him. "It's getting easier, though. Walking, that is. Things are starting to work right again." He flexed his leg as evidence. "Couldn't have done that a month ago."

Marcus laughed a little. "Yeah, looks like progress." The two men proceeded toward the door. As they passed the front desk, Frank's wife Margie waved at them.

"See y'all on Wednesday." Marcus couldn't help but smile back at her. Margie's enthusiasm for life was practically contagious. She often worked the desk in the office, and he always looked forward to seeing her during Cole's sessions.

"Seeya then, Margie." Marcus called back to her,

waving. Cole smiled in her direction and tossed up a
farewell wave of sorts before pushing on through the door.
Marcus had noticed in the last few weeks, since Cole's re-
emergence into society that he had little to no time for any
interaction with other people. His conversations with
anyone other than his son or doctor were brief, cold, and
typically void of anything besides surface discussion.

He had decided not to breach the topic with his father.
There was no need, he figured. Once they had both gotten
through the grieving process, they would try to pick up the
pieces of their lives and move on.

As Cole opened the car door and sat down, Marcus
realized he was no longer flopping into the seat like an
angry toddler. He seemed to have more control over his
muscles, and his movements were more precise. Silently, he
smiled, and sat down behind the wheel.

"Lunch?" he asked, closing the door and turning the
key.

Cole nodded. "Sure."

"Any preferences?"

His father shook his head and shrugged as he retrieved
his sunglasses from the cup holder and placed them on his
nose. The bright winter sun was blasting them, like ants
under the magnifying glass of a child. Marcus thought their
situation surprisingly similar to the ants'. At the mercy of a

cruel god, bathed in fire, they were unable to escape their crushing destiny. With thoughts of gods and insects rattling around in his mind, Marcus started the car and drove away.

The trip up the stairs leading to Marcus's apartment was one of the day's typical adventures. Every day, this seemed to be the most difficult part of Cole's existence. The three story climb was difficult, and tiring even for Marcus. The stairs shot up at a steep angle and were made of an ancient black grate, making the use of a cane impractical. As it was, the pair had to traverse the steps slowly, with Cole leaning on Marcus's shoulder the entire way. When they reached the plateaus that separated the various floors, they would lean against the rail and rest for a moment, gathering their strength for the next leg of the climb.

Today, though, it seemed to come a bit easier. Cole was relying less and less on Marcus to half-carry him up the squawking metal death trap, and was instead walking more on his own. Although the climb still took at least ten minutes, it was a decent sight better than the fifteen minute ventures they had had over the past few weeks while Cole had been staying with his son.

They had both found the house to be a sobering reminder of what they had lost, and had made the decision to put it on the market. Since then, they had been staying at

Marcus's apartment. It was cramped, but it was something. Cole slept in the bed, and Marcus on the couch. As always, they both went to their respective corners of the tiny apartment and performed their nightly rituals. Marcus spent the time reading or watching television, and Cole took the opportunity to pour over his plans for rescuing Katie.

Usually, at some point during the evening, Marcus would meander through the apartment, into the kitchen where his unfinished book was still lying on the table that no one seemed to use anymore. Some nights, he would simply look at it and turn away, suddenly dead to the world. Others, he would sit down and flip through the 500-odd handwritten pages. He would see his notes in the margins, things that he had circled or marked out, and entire sections that he had drawn large X's over, only to write out to the side, "NEVERMIND. KEEP THIS." Inevitably, though, he would get up from the table and go back to the living room, where he'd read or watch something that someone else had written, while ignoring as best he could the monkey that seemed to have taken up residence on his back.

Cole entered without sound, almost sheepishly from the other room, holding in his hands a manila envelope, packed tightly and overflowing with papers. The papers themselves were heavily inked, notes scribbled in the margins and clearly worn from being turned over and over what must have been hundreds of times.

"Marcus," he said, his voice cracking from disuse. He cleared his throat before continuing. "Marcus, we need to discuss the plans."

Marcus sighed. "What plans, Dad?"

A look of incredulity crept across his father's face. "To go get Katie."

Marcus turned the TV off and adjusted to look into his father's eyes. Not for the first time, it dawned on him how difficult these last couple of months had been for Cole. He looked as though he had aged ten years. His cheeks had gone gaunt, his eyes had sunken in, and his hair grayed at the edges. "Dad, we can't-"

"Can't what?" Cole cut him off harshly. His voice had taken on an edge since the night of the murders. Gone was the pleasant exterior, the shop owner that everyone loved. He was replaced by someone more suited to this new world.

"We can't go get Katie." Marcus braced himself. He knew that his words cut deeper than knives in his father's back.

But, to his surprise, Cole said nothing. He didn't speak a word before collapsing onto the couch next to his son. Gently, he laid the papers and folders on the coffee table and rubbed his eyes. His hand came to rest covering the weary, dried orbs. "What else am I supposed to do?"

Marcus placed a hand on his father's back. "We're doing all we can."

Cole brushed the hand away. "No."

"Dad, come on."

"No! I can do more!" With that, he stood, quicker than he had in the last three months, gathered his papers, and stormed back into the other room, slamming the door behind him.

Marcus laid his head in his hands. "Damn it." He said under his breath. "I have to go somewhere." He called to his father, then stood and walked out.

Outside, the sun was resting heavily on the horizon. Soon, it would dip down completely, drunkenly disappearing for the night, only to reappear bright and early in the morning. Marcus enjoyed this time of the evening. It allowed him to think more clearly, to slough away the pressures of the day.

Almost without thinking, he pulled the half-empty pack of Marlboro Reds from his shirt pocket and took a cigarette. Lighting it, he drew in heavily. The warm flavor of tobacco filled his mouth, trickled down his throat, and settled in his lungs. His coping mechanism had developed into a slightly more dangerous habit than he wanted to admit.

A couple more drags and he discarded the cigarette, flicking the butt off somewhere into the street. Hands in the pockets of his jacket, Marcus continued on. He had gone about a block and a half when he first noticed the car.

Black, long, and every window tinted, it rolled up behind him with an engine that purred like a Bengal tiger. Marcus glanced over his left shoulder at the vehicle. He was unable to make out the driver, but no sooner than he looked did they speed past him and away. It seemed odd, but Marcus chose to ignore it. He would have, at least, until he noticed it whirling around and coming back toward him. The car screeched to a stop at the curb. Marcus took a couple of steps back just as the passenger door flung open.

Marcus tried to take in the car. It was as dark inside as it was out. The leather interior was a deep red, reflecting the late afternoon sunset with warm, dark reciprocity. A moment after the door swung open, someone spoke from within that tomb.

"Get in." The voice was cold, flat, but with a hint of a smile. A smile devoid of happiness, but a smile nonetheless, like a maniac in an asylum bed, sweating through his insanity.

"Who are you?" Marcus took another step back. The man behind the voice leaned out now, barely into the light. He was just visible enough for Marcus to see that it was the man from the warehouse.

"Just get in, Marcus." The man smiled insanely.

For a moment, Marcus had considered turning and running. He knew, though, somewhere deep inside himself that the man would catch him, probably without even trying. "Why?"

The man locked eyes with him for a moment. In that instant, Marcus somehow felt deep in his bones that he had no choice in the matter. The man didn't speak again. He simply scooted over to the other window. As slowly as he could, Marcus ducked into the seat and closed the door behind him.

Almost instantly, a thick black covering came down over his face. Marcus tried to fight, but it was useless. The other man was far stronger and easily brushed him aside. "Now, I promise this isn't personal. But the boss says you can't know where he lives. So, you can't know." The rest of the ride took place in total silence, save Marcus's stuttered breathing against the interior of the bag.

After what seemed like hours, Marcus felt the car come to a stop. The man reached across him and opened the far door, shoving Marcus roughly from the car. He stumbled onto the ground, bracing himself as he fell. Under his hands, he felt the rough, scratchy terrain of a sidewalk. No sooner had he made this realization than he was dragged to his feet and instructed by a large hand on his elbow to walk. He felt his feet cross a threshold and the air turn warmer as he stepped inside of a building. Some light penetrated the bag over his head, but for the most part he was still blind.

Marcus's foot slammed into something and he stumbled to his knees on what felt like stairs. He felt carpet under his fingers this time, and decided that he was probably in a house. Again, he was pulled up and forced to walk. Though, this time he was more dragged than guided up the stairs, which seemed to go on forever. Marcus figured they went up at least three flights of stairs before they stopped. His shoulder ached from being pulled, and his foot throbbed. All this in addition to his heart, pounding away inside his chest like a hammer on a forge, made him feel like he might explode at any moment. The bag over his head was hot and stuffy and his own breath warmed it, making him even more uncomfortable. Though, he supposed that was part of the point.

A door creaked open in front of him, and suddenly the hand on his elbow disappeared. Marcus could feel someone behind him, untying the bag that covered his head and, in a moment, the darkness disappeared, giving way to a nearly blinding light. As Marcus's eyes began to adjust to the room, he was shoved into a padded chair, looking at a large, dark wood desk.

Across the desk sat a broad-shouldered, black-haired man, with a jaw like an anvil and eyes that looked far away from this office. A light stubble adorned his stress-wrinkled face, but otherwise he seemed well-kept. He wore a black dress-shirt, sleeves rolled to his elbows, and unbuttoned at the top. A tuft of graying chest hair spouted from the collar of his shirt. His shoulders were hunched as he leaned on his elbows, hands at either of his temples making blinders that surrounded his eyes. A tumbler holding a finger of dark brown liquor sat on the desk. It was with a weak gesture that he dismissed everyone else from the room. The door shut as they left.

Then there was silence. At least a full minute of it, tense as a hangman's noose. Marcus shifted uncomfortably in his chair, looking around the room. There were bookshelves lining the walls, all full of various sized tomes of different colors. Behind the desk was a well-stocked liquor cabinet. If the levels of the various bottles were any indication, Marcus assumed it saw fairly consistent use.

The man never looked up, even when he spoke.

"So you're Marcus?" His voice was thick and deep, a light accent dancing at the edges of his words. .

Marcus swallowed hard before answering. "Yes sir. I-"

"Cut the shit," the man interrupted, rubbing his eyes. "Call me Luke. The trained monkeys that work for me have been calling me 'sir' left and right."

"Uh," Marcus stammered about, unable to land on the

right words. "Okay."

"You're Marcus, I'm Luke. We're introduced." He downed the drink, then reached back to the liquor cabinet and retrieved a bottle before pouring another one. "Drink?" he asked, looking at Marcus for the first time.

Marcus shook his head, but Luke poured a drink anyway and slid it over to him. Luke offered a silent toast, and the two of them drank. The liquor was a whiskey, dark and bitter and on fire as it slithered down Marcus's throat. He coughed, and Luke chuckled humorlessly.

"Hurts, doesn't it?" Marcus managed a nod. "Yeah, I know. Packs a punch though." Luke reached into his desk drawer and retrieved a pack of cigarettes. He lit one and dropped the pack in front of Marcus, tossing over the lighter as he did.

Marcus was unsure of what to do, but lit a cigarette anyway and slid the pack and lighter back to Luke. The tobacco was rich and bold. Unfiltered.

The two sat in silence for a bit longer, smoke swirling about them and heating the room. Finally, Luke spoke.

"Do you know why you're here, Marcus?"

Marcus shook his head in a lie.

"You borrowed thirty thousand dollars from me."

Marcus cast his head down into his lap as fear threatened to reach out and grab his heart out of his chest.

The drink, the cigarette, it was all a set up for Luke to kill him.

As if he knew what he was thinking, Luke spoke, "Don't worry. I'm not going to kill you. If I was going to kill you, I wouldn't have had them put the bag over your head. The truth is, Marcus, I need your help. And, if I'm not wrong, you need a way to pay me back. Is that right?"

Marcus nodded.

"Well, I need someone dealt with. It won't be easy, but the man's done things that hurt my family. And I don't let people hurt my family."

A million thoughts raced through Marcus's head at once, but he only managed to voice one of them. "Sir – Luke – I'm not a bounty hunter. I don't know the first thing about it." His heart was pounding again. He couldn't give Luke what he wanted, and that meant that he was about to die.

Luke shook his head. "I know, kid. Trust me. I do. Normally, I'd just send one of my own guys. Unfortunately..." he trailed off, then seemed to search for his next words before speaking again. "...we've had some internal problems recently, and as such, I can't spare anyone right now." He lowered his eyes. "And this *problem* won't sit around and wait for me."

Marcus took a deep breath, tried to collect himself. "But you don't even know me." He winced as he said it, but it was out there now.

"Exactly. We don't know each other. You've got nothing on me. You don't know where you are, or who you're talking to. All you know is, I'm looking for someone, and I'm willing to wipe your debt if you find him." Marcus must have looked unsure, because Luke continued on. "Just, trust me. If you do this for me, you won't regret it. I'm someone you want on your side in this city." He leaned back in his chair, swirling his drink, and exhaled smoke in wobbling rings that danced up toward the room's meager light.

Marcus swallowed again and put his cigarette out in the ashtray on his side of the desk. "Who is it, anyway? What did he do?"

Luke leaned forward and grabbed a file from under the desk and tossed it down in front of Marcus. "He killed my brother."

As Marcus opened the folder, his stomach leapt into his throat. There, staring back at him from the other side of a photograph was Viggo Lassiter. Marcus felt his throat go dry and he kicked back the rest of his drink in one swallow, ignoring the burn. "This is the guy? He killed your brother?"

Luke nodded. "He was one of my guys. Promising. Then he went fucking crazy and skipped town. He fucked over some clients in the process and they retaliated by killing my brother and trying to kill me. Now, it's time for him to pay."

Marcus's mind reeled as things suddenly came into striking focus. Viggo Lassiter was on the run from something he'd done – no, he was on the run from *Luke*. And on the way, he'd broken into his family's home for some reason – *No,* Marcus thought. He was looking for supplies, or cash. Things went wrong, and now his family was dead. But what about Katie? Did Luke know about her? He had to find out.

"You don't know?" he said, so quietly Luke leaned forward.

"Know what?" Luke asked, his voice betraying the slightest tick of curiosity.

"You don't know what he did?" Marcus swallowed, choked back bile. He glanced at Luke, saw he was shaking his head 'no.' Marcus closed his eyes, pressed hard against the lids with his thumb and forefinger, but the image of Viggo Lassiter's face was burned into the black.

"He killed my family."

No one spoke for awhile. Luke leaned back, his chair squeaking in protest.

"Shit," Luke said. He poured two more drinks and slid one to Marcus, who took it in a hand, suddenly weak. "Tell me everything."

And Marcus did. He told him the whole story. When he was done, Luke nodded thoughtfully. "It sounds like we have something in common. Viggo Lassiter killed our family."

Marcus nodded, still staring at the open folder. The file was even more of an indicator that Lassiter was a sociopath: it detailed all of his kills, all of the people he had harassed for money, all of the hits he had carried out, in addition to other bits about his life and past. But Marcus couldn't stop nodding. "I'll do it."

Luke gave a grim nod. "It won't be easy. Viggo's good at what he does. He makes death look like an art. But with me helping you, you should be able to take him down. We'll work out the details tomorrow over breakfast, but you need to start thinking about what you need. Is there anyone else you need to take with you?"

Marcus didn't have to think about his answer. Even if he told Cole not to come, it wouldn't do any good. And he was walking better now, so Marcus figured he could be of some use.

"Just one. My dad."

Luke chuckled, but nodded again. "Okay, fine by me. Bring him with you tomorrow."

"Wait, where are we meeting?"

"They'll pick you up at nine at your apartment. Be ready when they get there."

Marcus almost didn't mention the other request he had,

but thought best to try. "Can you not send the tall guy with the crazy smile tomorrow?"

Luke laughed. "Sorry, kid, Leon's the best guy I've got to watch my back. He stays."

Marcus reluctantly nodded. "Tomorrow at nine."

"I'll see you then." Luke clapped his hands together and the door swung open behind Marcus. Without warning, the black bag slid back down over his head and he was enveloped in darkness again, being dragged from the room.

CHAPTER 16

Painted Sand

Cole sipped his coffee, never taking his eyes off the man that sat across from him. He had introduced himself as "Luke," but Cole wasn't sure he believed that to be his real name. Regardless, he'd managed to change Marcus's mind about going after Viggo Lassiter, and that's all that mattered in the end. Now, they sat across from each other in a corner booth at a diner across the city from Marcus's apartment discussing the "details," as Luke put it.

"Viggo isn't going to be easy to track down. He's got a big head start on you, and he's paranoid as all hell, so he's going to be waiting for someone. Now, he doesn't know who you guys are, so you have that working for you. He'll be expecting one of my guys, which is part of the reason I can't send any of them." Luke drank from his cup of water before continuing. "I know that this is out of both your comfort zones. But he's a bad guy, and he needs to be dealt with."

"And we're the ones you want to send?" Cole spoke up.

He shot his son a knowing look before turning back to Luke.

"Well, no. Not really. But you're my best option. My guys are all tied up here, and besides that, Viggo knows them all. Not to mention, you have an added incentive to deal with this effectively." Luke took a bite of his eggs and leaned back.

Cole sighed, as did Marcus. He had been informed of his son's outstanding debt to this man, but was still having trouble accepting that someone that shared blood with him could've been so stupid.

"Yeah, so I've heard."

Well, we do *have another incentive,* Cole thought, stifling the anger in his chest. *Sometimes it's best not to question why fate hands you an opportunity.* If this is what it took to get Marcus on board, then so be it.

Marcus chimed in, probably hoping to steer the discussion in a different direction. "So what's our plan?"

Luke nodded and leaned forward, lowering his voice. "Well, first of all, there's the matter of transportation, and crossing the border. You'll be taking an unmarked car down to Mexico. It's brand new, directly from the factory. Doesn't even have a VIN number, so don't get pulled over. Drive exactly the speed limit, all the way south."

"Wait," Cole interrupted, digging through his pockets and producing a memo pad and pen. He wrote down what

Luke had said. "Speed limit, no more." He mumbled. "Okay, go on."

"Right," Luke continued. "You won't get any weapons until *after* you get across the border. It'll be easier to get untraceable guns down there, and trust me, you don't want to have to deal with taking them across."

"No guns before the border," Cole scribbled as Luke talked.

"Once you're across and have some guns, I'll get you in contact with my main guy down there. If anyone has a trail on Viggo, it'll be him. From there, it's up to you." He leaned back before suddenly sitting back up and producing a phone from his inside jacket pocket. "I almost forgot this. Only use this phone if you need to contact me. No other phones whatsoever. Got it?"

Cole and Marcus both nodded. The younger Traeger took the phone and shoved it in his pocket.

"My number is programmed into the number 5. Just hold that down, and it'll dial me. Trust me, I'll always pick up." With that, Luke slid his plate back and tossed down his napkin before downing the rest of his water. "And that, gentlemen, is all I have to say. The car will be parked outside of your apartment this evening at seven. You'll need to leave by Friday."

"But that just gives us two days," said Marcus.

"Yes. I'm aware. Things are going to move very quickly now, and you have to move with them. Would you like a ride back to your apartment?" The Traegers both shook their heads. Luke nodded, then made his exit. The door chimed as he walked out, leaving the two of them sitting in the noise of the diner, the clatter of forks on plates surrounding them.

Marcus stood and then sat on the other side of the booth. "Are you ready?" he asked after a moment.

Cole breathed deep, then ran his hand back over his hair. "I don't know. This isn't really what I had in mind. I just wanted to get Katie back and bring Viggo to stand trial. I never wanted to do the deed myself."

"What's the difference?"

Cole looked at his son. "What do you mean?"

Marcus shrugged. "I mean, he's going to die either way, right?"

Cole shook his head. "That's not how it works. We're not killers, Marcus."

"He sure is!" Marcus stifled his voice to keep from yelling, but just barely. "It didn't bother him to kill our family. I don't think it should bother us to kill him."

"Revenge isn't our way." Cole set his brow and lowered his voice. He was nearly growling. "We're going to get Katie, not deal out western justice. We're not cowboys, and we're not bounty hunters. We're just regular people."

"Not anymore. That's not what we are. But either way, we have to bring him back."

"And that's what we'll do."

Marcus stood up in a huff.

"Where are you going?" Cole asked him.

"I'm going to get ready. We need to make arrangements, make sure there are no loose ends."

Cole looked down. "Yeah, I guess you're right." He looked back to his son. "I'll see you at home."

"See you there." And with that, Marcus headed for the exit. Again, the door chimed as he walked out.

And then Cole was alone. He finished his meal, then realized they had all left him with the check. He couldn't help but laugh at that, even as he paid. After he'd finished, he slowly made his way out of the diner to the sidewalk and hailed a cab. As he flopped into the seat, the driver turned and looked over his right shoulder.

"Where to?"

Cole closed the door before answering. "Miles Cemetery, over on Grandview."

The air was cold at the cemetery, and the ground hard on the bottoms of Cole's feet. He walked between the graves at his own slow pace, possibly slower than normal knowing what was waiting for him. The place was quiet, as cemeteries should be. There weren't any visitors that he could see, and the thousands of graves stood alone, as they had for so long. Finally, he came to the stones he had wished he would never see.

LILLIAN JACOBS TRAEGER

MARCH 14, 1965 – SEPTEMBER 23, 2012

A LOVING MOTHER AND WIFE, GONE TOO SOON

"And when you finally fly away, I'll be hoping that I served you well"

Cole couldn't help but laugh a little at the lyrics to Rod Stewart's "Forever Young," being emblazoned across his wife's tombstone. She had always loved that song, and he had never passed up an opportunity to tell her how much he hated it. Now, though, those words seemed to be in his mind constantly.

To the left of Lillian's stone was another one, a little smaller.

BRYCE TRAEGER

AUGUST 14, 2002 – SEPTEMBER 23, 2012

A LOVED SON, TAKEN TOO SOON

An engraving of a young boy kicking a soccer ball adorned the lower half of the stone, and someone had set super hero and wrestling action figures around the base. Cole had the strangest feeling wash over him as he pictured those little men watching over his son's grave, standing vigil. They were doing what he couldn't.

He collapsed to his knees and gripped the headstone, touching his forehead to the cold marble slab as a light rain pattered down around him and wet the dirt. "I'm so sorry," he wheezed. "I'm so sorry, I let you down." He heaved a breath, then sobbed again as his mind wheeled through a thousand images of Bryce; his wrinkled little body as the doctor handed him to Cole. His pudgy-cheeked smile as he toddled around the house. The young man he'd grown into. Kind, with a fiery temper. "You were so *good,*" Cole sobbed, snot and tears running together down his face and mingling with the rain as droplets fell to the dirt.

Some time later, he wasn't sure if it was minutes or hours, Cole was lying curled up between the graves of his son and his wife. Slowly, his joints aching from the cold and stillness, he sat up and looked at Lillian's stone. And when looking at her was too hard, he cast his eyes down.

"There are a lot of things I never said." His voice was raw from crying, and his head pounded, but he used the pain to force clarity. "Things I should've made sure you knew. I should've told you more that I was lucky to have you. I should've told you it killed me to not have Marcus around. I should've let you in more." He paused, unable to continue.

"We're going to get him," he managed to croak out when his voice returned. "We're going to get the son of a bitch who did this. We're going to bring him back, and he's going to pay for what he did." Again, he stopped, wiping tears from his eyes.

After he took a breath, Cole continued, his voice barely more than a whisper. "I'm so sorry I let this happen. It was my responsibility. I was supposed to keep you safe. I was supposed to –" Cole choked on his words and spat on the ground. His stomach was heaving, and the tears were drying against his face in the chill wind. "I'll keep Marcus safe." He finally said when his breath returned to him. "I won't fail him again. I promise." He climbed to his knees and braced himself on the headstone.

"And I *will* bring her back." This time, it wasn't sadness, but fury that forced tears from him. How he had any left, he didn't know.

When he finally stood, he turned and saw one last stone in the line.

COLE TRAEGER

OCTOBER 19, 1964 –

His eyes slid over the unfinished epitaph as his stomach bubbled with rage. He spat on the headstone and turned to leave.

It was late when Cole trudged slowly and shakily up the stairs to the apartment he shared with his son. When he pushed open the door, Marcus was sitting on the couch behind a fold-out table, upon which his novel in progress was propped.

"Making progress?" Cole tossed his coat onto a metal chair that stood to his left as he entered, a stand in for a coat rack.

Marcus sighed and rubbed his eyes. "No, not really. I don't know how to end it. I'm so close, though."

Cole took a seat beside his son on the couch and pulled the table over toward him. Gingerly, he flipped through the pages, reading the notes in the margins and looking over the story as best he could.

"I've never read one of your stories," he said after a moment. "I should've." He flipped the book closed and pushed the table back before turning to face his son. "I'm sorry about that."

Marcus looked surprised, but happy. "It's okay," he said slowly, as if trying to find the right words. "There'll be time when we get back."

Cole nodded, then reconsidered. The gravity of what they were about to do was settling on him. It was as if the world was sitting weighted on his shoulders, and like Atlas, if he shrugged, everyone might just fall off. "Actually, can I read some now? I think I'd like to just do it now." He looked into Marcus's eyes and saw something he hadn't seen associated with himself in a long time: anticipation.

"Yeah. Yeah, of course. Give me just a second. I'll go get some." Marcus stood and jogged into the bedroom. After a moment, he returned with a binder, packed so full, the papers seemed as though they could leap from their bindings. After he repositioned himself on the couch, he handed the binder over to his father.

Cole took it, holding it as though it were a precious child. It felt worn, beat up, but strong.

After a moment, Marcus spoke. "These are all my favorites, from back when I was kid, up until now." The two made eye contact again, and Cole flipped open the binder. They sat for a long while, reading and laughing and talking like they hadn't since Marcus's childhood. Before they knew it, time had crept on by in that sinister way that it does, leaving them both yawning and blinking.

"I think it's time for bed," Cole said, stretching his arms back behind his head.

"Yeah, you're probably right." Marcus was still chuckling from something that had been said a few minutes earlier.

Cole clasped his son on the shoulder, then stood. "Goodnight, son."

"Goodnight, Dad." Marcus looked at him and smiled. Cole flashed a smile his way and walked slowly but surely to his bed, tears welling in the corners of his eyes.

Cole and Marcus's last day in the city was spent gathering supplies and packing their clothes. They had decided to take one duffle bag each, stuffed full of whatever they thought they might need. When Friday morning rolled around, the two of them moved about the apartment gathering up anything that they could possibly need that wasn't already in their bags. And, by nine o'clock, they found themselves standing outside, in front of a car that was clearly more than a couple of years old, but didn't seem to be too road-worn. Cole figured it probably hadn't been driven very far before, and maybe hadn't ever left the city.

The license plate was from Iowa, and the vin number was conveniently scratched out. The car would be difficult to trace for anybody, and as long as they stayed under the radar, it wouldn't be an issue. Cole took a walk around it, just to make sure it was in working order. He kicked all the tires and felt the doors. The coat of grey paint was clearly new, as were the hubcaps. It was long, longer than it needed to be, and reminded Cole of something his father would've driven. All in all, it seemed to be in excellent condition.

Not too excellent, though. Luke had been careful that the car didn't look new. It was made to be sure that it never drew any attention to itself. Cole felt confident it wouldn't, so long as he kept it at or under the speed limit.

Marcus took a deep breath before he spoke. "I guess we're really doing this," he said, his voice shaking like a tin roof in a tornado.

"I guess we are." Cole's stomach was somewhere in his shoes at this point. His chest felt tight and his legs wobbly. But at the same time, he felt a sort of strength rising through his body. He felt better than he had since the attack, he was finally walking with some semi-confidence, and he had a purpose for his life. It was refreshing, yet terrifying. And now, he was setting out on a quest the likes of which he had never considered a reality. He turned to his son. "You know we might not come back from this, right?" The thought had crossed his mind numerous times since he had decided to go after his would-be murderer. It chilled him to the bone to think that there was a distinct possibility that neither one of them would return home. "And if we do," he continued on, deliberately. "We won't be the same."

Marcus breathed deep and slowly. "I know," he said after a moment. "But I don't think we have a choice at this point."

Cole clasped him on the shoulder. "I'm not sure we ever did."

PART TWO

BLOODY TREES

CHAPTER 17

Resurgence

Viggo held tight to the little girl's hand. The village was small, but even the walls had eyes in a place like this. He didn't figure it likely that the American authorities had any inclination of where he was, but even so, the risk was too great.

"Come on, Sis." He had taken to calling her 'Sis' when she wouldn't tell him her given name. It was personal enough, he decided. He didn't need to know her name to take care of her. She didn't call him anything, but she was finally talking a little now.

Most of the drive to Mexico had been uncomfortable silence and AM radio. Somewhere in North Carolina, Viggo decided he preferred the silence to static-laced broadcasts of The Oakridge Boys.

All along, he had thought that the plan would come upon him when he got to Mexico. As it turned out, he was right. He just didn't like the plan very much. But this was where he had ended up, so it was as good as anywhere, he supposed.

The cantina was full. No surprise, it was supper time. "Are you hungry?" he asked without looking.

The girl said nothing, but he figured her head was shaking. She did that a lot. He looked to her.

"You have to eat something."

She shook her head again, her eyebrows furrowed into that same stupid, stubborn look she always had when he asked her something.

"Fine, then. Don't. I'm going to eat." Viggo wasn't hungry, but he knew it was probably time to eat. As he approached the bar, he squeezed the soft little hand even tighter. She gave a bit of a squeal and a tug, but he held tight. "Dos tacos." Viggo said to the bartender. He felt stupid speaking Spanish, especially given his lack of an accent.

The middle-aged brown skinned man nodded and yelled something to the cook, too fast for Viggo to catch. He knew it looked odd to not sit, but he couldn't risk it.

After a half hour, though, he finally gave in and took a seat at the bar, setting the girl in the chair next to him. For a while longer, probably close to an hour, the bar swirled around Viggo in a blur of mariachi music, warm beer and the smell of cooking meat. The place was nearly empty when the door swung open and caused him to look up.

The man was large, over six feet tall and weighing something close to 250 pounds. A long black revolver hung from a gunslinger's belt on his hip. A thick, dark mustache adorned his face and a worn old cowboy hat sat on his head. He removed the hat when he entered the establishment, revealing a mop of jet-black hair, plastered onto his skull by sweat. He ran his hands through the greasy mass and loosened it up.

Like something out of an old western, the man moved to the bar with a swagger that didn't seem to Viggo like something he'd picked up along the way. No, he decided. This was a true-born narcissist, living out a cowboy fantasy.

Fantasy or not, though, that revolver could put a swift end to all of Viggo's plans. All it would take is one half-decent draw, and it would all be over.

The large man sat down roughly at the bar, leather boots squeaking as he did. The bartender walked over and asked for his order.

"Maker's." The man's voice was rough, with a thick accent that Viggo could only describe as being 'country.' He scratched his mustache and took his drink with a nod. Kicking back the glass of bourbon in one drink, he turned to Viggo and spoke directly.

"You the guy I'm looking for?"

Viggo steeled himself and looked into the man's eyes.

"Depends."

The man huffed. "Depends. Fuckin' diapers." He swallowed before continuing. "You're the guy." He looked around, his eyes eventually settling on the girl.

"This her?" he asked.

Viggo gulped down a breath and tried to keep the fire in his chest from consuming him completely.

"Yep."

The cowboy nodded and swallowed. "Alright, then. Let's go." And without another word, he stood, turned on his heel and headed for the door. Viggo grabbed up the girl and hurried after him, in spite of her complaints.

The man walked to a red Jeep splattered with mud and missing its doors. He grabbed hold of the top of the vehicle and swung up into the driver's seat like he was mounting a horse.

"Y'all just follow me," he yelled to Viggo, who was making his way to his own car. Once Viggo had plopped into the driver's seat and the girl had climbed in the back, the little all-terrain vehicle was off and running. Viggo struggled to keep up.

They flew out of the village and onto an old sandy highway that headed straight out into the desert. They drove for nearly an hour before stopping. The sun had already set, and the cool desert night flowed over Viggo's skin as he exited the car. The girl hopped out of the back and stood beside him.

The cowboy swaggered out of the Jeep and over to them. He put his hands on his hips and stared at the girl for a moment, then spat before kneeling down to look her in the eye.

"What's your name?" he asked.

She said nothing, only stared at him.

"Girl, I asked you your name."

Still nothing.

The cowboy ground his teeth together. He spat into the sand again. "One more time. What's your name?"

This time she shook her head and he backhanded her. The girl's small frame went sprawling into the sand as she screamed. Viggo knelt to her, turning his back on the cowboy.

"Hey, Sis. Hey, you alright?" he asked, as softly as he could. She was crying into her hands, facedown in the sand. Viggo stood and turned to the man. "What the fuck was that?"

"She's gotta learn to talk. People like it when they talk." The cowboy stood and resumed his hands-on-hips pose.

"She's a kid, man. She'll get there. Jesus." Viggo rubbed his brow. "Look, just don't hit her again. Alright?"

The cowboy spat. "No-can-do. If she won't talk, she gets

hit. Look, she's got plenty of time before they put her to work. A couple years, at least. I'm sure she'll get the hang of it by then."

Anger bubbled up in Viggo's chest. "What do you mean, 'put her to work?'"

The cowboy chuckled. "You know goddamn well what I mean. This was your idea, pal."

"She's supposed to be a cleaning girl," he said. "They're going to let her clean the boss's house."

The cowboy laughed now, his jubilee nearly drowning out the girl's crying. "They lied to you, son. The girl for the guns and safe passage across the pond. That's the deal. Nothing's guaranteed about what she'll be doing."

Viggo wondered if he could kill the cowboy before the revolver was in his face. The man's large hand was already resting on the gun's hilt, so he didn't like his chances. But soon, he decided, he'd see this man dead. For now, though, a part had to be played.

"Fine," Viggo said with a sigh. "I just wish someone would tell me the fucking truth for once."

"No such thing, man. No such thing." The cowboy checked his watch. "They should be here by now."

Viggo was getting anxious. He was right, someone should've come to pick them up. He turned to look back the way they'd come. No sooner had he turned his head did he feel the cold metal barrel of a gun to the back of his head. He put his hands up.

"Alright," the cowboy drawled. "Now you're gonna drive us the rest of the way."

Viggo didn't respond until he heard the chilling *click* of the gun's hammer being pulled back.

"Fine, man. Fuck."

Viggo drove until after dark down a barren desert road. They mostly rode in silence, aside from the cowboy's humming along to the radio. The girl fell asleep in the back seat not too long into the ride.

A couple of hours after dark, the cowboy held up his hand. "Stop here and flash your lights." Viggo did as he was told, and after a beat a car he'd not been able to see previously flashed theirs back from off the road. Then they pulled onto the road in front of them and continued on.

"Follow them," the cowboy said. And again, Viggo did as he was told. They drove on another ten minutes before he began to see the edges of what appeared to be a compound. As they approached the front gate, the car in front slowed. Someone appeared at the gate and began yelling back and forth in Spanish with the person in the car. Viggo could see both parties gesturing toward their car at points in the conversation.

After a minute or so, the gate swung open and both cars

drove through. Once inside the fences of the compound, Viggo was blinded by spotlights being shined on his car. The cowboy was already getting out when the doors of the car were pulled open and Viggo was pulled out of it. He turned his head and saw someone grabbing the girl and dragging her from the car, as well.

"Leave her alone!" he yelled, but no one heeded him. He turned to the man who had hold of him and brought his right fist into his jaw. The captor stumbled back, dazed. Viggo turned his attention to the flannel-clad man who had the girl. Another right hook sent him to the ground, the girl on top of him.

Viggo bent to pick her still-mostly-asleep body off the ground, but was grabbed from behind around his chest. His assailant pulled him backward, until he snapped his head back into the man's face. He felt his nose break under the pressure of the blow. The man went stumbling back into the dirt as Viggo lunged at the nearest person he could find.

He tackled them into the dirt, then rose to his knees, balling his fist and raising it above his head. As he began his downward swing, though, he saw his victim's hand, fingers curled around a small chrome revolver that was aimed directly at his head. He stopped cold, and as he looked around, he saw them.

Thirty men at least, standing in a circle around him

with their weapons drawn.

Goddamnit. Viggo released his fist and raised his arms. A half-beat later, someone came up behind him, seized his wrists, and tied them together. He was hoisted to his feet as the man beneath him scurried away. The cowboy scooped up the girl, who had woken up and was staring in fear at the large group of men with guns. One of the men stepped in front of Viggo, facing him.

He was Latino, tan and lean. His hair, jet black and curly, was combed tight to his head and slicked back. His face was clean-shaven and his eyes dark and hard. He wore a flannel button-down and jeans, belted tight, and cowboy boots.

"My name's Jorge," he said, his accent nearly nonexistent. "You must be Viggo."

Viggo remained silent, staring unblinking into Jorge's eyes.

"I'll take that as a yes. And I'll assume that *she*–" he pointed to the girl, now being held firmly by the cowboy, "is the girl you told my people you had."

Viggo remained silent.

Jorge sighed. "Okay, then. Boys, take them inside."

Viggo was dragged through the compound's yard and into the large concrete building that the fence surrounded. Inside, he saw a great room that didn't seem to fit the outside of the building. Grandiose and elegant, the room was straight out of a mansion in Beverly Hills. As he was taken further into the compound, every subsequent room felt the same. He eventually found himself seated at a dinner table that was made of solid mahogany and trimmed in gold. His chair was plush and comfortable.

Viggo's hands were cut free as Jorge walked into the room. The cowboy followed, the girl following behind, eyes wide as she scanned the opulent room. When all of them were seated, Jorge spoke.

"Shall we eat?" Servers proceeded to bring in the first course. A bowl of hot tortilla soup was placed in front of each of them. Viggo looked around incredulously. The cowboy attacked his soup like it owed him money. The girl stared at the bowl and slowly picked up a spoon. Jorge was stuffing a napkin in his shirt collar and picking up a spoon, but his gaze was still locked on Viggo.

Viggo looked at the soup and took a sniff. It didn't *smell* poison. Though, he had to admit, he didn't know what he was looking for. He slowly picked up the spoon and scooped a bite into his mouth. He hadn't realized how hungry he was until he actually tasted something. The rest of the soup went down quickly, as did the following two courses.

There was very little conversation during the meal. The occasional joke by Jorge broke the silence every once in a while, but for the most part, they kept quiet. Viggo couldn't help but notice how different it was than meals he'd shared with the Scolessas. He hadn't been invited to the big table very often, but whenever there was an occasion to celebrate, there was a sense of welcome and family. Viggo felt none of that here. The enormous dining chamber was as intimidating as it was gaudy, and Jorge looked to Viggo like a man who would sooner kill him than strike a deal with him.

It was during dessert, a salted caramel flan with blackberries, that Jorge decided to talk business.

"What do you want for the girl?" He asked, bluntly. His eyes never left his plate, as though he was discussing the weather.

Viggo swallowed and cleared his throat. "I need to get to Europe. I know you have shipments that go there. Just get me on that boat, and I'll do the rest."

Jorge laughed. "Ship captains don't often take kindly to passengers who travel for free."

"I figure your captains take kindly to whatever you tell them to take kindly to." Viggo took another bite while he waited for Jorge's response.

"You're asking me to transport you across the ocean, crossing international borders, smuggling a fugitive into Europe, for what? One girl?" He laughed again as he took a bite. "Doesn't seem like a fair trade to me. Do you have anything else you can offer?" His eyes glinted knowingly.

Viggo's mind was racing. *There's no way he knows about the money,* he thought. He had buried the duffel bag of cash just after sneaking over the border, taking only enough for what they needed. *It's a hundred miles away. There's no fucking way.* He steeled himself.

"The girl's what I got. She's young, she'll make a good worker for you."

"Oh, I'm sure she would," Jorge said, smiling. "In time. But there are many girls like that."

"She's American, man."

"So are you." Jorge placed his fork on his plate. "One American girl is not enough. Sure, she would be worth fifteen, maybe twenty-thousand. But smuggling you across the ocean and into Europe?" He made a *tsk* noise. "That would cost you closer to a million. Maybe two."

Viggo was outraged. "A *million goddamned dollars?* Are you shitting me?" He was shouting now.

Jorge stood from the table and ripped a Glock nine-millimeter pistol from the holster at his side, leveling it at Viggo.

"You will watch your tongue at my table, or I will cut it out, *gringo*." His voice was ice, and his eyes had yet to show any fluctuation in his mood.

Viggo returned his stare, determined to give him no fear. "It's horseshit."

Jorge waited a moment before holstering his pistol. "That, my friend, is your opinion. Still, it is the deal."

"There's no deal, then." Viggo stood, then took a step to retrieve the girl.

"So be it."

The cowboy stood and drew his revolver. Viggo froze. The doors to the room flew open as the men who had met them at the gate stepped through with all kinds of weaponry pointed squarely at Viggo.

Jorge sat and resumed eating his flan.

"Then we will take you both."

CHAPTER 18

The Long Road Ahead

Marcus looked out the window. The clouds rolled by on a bright blue canvas of sky over the flat Texas desert. The car was a smooth ride with comfortable leather seats, but Marcus couldn't help but fidget more and more as they drew closer to the Mexican border.

"Sit still," Cole said. "Relax."

Marcus scoffed. "Right. I'll just kick back and chill out. No reason to stress."

"Look, I just mean that you need to take a deep breath and do your best to not worry about it," Cole smirked. "You'll have more than enough to worry about soon enough, I figure."

"Oh yeah," Marcus exhaled. "I'd guess you're right about that."

They had been on the road for more than a day at this point. They had stopped only a couple of times since leaving the city. Their conversations had run the gamut. Mostly, they talked about the old days, but of course, old wounds reared their head.

"I did *not* kick you out," Cole was saying. "You left all on your own."

Marcus chuckled and shook his head. "So it's still the same shit with you? After all this time? After everything that's happened?"

His father turned to him, his bright green eyes ringed with red from lack of sleep. "Don't use their deaths as a prop for your own insecurity," he seethed, and Marcus was instantly teleported back to the days before he'd left home. "You don't get to do that to me."

Marcus sighed, looked skyward. "I'm not doing anything *to* you, Dad," he said exasperatedly. "I'm just saying, can we please try to move on? I thought that's what you wanted. Isn't that why you brought all this up in the first place?"

"I wanted to get it out in the open, air it all out."

"Well it's certainly out there now!" Marcus threw his hands up, and both father and son huffed simultaneously.

"Look," Cole said after a couple minutes of silence. "I just don't want any baggage between us if..." he trailed off.

"If we don't come back?" Marcus finished the thought. "Yeah, I know."

Cole sighed. "I'm sorry. Regardless of whatever disagreements we had, you're my son." He swallowed hard.

"And I should've been there. No matter what."

Marcus looked down at his lap, unexpected emotion welling in his throat. "Thanks, Dad." He took a deep breath, then continued. "I'm sorry, too. I walked away when it got hard. And I could've come back. Mom all but begged me to come home. But I didn't." Tears gathered at the corners of his eyes. "If I had, maybe...I don't know, maybe it would've been different."

Cole's hand grabbed him by the shoulder and gave him a shake. Firm, but not painful.

"You can't go there," he said, his voice thick with emotion.

Marcus looked at him and saw a haunted distance in his eyes.

I can't go there, Marcus thought. *But you've done nothing else.*

They also discussed the plan, and what they would do when they found Viggo. Luke had assured them they'd be loaded to the hilt with weapons and cash once they crossed the border, but when it came right down to it, they were both completely untrained. And if it came to a real fight with Lassiter, neither of them felt very confident about their ability to incapacitate him.

Marcus and Cole also argued for several hours about

the decision to kill Viggo or capture him. Cole was hell-bent on capturing Viggo alive and bringing him back to the United States to be prosecuted, but Marcus felt he was trying to be more realistic about things by pointing out that they may have to kill him. Cole refused to accept it, though.

And still, much of the ride had been spent in silence, either while one of them was asleep, or when the conversation simply ran dry. In those times, Marcus was left to his own thoughts, which often strayed to his mother, brother, and sister. Truth be told, he hadn't taken much time to think of them in the weeks after he lost them. He'd had to worry so much about simply getting by, and then trying to mend fences with Cole, and now going on a manhunt to Mexico. There just hadn't been time.

Now, though, trapped in a car for hours on end, he was left to their ghosts. His mother was the one that haunted him most. She had been a loving woman, if stern. But she had always gone out of her way to make up for Cole's harshness. Never in his life had Marcus doubted her love for him, even if he couldn't understand now how she put up with him while he was growing up.

Their last conversation was what Marcus thought about the most. He had called her to apologize for his outburst when she'd come to see him for Thanksgiving, and she had taken the opportunity, of course, to remind him of how much she felt he needed to fix things with his father. He could still hear her pleading.

"Please, Marcus, just talk to your father," she had said. Her voice was strained by emotion, and he knew how important it was to her that he hear her out.

"It's not me that won't talk, Mom. He doesn't want to hear it." Marcus was stalwart. He was sure of how he felt.

His mother had sighed before responding. "It looks to me like you're the one who doesn't want to hear it."

He scoffed. "Right, I'm sure."

"God, you two are so much alike," she said exasperatedly.

"Oh, don't say that, please. I'm nothing like him."

Now she was the one scoffing. "If you'd known him when he was your age, you'd feel differently. You're both bullheaded and prideful to a fault, and neither one of you likes to hear that you're wrong." She allowed a beat of silence for her words to sink in. "But you *both* are. I tell him all this stuff, too, but neither one of you will listen to me."

Marcus didn't have a response.

"Look, Marcus, I'm sorry. I know he's hurt you. But even though you don't see it, you've hurt him, too. You've both shed blood here. Please, just let it go."

Marcus thought for a moment before sighing. "Fine. If it'll make you happy, I'll give him a call this week."

"No," she said sharply. Marcus was taken aback by her tone. "No phones. You're coming here for dinner. Next Saturday. Kapische?"

"Mom, I–"

"*Kapische?*"

Marcus sighed. "Fine."

"What are you thinking about?" Cole's words ripped Marcus from his thoughts.

"Nothing," he lied.

"Really?" Cole raised a brow inquisitively.

Marcus blew air out his nose. "Mom."

"Ah," Cole responded. After a beat, he continued. "Me, too."

"Do you think about her a lot?" Marcus asked.

Cole swallowed. "Literally all the time."

"Are you afraid?" Marcus had wondered since this all began. His father didn't show much emotion, but it had to be in there somewhere.

Cole seemed to consider his answer. "Of Lassiter? No. I'm scared of what comes next. After we get Katie back. Or, after we don't. At some point, I have to go back to just living. Get back to normal somehow. Do I go back to the store? I don't know. Maybe I'll come to Mexico myself and just live down here. There's a lot to think about. What about you? Are you scared?"

Marcus tried to phrase his answer as best he could. "I'm scared of not finding Katie. And I'm scared of losing Viggo, or not finding him. And, yeah, I guess I'm scared of when this all ends. So, yeah, basically. I am."

Cole nodded. "Yeah, I get it." He reached over and grasped Marcus by the shoulder. "We're gonna be okay. Alright?"

Marcus looked at his father. "Yeah. We'll be fine."

They crossed the Mexican border without incident later that night. Once across, they drove to the nearest town and found a McDonald's. While sitting in the car in the parking lot, Cole used the cellphone Luke had given them to call and let him know they'd made it across the border.

"Great," Luke said from the other side of the call, over speakerphone. "So now you need guns."

"That's what we were hoping," Cole said.

"Go to La Concha," Luke said. "It's a town, maybe an hour and a half from you. It's on the map. There, find the restaurant *La Tapatia* and ask for Morales. He'll know you're coming. You won't owe him anything. I've taken care of it. Check in with me after you have the guns and we'll discuss the next step." And with a *click*, he was gone.

"Well," Cole said. "I guess we've got some more driving to do."

The pair ate before getting back on the road, and

Marcus fell quickly to sleep as the Mexican countryside stretched out in front of him.

Cole rubbed his eyes as he glimpsed the nondescript sign marking their entrance to La Concha. The town was small and cramped, much like Cole had expected a Mexican village to look. The porches of buildings they passed were dimly lit, and citizens roamed the dirt streets, paying little mind to the American car.

Cole reached over and shook Marcus by the shoulder. He snapped awake.

"What? What is it?"

Cole regarded him with a raised brow. "We're here, that's all. I need you to help me look for the restaurant."

Marcus nodded as he took a deep breath and rubbed his eyes.

La Tapatia was tucked away in a back corner of the town, hidden from view to anyone who didn't know to look for it. From what they could determine, it was a sort of steakhouse and bar, but the inside didn't resemble any steakhouse Cole had ever been to. He approached the bartender and asked in carefully enunciated English where Morales was.

"Where is Morales?" Cole asked, probably slightly louder than needed. He looked at Marcus and saw him cringe.

The bartender shook his head.

Cole huffed before continuing. "Morales. I need to see Morales." The bartender did not respond. "Please," Cole pleaded. "I need to see him."

"Couldn't be more out of place if we tried," Marcus grumbled from behind him.

After a moment, the bartender sighed and stepped to one side of the bar. He pointed to a man in the back of the restaurant, slight and unassuming, sitting quietly and reading a book. Cole thanked him, slipped him a twenty-dollar bill and walked in the man's direction.

"Excuse me," he said when he arrived at the table. "Are you Morales?"

The man continued reading, never looking up. "Yes. How may I help you?"

Cole was surprised to find Morales had no accent. He was clearly American-born.

"Luke Scolessa sent us," Cole said.

"Ah," Morales sighed. "Good to know. I was wondering when you'd arrive." He placed a bookmark in the tome as he snapped it shut, then laid it on the table and gestured to two empty chairs. "Please, be my guests."

Cole and Marcus exchanged a glance with one another as they sat.

Morales took off his reading glasses, folded them, and put them in his shirt pocket. He wore a loose-fitting checkered button-down shirt with the sleeves rolled up, and khakis with dress shoes and brown socks. He rubbed his chin, then spoke.

"I have guns for you. Luke told me you wouldn't need or be able to transport any heavy-duty hardware, so I got you some smaller, more portable options." He reached down and produced a backpack from under the table. He sat it on the table and unzipped the largest compartment. From it, he produced a small chrome-plated revolver, a nine-millimeter handgun with two magazines, and two boxes of ammunition for each gun. "I have one more thing for you, in the back." Morales stood and walked briskly to the restaurant's kitchen. He returned a moment later with a large duffel bag. He placed it on the floor and unzipped it, producing a 12-gauge pump-action shotgun. "Keep this in your car. You never know when you'll need something with a little more punch." He rezipped the bag and left it at Cole's feet.

"So, is there anything else?" he asked when he had reseated himself.

Cole and Marcus looked at each other.

"I don't think so," Marcus said, sounding unsure even as he did so.

Morales nodded. "Inside the bag, you'll find holsters for your handguns. Keep the magazines for the nine mil loaded and ready to go. There's a reloader for the revolver, too, in case you need to reload fast. Familiarize yourselves with these guns. Get some target practice in, if you can."

Marcus was nodding and standing to leave, but Cole had to ask.

"Did Luke tell you why we need these?" he asked. Cole thought if Marcus could've teleported away from him, he would've done it at that moment.

Probably thinks I'm pushing our luck, Cole thought.

Morales leaned back in his chair. "Something about finding a man for him. I don't ask many questions when Luke tells me to get guns ready."

Cole hesitated slightly, but continued on. "We're looking for a man named Viggo Lassiter. Do you know him?"

Morales rubbed his jaw. "I know *of* him. Truth be told, I'd rather not get involved in whatever business brings the Scolessas south of the border."

Cole held his hands up in surrender. "No, no, I don't want you to get involved. But if you have any idea where he is, it could really help us out."

Morales sighed. Marcus's head was darting around, looking at every door in the place.

"I believe he was headed further south, to seek out passage to Europe, if what I hear fourth-hand from the bartender is true." He took a drink of a glass of water that sat next to him. "If he did, then he probably sought help from one of the cartels that runs shipments across the Atlantic. Biggest one is *Moncada Lavilla*."

Marcus sat back down, leaning in close. "Drugs?" he asked. Now it was Cole's turn to cringe.

Morales scrunched his lips and nose. "Drugs, yes. But not *only* drugs. He deals in a more...exclusive type of product, as well, if you get my meaning."

Cole could see the muscles of Marcus's jaw working as he took in Morales's words.

"You mean...you mean people?" Cole couldn't stop his voice shaking.

Morales nodded, and Cole's stomach shot through the floor. He looked at Marcus and immediately knew they were thinking the same thing: they needed to find Katie, and quickly.

CHAPTER 19

The Passing Days

Viggo's tongue was parched, and his wrists had rubbed raw from the restraints holding him bolted to the wall. His eyes had adjusted to the darkness fairly quickly, so he could see most of the dingy basement he was being held in. It was damp, and made humid from the warm breeze that floated in from the barred window set just above Viggo's head. He was sweating profusely, and his mouth had run dry days before. The meager sips of water and scraps of food they brought him were barely enough to keep his heart beating, but the rage that burned in him did that well enough for them.

The door at the top of the stair swung open, and Viggo steeled himself as best he could. The cowboy who'd brought him here walked down the stairs with a heavy sort of gait, swaying from one leg to another as he went. His right hand rested on the hilt of his massive revolver, the other with a thumb in the waistline of his pants, just over his belt buckle. He swaggered down to Viggo like a twisted take on John

Wayne and stopped in front of him, squatting.

"How's it going?" he asked, a stupid half-smile dancing on his lips. He was chewing gum and the loud *schlap, schlap* noise kept time in the cadence of his slow drawl.

Viggo looked around and shrugged as best he could with his hands manacled. "How do you think it's going?"

The cowboy chuckled and punched Viggo in the stomach. As he gasped for breath, Viggo could hear the big cliche laughing. "Oh, man. You're gonna make this hard, huh?"

Viggo breathed as deep as he could. "Go fuck yourself."

The cowboy nodded, then backhanded him across the face with surprising speed. "You're gonna learn to keep your goddamned mouth shut, son."

Viggo licked the blood from his lip before responding. "I'm sure that works for people who are scared of you. Probably worked for your piece of shit daddy–" He was cut off by a right hook that caught him across the jaw and made him see stars.

"Speak ill of my daddy again and I'll rip your goddamned heart out, yankee motherfucker." The cowboy hocked loudly and spat a ball of mucus on Viggo's chest, then stood, turning on his heel and heading back up the stairs and out the door.

As Viggo drifted in and out of consciousness, he thought

of how good it would feel to rip that revolver from his holster and empty it into the cowboy's face.

Hours or days passed before Viggo saw the cowboy again. This time, another man, short and stocky and wearing a scowl, accompanied him. Viggo studied them as best he could in the dark, but most details escaped him. He could tell the short man wore a thick black beard, but beyond that, most escaped him.

"This–" The cowboy gestured to the other man as he spoke. "--is Richie. Richie is gonna do his best to teach you some respect. Try to quell that unruly mouth o' yours."

Viggo looked to Richie. "Fuck you, Richie."

That was met with a swift kick to the ribcage from the cowboy. "Now," he said as he straightened his gun belt. "I'll leave you boys to it." And he turned and left, thudding back up the stairs with his heavy walk. Richie approached Viggo slowly and knelt. "I'd shake your hand," he said with a thick Mexican accent. "But it seems they're tied behind your back."

"Yeah," Viggo coughed. "seems that fucking way, doesn't it?"

Richie punched him in the face, and Viggo could've sworn he felt something break. But, when he worked out his jaw and stretched his facial muscles, everything seemed to be working.

"What the *fuck*?" Viggo exclaimed.

"You will not speak sarcastically when you are around me," Richie said, matter-of-factly. "I am here to teach you respect, and sarcasm is not respectful."

"Alright, man, fuck." This time, Richie punched him in the side, and Viggo knew he felt a rib crack.

Richie stood. "I'll be back every couple of days until you decide to listen to me and stop getting beaten." He turned and pounded up the steps, his footsteps betraying as much emotion as his voice.

Viggo laid over on the floor in the fetal position and tried to sleep, but his pounding head and abdomen made it difficult to think of anything else.

True to his word, Richie arrived every so often to ask Viggo some questions and pound on him. Eventually, Viggo realized he could mark the passage of time a little by the beatings. By his count, he had been held prisoner for around twenty days. His restraints had been removed not too long ago. Now, he was only tied up for his sessions with Richie. He still lived in darkness and shat in a bucket, though. And he hadn't had a bath in all the days he'd been in the basement.

He also had yet to see Jorge in that time. Richie, he saw often. The cowboy made the occasional appearance. Maids brought Viggo his food and cleaned the bucket he used for waste. But not once did Jorge show his face.

Motherfucker, Viggo thought. *When I get out of here...* He let the thought trail off because he knew it was all too likely that he would never leave this basement. Jorge had given no indication when he took him captive as to when he would be set free, or *if* he would be set free.

They had placed a bag over his head before transporting him, and he knew he was in a car at some point, so chances are, he was some distance away from Jorge's compound.

Bastard still could've come to talk to me. Took me captive, then just left me to rot in here. Fucker.

Not for the first time, Viggo wondered why Jorge had bothered with this. He could've turned Viggo away and kept the girl. Hell, he could've just shot him in the face and been done with it. But instead he'd taken him captive, and was sending Richie to soften him up, break down his walls.

He'd seen the Scolessas take prisoners before. He'd watched Mal cut ribbons from their flesh while they screamed anything they thought he wanted to hear. But they'd never done this. This seemed too sloppy for a cartel as well-organized and feared as the *Moncada-Lavilla*, and his life might hang on the balance of his figuring out what they wanted from him.

He chuckled to himself with no mirth. *Life?* He thought.

What life? Even if I get out of here, where the fuck am I supposed to go?

He knew it was true. He wasn't getting to Europe without the cartel's help. And besides, Europe was no place for him. He knew that. Maybe he could find some sort of life worth living further south? There were places men like him could find a home, he knew. But still, what would be asked of him, to keep that home? Would he do it?

As if I have any lines left to cross, he thought bitterly, the image of Cole Traeger's son's dead-eyed stare floating up through his mind. He saw those bodies a lot, when he tried to sleep. And for what? Just so he could end up here? And then the girl...

Viggo dropped his head and squeezed his eyes shut, desperately wishing the thoughts would stop. The catalogue of his sins cascaded open on the back of his eyelids, though, and the tears came unbidden to roll down his grimy cheeks.

Viggo wasn't sure how much time passed before the basement door banged open above, and he could hear the sounds of a celebration taking place upstairs; music, laughter, cheering, and screaming greeted his ears. The cowboy half-walked, half-stumbled his way down the steps. Upon reaching the bottom, he stumbled over to Viggo's bucket, unzipped his pants, and let loose a torrent of piss. Viggo wrinkled his nose at the smell. When he was done and had zipped himself back up, the cowboy meandered back toward the stairs, then abruptly lost balance. He leaned against the wall, then slid into a sitting position on the basement floor.

Viggo approached him cautiously, expecting him to stand up and beat the shit out of him, as he seemed to like doing. As he drew close, though, he realized the cowboy had a stupid grin on his face, and seemed altogether happier than he normally did when he came to the basement.

"Man," he said, slurring his words stupidly. "What're you doing?"

Drunk motherfucker, Viggo thought.

"I'm sitting in this dingy-ass basement, thinking of how sweet it's gonna be when I blow your brains out with that fucking ridiculous gun you've got on your hip." Viggo smiled as he spoke, but he felt no satisfaction. *Just playing the part,* he thought.

The cowboy reached for his gun...and *laughed.* He unholstered the metal beast, not to shoot, but to examine. He held it up and Viggo saw the little light that bled into the basement glinting off the black steel body and gold-embossed hilt.

"It *is* pretty, ain't it?" The cowboy asked, as if they were old buddies. "I got it off a gun runner, used to pass through here sometimes. Said he had it custom-made by some gunsmith over in the Middle East. That's probably bullshit, though."

"Yeah, probably," Viggo said, slightly stupefied by the cowboy's sudden change in demeanor.

"Still a sweet-ass piece, though." He smiled, then closed his eyes and drifted into a drunken stupor.

Viggo approached the cowboy carefully, like he was a bomb that might go off any minute. His eyes slid down to the gun belt at his waist, then over to that gold-embossed grip peaking out from the top of his holster. Slowly, so slowly, Viggo reached down and slid the gun free. The cowboy never moved as Viggo stood back and exhaled, his heart leaping into his throat.

He was holding the gun, his ticket to escape. He could end this miserable sack of shit right now, claim his victory over...he realized at that moment he didn't even know the cowboy's name. He shrugged. It didn't matter. He wasn't even human to Viggo, not really. Just a stupid mustache and a mean streak.

Viggo aimed the gun at the floor, gripping it with both hands and staring down the sights. Slowly, he swung his aim over, until he was looking directly at the cowboy's face. He was drifting in and out of drunken sleep, so he barely took notice of his own gun being aimed at his head.

Viggo pulled back the hammer. *I could do it right now.*

His finger moved to the trigger as images of the cowboy's brain splattered against the wall flashed through his mind. Just as he was about to pull the trigger, an uproarious cheer came from upstairs and he was reminded of how outnumbered he was. To kill him now would be a definite death sentence. Maybe for the girl, too, depending on how spiteful they felt. Reluctantly, he released the hammer and shook the cowboy to consciousness.

"It's a nice gun," he said, handing it back.

"Hell fuckin' yeah, it is." His speech was slurred and his accent was thicker than ever. Groggily, he holstered the revolver and pulled himself to his feet. Then he drunkenly ascended the stairs and went back through the door he'd come in through, leaving Viggo again in total darkness.

In Viggo's time in captivity, which he now estimated at more than a month, he had been allowed to bathe only twice, and his hair and beard had not been trimmed. Though he couldn't see himself, he assumed he looked like some sort of vagabond who'd spent the last month in the desert or on a train car.

Richie's visits had become less frequent and less torturous as Viggo had learned to simply agree to his terms when he came. Now, they spent much of the time talking, and Richie sometimes brought him extra food or water.

Viggo had gathered enough information from talking to Richie to learn they were hoping to rehabilitate him and use him to strike at the Scolessas and take control of their organization in the states. Or so he thought; it was impossible to read Richie, so he knew it was possible he was being fed a line of bullshit.

But he had no choice other than going along with it, at least for now. And he wanted them thinking he was compliant. It had become clear there was no shooting his way out of this, no one-man army was walking out of this place alive. He would either have to play along long enough to escape, or hope something caught them off-guard enough to give him a chance to do...something. He wasn't even sure what it would look like.

Viggo wondered about the girl, and what had become of her. He hoped she was being taken care of, but he feared they'd already begun conditioning her for her new line of work. Many times since his captivity had begun, Viggo had cursed himself for being so stupid as to believe the cartel when they told him she'd be used for house service. He had let his anxiousness to get across the Atlantic get the better of him and he'd become careless.

The girl was still a mystery to him in many ways. In some ways, he considered himself responsible for her. He knew it would've been easier to just kill her with the rest of her family, but he couldn't bring himself to do it. Viggo never relished in killing, but he accepted its necessity when he had to. Killing innocent children had never been something he chose to do, though.

But I did, he thought to himself, drowning out his own lies. *I killed that boy for no reason.*

The basement door flung open and banged against the wall, jarring Viggo from his thoughts. The cowboy and two other men entered, tromping down the steps angrily. Even in the dim light, Viggo could see the scowls adorning their faces. The cowboy approached him and, without hesitation, punched him in the face, knocking him back against the wall, where the other two men seized his arms. Viggo shoved his shoulder into the one on his right in an attempt to wrench his arm free, but found himself staring down the barrel of the massive revolver he'd held in his hand only a few days prior.

"Don't fuckin' move." The cowboy chewed a gum as he spoke. "Who did you tell you were coming here?"

Viggo stared at him, dumbfounded. "No one."

The cowboy cocked the hammer of the revolver, and Viggo saw the wheel slide into place. "I'll ask again – who the fuck did you tell you were coming here?"

Viggo stared into his eyes. "I didn't tell anyone. It's just me and the girl."

The cowboy stared at him intently for what seemed like an hour, then released the hammer and holstered the gun. "Fine. We'll see if *they* can tell us, then." He turned and walked back up the stairs, the other two men dragging Viggo with them as they trailed him. As they passed through the door at the top of the steps, Viggo's eyes burned from the lights. He wondered how long he'd really been down there. Maybe his count was off; maybe it had been two months, or three. He feared he'd never know for certain.

"Where are we going?" he asked the men holding his arms. "Hey, man, just tell me what's going on?" Neither of them responded. Viggo realized they might not speak English.

They dragged him through the building, following the cowboy's footsteps. One thing stood out to Viggo among the many concrete walls and hallways. There were no other people anywhere. After a few minutes of walking through the building, they pushed through a set of double doors and Viggo found himself outside in the desert sun. He saw a ring of armed men in front of them. He was pulled through the throng to the center and thrown roughly to the ground.

Viggo pulled himself to his knees and found himself staring at two other people, also on their knees, with black hoods on their heads. Their hands were tied behind their backs, like his had been when he first arrived. He looked to his right, and saw the cowboy talking with someone, his back turned to Viggo, obscuring the other man's face. Still, Viggo felt he knew well enough who it was. As the cowboy stepped away, his feelings were affirmed.

Jorge Lavilla stood, gun holstered on his side, looking as ice cold as the night of Viggo's dinner and subsequent capture. Viggo glared at the cartel leader, hoping he would strike something at the man, something resembling fear. Jorge barely seemed to notice him for nearly a minute. When he did look Viggo's way, he smiled and proceeded to walk over and stand between Viggo and the other two men.

"It seems your friends have come to rescue you," he said, still smiling.

Viggo shrugged. "They're not with me."

Jorge narrowed his eyes. "So you say. Still, I feel as though you are lying."

Viggo scoffed. "And why is that, exactly?"

Jorge's smile widened, exposing his perfect teeth. "Because they said they were looking for you." He drew his gun from its holster.

Viggo's stomach dropped. *The Scolessas.* "Look, Jorge, I don't know them."

The thin Latino man with no accent laughed. "Do you often have men you don't know looking for you?" He pointed his gun at one of the hooded men. "Let's see how you feel about me shooting one of them." The men were shaking their heads, mumbling something. "Well, actually, let's see what *they* have to say."

Jorge reached down and pulled the hood off one of them. The man underneath was no more than twenty years old, long brown hair tousled and mussed. A thin beard grew on his cheeks. His mouth was gagged with a tied rag. There was something familiar about him, but Viggo couldn't place it. Jorge knelt, holstering his gun and removing the gag.

"What were you saying?" he asked the man.

The young man was breathing heavily. "We're...we're not with him."

Viggo sighed in relief as Jorge's smile changed to a look of confusion. "Then why did you say you were looking for him?" he asked.

The young man swallowed hard. "We're here...to take him home. He...he killed our family."

Viggo's jaw tightened as he ground his teeth. *No fucking way. No* fucking *way.*

"Oh!" Jorge exclaimed. "Well, isn't this interesting? They aren't here to *free* you!" He was laughing, on the verge of hysterics. "They're here to *capture you!*" He bent over, putting his hands on his knees as he laughed. He pointed at Viggo. "You *do* have a way of pissing people the *fuck* off, don't you?"

Viggo was staring at the kid, at a loss for words. "Take the hood off the other one," he said.

Jorge's laughing ceased. "What?" he asked.

"Please," Viggo said, his voice shaking with fear of what he would find. "Take the hood off the other one."

Jorge shrugged. "Fine by me." He reached over and ripped off the other man's hood.

Viggo nearly passed out. Cole Traeger stared at him with eyes full of hate.

CHAPTER 20

One More Day

Cole held the small chrome-plated revolver, turning it over in his hands as Marcus drove. The sun was rising over his right shoulder, and he knew they had another couple of hours to go, at least. The map he was consulting said they were about a hundred miles out from the town nearest the *Moncada Lavilla* cartel's territory. Morales hadn't been able to tell them the exact whereabouts of the cartel's compound, but he thought they would stand a decent chance at finding them in the town of *San Juan el Baptiste.*

"Find a man named Nestor Gaviria," he had told them. "He will be able to lead you to the cartel's compound."

Cole and Marcus had agreed and hastily begun leaving, but he had stopped them, with a warning. "Understand me," he had said. "Even *if* you find the *Moncada Lavilla* cartel's hideout, chances are you will not find the man you are looking for. Either he bartered safe passage to Europe, or he's dead. Either way, your trip down here and all the risk you took upon yourself may be for naught."

Cole had nodded before responding. "We know. We still have to try."

The road that led to the town had proved to be as difficult an opponent as they'd faced to this point. Winding through hilly, unfamiliar territory that grew more and more treacherous as they went, they had been forced to take it slow, which served to unnerve Cole even further.

"Goddamn it, I wish we could go faster," he said, grumpily placing the small revolver in the cup holder.

Marcus sighed. "Dad, we're going as fast as we can. Viggo already has a month's head start on us. You know there's no guarantee we'll ever find him."

Cole grunted. "I know. Still, even if he's long gone, this is our *only* chance of getting Katie back." He cringed a bit at the speaking of his daughter's name. Cole had tried to limit the usage of her name since he had lost her. It made it easier to cope with her not being there. And, he hoped, it helped prepare him for the very real chance of never finding her.

Cole shook his head, trying to rid himself of the thoughts of losing his baby girl forever, and instead turned his attention to the Mexican countryside rolling by his window. Lillian had always talked about coming down to Mexico for retirement. He had laughed her off back then.

"Retire?" he'd ask incredulously. "You mean you're actually planning to do that at some point? Must be nice."

Well, we're here now, honey. He rubbed his brow and closed his eyes, trying to get some sleep before they arrived. Though it took almost a half-hour, even with the exhaustion he was facing, he managed to finally drift off as the sun rose fully into its place in the sky.

He dreamt of Lillian, and their children. They were young again; Marcus was no older than thirteen. Bryce was five, and Katie was still a swaddled newborn. They were playing in their backyard, and the sun warmed a breeze that tousled Lillian's hair around her face. She smiled at him through the thick, brown hair, and he felt the warmth of her love surrounding him.

When Marcus shook Cole awake, the sun was fully risen and beating down on them from above.

"Dad," he said. "We're here."

Cole looked blearily out the windshield. The small Mexican village of *San Juan el Baptiste* was nestled in a valley between two diminished peaks. It seemed quiet enough from a distance, but Cole knew it held something darker in its depths.

"Alright," he said. "Let's find Gaviria."

As they turned onto the town's main throughway and looked for a place to park the car, Cole couldn't help but wonder what Gaviria would tell them. Would he take them to the cartel? Would he just tell them where to find them? Would he turn them over as hostages? Not for the first time, Cole regretted bringing Marcus along, though he didn't believe for a second he could've stopped him. Still, if anything happened to Marcus...

Cole pushed the thought from his mind and tried to focus. Marcus found a parking spot and they left the car, proceeding on into the town on foot. As they went, Cole tried to think of where they might find Gaviria. He decided to try asking some of the people on the street first, but his questions were mostly answered with silence, or the occasional rude gesture.

Until a man, maybe mid-twenties, had perked up at the name. He gave Cole and Marcus an appraising look, then nodded.

"I can help you find him," he said in heavily accented English. "Do you have a car?"

Cole and Marcus exchanged a glance, probably too obviously excited, then nodded. Marcus lead the way back to the car, and Cole walked just behind, taking the opportunity to get to know their new acquaintance.

"What's your name?" he asked the man, taking in the measure of him. He was average height, maybe an inch shorter than Cole, with tanned skin and dark hair, a light stubble on his cheeks and a goatee sprouting from his bottom lip. He wore khaki shorts and a tank top, showing arms of corded muscle, ringed with tattoos. He smiled at Cole, flashing a mouth of white teeth.

"Santiago." He extended a hand, which Cole shook. "But call me Santi."

Cole nodded. "I'm Cole." He gestured toward Marcus. "That's my son, Marcus."

At the mention of his name, Marcus shot a glance over his shoulder, and Cole instantly realized his mistake.

Real names, he thought with an inward groan. He chastised himself mentally for slipping up, but it was done now. He had to hope this new ally was trustworthy. Trustworthy, and not a member of the damned cartel himself.

But Santiago seemed the opposite of what Cole expected to find in a cartel gang member. He was kind, well-spoken, and laughed easily as Cole recounted their drive down. He made sure to leave out any details about Luke or their reasons for making the trip, telling Santi they were just coming down to visit some old friends, but the young man still seemed genuinely amused.

"Well, you've chosen an interesting place to vacation," he said when Cole had finished talking. They were nearly back to the car now. "San Juan el Baptiste isn't exactly *inundado de turistas.*" He slipped into that sort of Spanglish dialect constantly, leaving Cole to decipher his meaning. As he fumbled with this phrase, though, Marcus spoke up.

"Not a lot of tourists," he said from ahead of them.

Cole nodded, understanding. "Right. Well, when we find Nestor, we'll be on our way somewhere a little bit... beachier." And some part of him wished it were true.

Santi nodded as they turned off the street, into the small parking lot where they'd left the car. "So," he said. "You know Nestor well?"

He'd asked the question innocently enough, but Cole caught something in his voice that gave him pause."Not me," Cole said, trying to think of some other plausible reason he'd be looking for the man. "My late wife was family to him. Distantly, but still. Before she died, she asked us to bring her ashes down here and spread them." Marcus had bristled at Cole's use of the phrase "late wife." Truthfully, he'd nearly vomited getting the words out, but Santi seemed to have bought the story, nodding along agreeably.

As they reached the car, Marcus removed the duffle bag of guns and cash from the back floorboard and tossed it in the trunk, making room for someone to sit in the back seat. Santi climbed in the back, and Cole took over driving.

"Alright," Santi said, scooting over to the middle of the

bench seat and perching his elbows on the front two seats. "Pull out of here and take a left."

Following Santi's directions, Cole navigated the car along the town's streets, then headed out of town, following a road cut into the side of a mountain. Cole was careful not to look over the edge. Eventually, Santi directed him off this road as the terrain gradually shifted from mountainous to a thick forest.

"He lives all the way out here?" Marcus asked as they drove further into isolation. They had been driving for a couple of hours at this point, and Cole shared his son's trepidation. Not for the first time, he wondered if he'd made a horrible mistake.

Santi just smiled. "Yes," he said, flashing those white teeth again as he lounged in the backseat. "Nestor *es un muy reservado.*"

Cole didn't know much Spanish, but he gathered the meaning. Nestor was a private man.

He better be, Cole thought, bile rising in his throat.

Not much further down the road, Cole came to a stop in front of five men, all outfitted with body armor, holding rifles. His heart leapt into his throat as he hit the brakes. One of the men approached the driver's side window and knocked lightly. Cole rolled it down, noticing the others taking up positions in the front and back of the car.

The man leaned down and looked in their window, taking in the odd trio. A black wrap covered his face below his eyes, and those orbs gave nothing away.

Cole's stomach trembled. He was glad to be sitting down, as he was not sure his legs would've held up under that gaze, and that gun.

The man spoke in Spanish, his voice low and cool, his eyes sliding over the three men in the car. Cole stammered, turning to look at Marcus, who shrugged. Then Santi leaned forward and took the reins in the conversation. He and the armed man exchanged a few sentences, of which Cole understood nothing. Then they both chuckled and the man stepped away from the window, signaling them forward.

As they rolled past the checkpoint, Cole exhaled and turned to Santi.

"Thank you—" he began, but was cut off by Marcus's eyes, fixated on Santi. As Cole's gaze moved toward the backseat he saw why.

Santi's face bore the same placid smile he often wore. But his hand held an enormous serrated knife to Marcus's throat.

"Alright, Cole," he said, his voice even. "Pull over here, and I won't have to open your son's throat."

Cole's stomach rolled as his eyes met Marcus's. He saw

fear there. His son was afraid and the cold feeling in his gut told him he'd done this to him. Santiago held the knife, but Cole had put them in his grasp.

Cole pulled the car over on the side of the road and put it in park.

"Get out and leave the keys in *el encendido*." Cole assumed that was the ignition, so he did as told and found himself standing on the outside of the car. Santiago and Marcus were climbing out from the passenger side. Marcus moved around the front of the car, the knife pointed squarely as his back. Santiago walked him toward Cole until they were standing side by side, facing him.

"Open your wallets, give me everything you have," Santiago said.

Cole put his hands up in what he hoped was a peaceable gesture "Wait a second—"

"Now!" Santiago screamed, jamming the tip of the knife toward Marcus's throat and pricking him, drawing a thin line of red. It ran down his neck and disappeared below the collar of his shirt.

Rage flared in Cole and he tamped it down. *The best thing I can do for Marcus is cooperate with whatever he says,* Cole thought. For now. He did as Santiago asked, giving him all his cash and credit cards. Marcus did the same. Santiago smiled as he pocketed everything.

"Alright, *muchachos*," he said, backing toward the car. "I'm gonna take this, too. Have fun finding your way back to town." And he laughed, a grating sound that drove Cole to think about leaping on the car, trying to rip Santiago's throat out with his teeth, something, *anything*.

But he didn't. Santiago pulled away with their car and all their guns and money, not to mention anything of their pride. Cole and Marcus stood there in silence for a long while, saying nothing. Marcus's hands balled into fists at his sides, knuckles turning white. Cole took a step toward his son, opened his mouth to say something. And Marcus rounded on him, eyes wide with fury.

"Goddammit, Dad," he began, his voice a hoarse whisper escaping through gritted teeth. "What were you thinking? You might as well have handed him the keys to the car on the street!" He was clearly struggling to keep himself from screaming. The armed men from the checkpoint were still close by, and that could only make things worse.

Still, Cole's own anger and bruised ego were rising. He shoved a finger in Marcus's face. "Don't blame me," he seethed. "I'm not the one who ended up held at knifepoint."

Marcus scoffed and threw his hands in the air, then let them fall to his sides. "It's always my fault, huh? Even when you're the one driving the *fucking car*."

"You could've spoken up whenever you wanted, you know," Cole shot back. "Anytime you felt like things were off. But no, you sat right there and said nothing. Because you're lost in all this crazy shit, just like me!"

Marcus's eyes went wide and he pointed a finger toward Cole, advancing a step. "What am I supposed to do, have an argument about this in front of a stranger?" He adopted a mocking tone. "Oh, hey Dad, don't forget to be careful about who we trust, we are looking for a cartel, after all." He rounded on Cole again, inches away now. "I didn't think you had to be reminded to be fucking careful."

Cole was out of retorts, so he unsheathed an old favorite, dropping his voice to its most sinister whisper. "Don't you take that tone with me, Marcus."

Marcus laughed. "Figures."

Cole opened his mouth to speak again...and stopped short, suddenly aware of how stupid they must look; how stupid *he* must look. He dropped his eyes, then rubbed them with his palms like he was trying to grind them down to nothing.

"Oh what's the point?" He turned from Marcus. "You're right. It was stupid." Another pause as he worked up the words. "I'm sorry."

Marcus said nothing for a moment, then sighed. "Me, too."

Cole turned back to him and gestured to the road. "Come on," he said. "We'd better start walking."

They walked for what Cole thought must have been a couple of hours before a passing truck picked them up and gave them a ride back to town in its bed. The trip was mostly quiet, Cole not feeling the need to fill the silence with more apologies, and Marcus trying to rest as the truck jostled along. After they were left back where they began, Cole turned a corner and spotted a phone booth, complete with a phone book, and had an idea.

He was surprised to find one in such a remote location, but chose not to look a gift horse in the mouth. According to the book, Nestor Gaviria lived at *Al Nueva de Centrar No. 45*. Once he had the address, it was as simple as finding it, which only took an hour or so; *San Juan el Baptiste* wasn't much of a town at all, it turned out – just a collection of a few streets and buildings.

Hesitantly, Cole knocked.

For a while, there was no answer. They were about to turn and walk away to go look for him elsewhere when the door flew open, and they found themselves face to face with a squat man, clothed in a dirty undershirt and jeans. He was balding on top, but what hair remained had grown long, nearly to the middle of his back. He stared at them intently, then spoke.

"What you need?" he asked in broken English.

"We're looking for the *Moncada Lavilla* cartel," Cole said.

Gaviria fell into a fit of snorting laughter. "Why?" he asked between heaves. "Why you *want* to find them?"

Cole looked at Marcus, and he took over.

"They have my baby sister," he said. Gaviria's laughter stopped. "And we think they know where the man who kidnapped her is."

The short, balding man sighed. "If they have her," he said. "You not get her back."

"Please," Marcus said, his voice taking on a pleading tone. "You have to help us. You have to let us try."

"Look," Gaviria said, extending his palm toward the two of them. "I can't tell you much. All I say is, you ask about them too much, they will find *you*."

A realization dawned on Cole. "Can you make that happen?"

Gaviria's eyebrows furrowed as confusion overtook his face. "You want me tell them you asking about them?" he asked, incredulous. "Why?"

"Yeah," Marcus said, sounding unsure. "Why would we want that?"

"Because," Cole said, maybe a bit too excitedly. "Then

we won't *have* to find them. They'll come to *us*."

"So they can kill you!" Gaviria exclaimed.

"Exactly!" Marcus echoed. "They'll kill us!"

"If we're trying to take away something of theirs, they're going to try to kill us anyway," Cole explained. "Maybe we can talk to them. Maybe we can convince them to give her back."

Gaviria snorted. "You will not do that."

Cole ignored him. "It may be our only chance. We can wander all over Mexico looking for them, or we can get them to come straight to us." He turned to Marcus; he knew what he was asking of his son. "You don't need to do this with me."

Marcus sighed. "Technically speaking, I'm the reason we're here. I don't get to walk away. Besides," he breathed deep, then exhaled. "What would I go back to? And you're right, this is our best shot at getting to her before she's gone for good." He turned to Gaviria. "Will you tell them?"

Gaviria wagged his finger at both of them, but Cole thought he caught an underlying tone of begrudging respect. "You both crazy. I will call, but you both crazy."

"Tell them we're looking for Viggo Lassiter," Cole said before turning to walk away. "That ought to get their attention."

It didn't take long for the cartel to find them. They decided to wait in a local pub and get something to eat. Cole couldn't ignore how strange it felt, having dinner and waiting for a ruthless drug and human trafficking organization to come capture them and drag them away to their compound. Still, he felt they'd made the right decision.

Right up until the doors to the bar flew open and four men walked in, tattooed and carrying varying types of guns. Two men carried pistols, one wielded a sawed-off shotgun, and the other was holding what Cole thought was an AK-47. The sight of them made Cole's stomach sink through the floor. He was half expecting them to open fire as soon as they walked in, but the bartender pointed the two of them out when questioned, and the men strolled directly to them.

The one in the front spoke for them, in clear English. "So, I hear you boys are asking about someone I know."

Cole glanced to Marcus and saw sweat beading over his brow. He turned back to the cartel member. "We're looking for Viggo Lassiter."

The man smirked. "Yep, that's the one. Well, we've got him. But, uh...I'm afraid you won't be able to see him. At least, not like you want to."

Cole clenched his jaw. "Why's that?"

The cartel member laughed. "He's locked in our basement right now. And I figure you'll be in a similar spot pretty soon." He took a drink of Cole's soda, then smiled again. "We appreciate you two making it easy on us." He snapped his fingers and barked an order in Spanish. The other man wielding a pistol and the one with the shotgun stepped forward, producing black sacks that had been tucked into their waistbands.

Cole felt his muscles tense. "What are you doing?"

The man who'd been speaking laughed and rubbed his jaw. "Taking you to the boss. That's what you wanted, right?"

Cole looked at Marcus one last time as the black hoods slid down over their heads and immersed them in total darkness.

Cole could feel the bumpy road beneath them for what felt like forever. He figured they were driving off-road, maybe through the desert. When the car finally stopped and he was pulled from it, he could feel the hot sun beating down on the back of his neck, and assumed it was late afternoon. If so, they would've been on the road for about three hours since the pub. He was made to walk a short distance, then shoved roughly to his knees. He could feel Marcus beside him, and his heart began to pound violently against the inside of his chest.

What have I done? he thought. *I promised Lillian I*

would take care of Marcus and get Katie back, and find Viggo. And now, I'm going to get us both killed. He tried to breath, but the thick black hood was keeping him from catching his breath fully.

He could hear people talking, a lot of them. They were all around him. It was chaotic noise, but it helped drown out the thoughts invading his head, so he welcomed the chatter. Then, as suddenly as it had begun, the noise stopped, and a singular voice spoke. It was a man, and Cole could tell he was Latino from the very thin accent that he could hear.

"It seems your friends have come to rescue you," he said.

Cole wouldn't have used the word "rescue," but he supposed it still mostly applied.

Another voice spoke, gruff and harsh, yet smooth at the same time. "They're not with me."

Cole's heart calmed. This was it, the man he'd come so far to find. The Boogeyman that invaded his dreams and stole his life. It was Viggo Lassiter. It had to be. Suddenly, Cole found himself resolute in his decision. He was mere feet away now. Anything could happen.

The two went back and forth for a while, until the first man threatened to kill either Marcus or Cole. Cole couldn't tell who the gun was pointed at, but it didn't matter; in his mind, his plan had worked, and they were nearly face-to-face with Viggo.

Suddenly, he heard Marcus speaking. There was fear in his voice, but Cole knew he felt the same. After another few moments, Cole felt someone grabbing the top of his hood. He steeled himself. As it was lifted, he found himself nearly blinded by the sun. Still, he forced himself to stare forward, and found Viggo Lassiter staring back with eyes full of fear.

CHAPTER 21

At the Border of Heaven and Hell

Marcus looked to his father first, then to the man he assumed was Viggo Lassiter. He looked like someone who'd been kept captive. His hair was grown out, dirty and matted. His beard was unkempt and messy, his skin covered in a layer of grime. Still, his eyes were sharp. It was clear to Marcus that he was still alert, no matter how long he'd been kept hostage. Now, though, he looked almost slackjawed. As though the sight of Cole had knocked the wind out of him.

"It looks to me as though you two *definitely* know each other," the man who'd been speaking said. Marcus thought he'd heard Lassiter call him 'Jorge.'

Cole nor Viggo made a move to speak, so Marcus took it upon himself.

"We've been looking for him," he said. "But we don't *know* him."

"Well, that's very interesting," Jorge said. "I don't often go looking for people I don't know."

Again, Cole and Viggo sat with their eyes locked, neither wanting to look away.

A large man, who looked American, walked up to Jorge and whispered in his ear. The man was wearing a cowboy hat, and a huge black revolver hung from his hip. Marcus would've found the ensemble humorous if he wasn't so scared of it.

After a moment, the man stepped away and Jorge spoke again. "Let's move this discussion to a more private location, so we can talk freely." He clasped his hands together. "I have a feeling we will be talking for quite some time."

Marcus, Cole, and Viggo were hauled to their feet by armed men and dragged inside the cartel's compound. As they passed through the building, Marcus couldn't help but notice how *big* it was. This was clearly a major operation. It dawned on him that they were essentially going up against a small army.

The three of them were taken to a small dank room in the back of the compound and left under the guard of three armed men. They were made to kneel, but their hands were unbound. Each of them had a high-powered weapon pointed at their head, and they sat in silence.

Marcus glanced at his father's face and saw it was still twisted into an angry scowl. He stared straight forward at the wall, his hands resting on his knees. On his other side, Marcus saw Viggo's eyes, clearly working on an idea of some sort. He looked at the floor, but his fingers drummed against his legs endlessly, keeping some pattern no one but him could hear.

"Hey," one of their captors said, advancing to Viggo. "Stop that." He gestured at the drumming fingers with the barrel of his AK-47. Lassiter cast his eyes up into the guard's, and for a moment, Marcus wondered if he was about to strike the man. But he simply looked back down and clasped his hands together.

The three of them sat there under guard for a long while, though Marcus couldn't say how long exactly. The room was windowless,with only a single swinging lightbulb over their heads. He figured it had to be at least an hour or two. After the first thirty minutes or so, Marcus found his heart had slowed and the realization set in that they had actually found Viggo Lassiter. He'd had his doubts, but somehow, they'd actually done it.

What now? He thought. *We're here, he's here, but there's no way we're walking out of here with both him and Katie.* He pinched his nose between his forefinger and thumb and sighed. A quick glance at his father showed no change. Cole Traeger had yet to move, save breathing. He'd done nothing but stare straight forward and scowl for the entirety of their time in the room.

Without warning, the door to their cell swung open. The man Marcus had made note of earlier, with the comically oversized gun, stepped inside.

"Boss is ready for ya," he said, a thick southern accent pouring out of his mouth like gravy. The three of them were made to stand and marched out of the room at gunpoint, Cole first, then Marcus, then Viggo in the back. They were paraded through the building, around corners, and down hallways for what felt like hours, until they eventually came to a lavish dining room, standing in sharp contrast to the bland concrete running through the rest of the compound.

"What the *fuck*?" Viggo spoke from the back of their line as they entered the room. Marcus sat in a chair that had been pulled out from the table, at the behest of his armed escort. "I've been here the whole fucking time?"

Marcus turned as he pulled himself up to the table to see Viggo with his hands on his bony hips, his head swiveling from side to side, taking in the room. One of the men gestured to a chair for him, but he either didn't notice or didn't care. "You've gotta be fucking kidding me." He turned to the man pointing at his chair. "You assholes drove me around for an hour with a bag over my head just to fuck with me? Fuck *that*, man."

The armed guard was still gesturing. "Sit."

Viggo leaned in, inches from the man's face. "Fuck you."

The butt of the shotgun caught him across the jaw, sending him forward onto the massive, ornate, gold-trimmed table. Before he could rise, the barrel of the gun was at the back of his head. Marcus held his breath.

Don't kill him, he thought. *Don't fucking kill him.*

Cole must have had the same thought. He was halfway out of his chair when one of the men caught him by the shoulder and roughly shoved him back down.

"You wanna die?" The man with the gun was asking Viggo. His accent was thick, and the words sounded all jumbled together, emphasized in the wrong way. "Do it one more time, *gringo*."

Viggo was leaning with his hands on the table, and what muscles he had left after whatever he'd been through were tensed. His teeth were gritted, but after a moment, he closed his eyes and raised his hands.

"Fine. But that's a fucked up thing to do, and you can tell Lavilla I said so." The man behind him grabbed him by his shoulder and guided him to a chair on the other side of Cole, all the while never moving his gun.

"There ya go. Nice and easy." The man dressed like a cowboy spoke from the other side of the room, hand on the huge black revolver. "Don't wanna cause trouble." Viggo didn't respond, but his anger was palpable.

Marcus made note of the name Viggo had mentioned; Lavilla. *Jorge's last name?* He thought. That would make him one of the heads of the *Moncada-Lavilla* cartel. Marcus suppressed a shiver and glanced back to his father. Cole's eyes never left Viggo, and Marcus could see his knuckles had gone white, gripping his chair.

Marcus remembered to breathe, then let himself relax as much as possible and take in the room. They were all seated on the same side of a huge carved wooden table. It was embossed with what appeared to be gold and sat in the center of a large room that looked like it belonged in a French chateau. The walls were white, with columns lining the sides of the room. At the far end of the room, an enormous ornate stone fireplace had been carved into the wall, statues of lions on either side. Pink, gold, and white designs were painted all around the space, and the ceiling was adorned with a huge painting of Michelangelo's *Creation of Adam*. Marcus noticed, though, that Adam in this version of the painting was Latino, and bore a striking resemblance to Jorge Lavilla.

At that time, the only door leading into the room burst open and the man himself strode through. Jorge had cleaned up since their meeting outside. His jet black hair was slicked back and shined from pomade. His beard had been trimmed and neatly shaped. He wore a simple white button-down shirt, the top three buttons undone, sleeves rolled up to his elbows, with crisp blue jeans and brown cowboy boots shining like a mirror in sunlight. As far as Marcus could tell, he was unarmed. He walked through the room, taking long strides, his perfect white teeth displayed in a warm smile. His eyes, though, showed no smile in turn. They were dark and hard as peach pits and jumped from man to man. First, they stared down Viggo, then Cole, and finally set their sights on Marcus. He stared back for a moment, but found himself unwilling to bear the weight of that gaze and looked down at his hands in his lap.

The cartel leader took a seat directly across from Cole, then waved to his men. "Leave us," he said with no hint of an accent. Without a moment of hesitation, the armed men streamed back through the door. All except the man with the revolver. He leaned against the wall behind his boss, sucking on a wad of tobacco with his thumbs stuck in his belt.

Lavilla took each man in turn again with his gaze, then folded his hands on the table and smiled. "So," he said. "I'll start with a simple question. Why are the two of you–" he jammed two fingers at Marcus and Cole. "looking for this piece of shit?" A thumb in Viggo's direction punctuated his question.

Marcus looked to his father, who sat with his arms crossed and still showed no signs of speaking. A beat passed as he considered his options. With a sigh, he turned back to Lavilla.

"He killed my mom and brother," he began. "He almost killed my dad. And he pissed off a lot of people back home."

Lavilla nodded. "So you want revenge? I can give you revenge." He snapped his fingers and the man behind him drew the massive revolver from the holster on his hip and leveled it at Viggo.

"Hey, wait," Viggo said. "Fuck, man. Hey, *fuck!*"

The man pulled the hammer back as Cole stood. "Wait!" He leaned in front of Viggo and faced his palm to the huge gun. "Don't!"

Marcus felt his heart pounding against the inside of his chest as he looked to Lavilla, who he found to be nodding.

"So, not revenge then." He shrugged. "Fair enough." The cowboy holstered his gun and went back to leaning against the wall. "So there's more to it?" He looked back to Marcus.

Marcus closed his eyes and breathed deep. "Yes." Cole was sitting again, and Marcus looked to him for direction again. This time, he was far less stoic. His eyes were wide, his chest heaving, and his hand was rubbing his jaw. He glanced at Marcus, meeting his gaze, and nodded.

"He stole my daughter," Cole said matter-of-factly.

Lavilla's eyes widened as he leaned forward on his elbows. "Your daughter?" He glanced at Viggo, who Marcus noticed seemed to be trying to shrink into nothing. "You didn't." Lavilla laughed. "Oh, wow. That is *low*, my friend. Even for you." He leaned back and crossed his arms, then signaled to the cowboy. "Tell the kitchen we'd like four slices of cheesecake and some coffee, please." The man swaggered off with a nod as Lavilla turned back to Cole. "I've got something you'll want to see."

Marcus glanced at Cole and found him visibly uneasy. His fists were clenched and his muscles tensed. When he spoke, his voice was quiet and shaky.

"What is it?"

Lavilla smiled again. "Just wait. Don't want to ruin the surprise."

The next three minutes crawled by in agonizing fashion. Marcus felt flush, his heart pounding. His breath was shaky and uneasy, and he knew Cole had to feel the same. He looked at Viggo several times and saw he had gone white and leaned back in his chair, his hand covering his eyes.

For the first time, Marcus noticed his smell. Viggo smelled as though he'd not seen a shower in weeks, a moldy odor emanating from him like spoiled meat, sweat, and piss.

It made his stomach turn, so he too leaned back as much as possible and tried to look somewhere else.

Without warning, the door swung open again, and the cowboy walked in. Behind him came three serving girls with slices of cheesecake that they placed in front of Jorge, Marcus, and Cole. As they left the room, Marcus found himself holding his breath again, waiting for the proverbial other shoe to drop. Fear gripped his chest as the whole world shrunk to the size of that door.

When Katie walked in, she was dressed in the same black and white uniform as the other serving girls. Her brown hair had grown long, and was braided down to the small of her back. She carried a serving plate with a slice of cheesecake carefully with both hands. For what seemed an eternity, she crossed the threshold and doddled over to the table, where Viggo sat, cake-less.

Marcus felt his throat on fire as hot tears came flooding from his eyes. He stood, unable to stop himself. Cole was on his feet, too.

"Katie!" his father called out. She looked up, focusing her eyes. "Katie, it's Daddy!" Recognition came to her slowly, but it came all the same.

"Daddy?" She asked meekly. The plate crashed to the floor. Her eyes drifted to Marcus. "Bubba?"

Marcus couldn't muster words, only a nod of his head.

His heart was slamming against the inside of his chest as he wiped his tears away.

Cole was crashing clumsily past Viggo when Marcus looked at him next. Marcus tried not to give the murderer any more victory in this moment than he had to, but he noticed Viggo hadn't yet looked at Katie.

Cole was a foot from Katie when she reached her arms out to him. As they collided, he scooped her up, gripping her tight to his chest. She buried her face in his shoulder and cried.

"I found you," Cole whispered to her between sobs. "I found you, baby. I'm so sorry."

Marcus took a step toward his father and sister before he heard Lavilla speak again. "Alright, alright," he said. Marcus's stomach dropped as he turned and saw the cowboy advancing on Cole and Katie. "That's enough of a reunion." Cole must have not heard, because he didn't look up until the cowboy had his hands on Katie.

"Hey, what are you–" Cole stammered as he realized what was happening. "Hey, no, wait. Wait! *HOLD ON!*" He screamed, but the cowboy kept pulling on her. Katie screamed, piercing the air with her high-pitched protests and wails, but the cowboy kept on pulling her, wrenching her from Cole's grip as he tried desperately to hang on.

Marcus looked first to Jorge and found him looking

annoyed, if anything. Viggo Lassiter had looked up, but offered no protest.

Luke's warning to Marcus came unbidden to his mind.

"He makes death look like an art," is what he'd said. As Marcus looked at him now, he wondered where that monster was. Anger flared in his throat and he swallowed his disgust as an idea blossomed in his mind, fed by the desperation of Cole's cries and Katie's wails.

Marcus shook Viggo by the shoulder. "Hey!" he said, trying to speak over the commotion. "Do something!" Viggo cast his eyes up into Marcus's.

"I can't," he said.

Marcus swallowed his anger again, forced himself to carry on. He wrapped a hand around the back of Viggo's head and wrenched him up, making him look at what was happening.

"Look at this," he seethed in the murderer's ear. "You're the only one who can do anything to help her right now." Viggo's eyes flicked over the scene with a calculating precision, then rolled over to meet Marcus's gaze. "And you know you owe us," Marcus added, though the words brought tears to the corner of his eyes. There was no way to quantify what Viggo Lassiter owed him, but if it made him get off his ass now, it would be worth the understatement.

Viggo looked to Jorge, who was watching the chaotic

dance between Cole, the cowboy, and Katie with a bemused grin, lifting a forkful of cheesecake to his mouth. He swallowed, then stood. "Get the girl and get down," he said, his voice deathly quiet, but resolute. "Don't hesitate."

Marcus nodded, then swallowed hard and tried to forget the pit in his stomach and the fire in his throat. He followed Viggo out from their places behind the table, and tried to keep his wits about him. The cowboy had Katie by the waist, pulling on her, while Cole had her up around the shoulders.

"Let her go!" Cole roared through his tears. "She's my daughter, let her go!"

The cowboy didn't speak, only grunted as he pulled at Katie, who continued to scream bloody murder. Viggo strolled to the cowboy with long steps and without hesitation, clocked him with a right hook. He let go of Katie and stumbled back for a moment.

Cole careened backward as he let go and landed on his back, holding Katie as tightly as Marcus felt was possible. It took only seconds for Cole to roll over on top of her. Marcus looked back to Viggo in time to see him catch the cowboy's hand as he drew his revolver, wedging his thumb between the hammer and firing pin. Marcus prayed silently that he was strong enough to withstand the larger man.

Viggo snapped forward and cracked the cowboy in the

face with his forehead, knocking him slightly off-balance, then used the opportunity to shove him against a wall and draw his arm back for a punch. That punch, however, found the solid concrete wall as the cowboy slid under it.

"*FUCK!*" Viggo screamed as he drew his hand back, shaking it. The cowboy headbutted him now, sending his own hat tumbling to the ground. Viggo stumbled back, releasing his grip on the gun.

As the cowboy lifted the gun and brought it to bear on Viggo, light glinting from the black barrel, Marcus felt his heart sink. But Viggo managed to duck and roll over his right shoulder as the larger man squeezed the trigger.

BOOM. The gun kicked hard, the barrel bucking several inches. Marcus grunted, his ears whingeing from the sound as it echoed off the walls. Katie was screaming, muffled by Cole's body and the gunshots dying in the corners of the room.

Viggo came to his feet, already mid-tackle. He caught the cowboy under his ribs, but was too weak to lift him off the floor. Still, the impact was enough to drive the wind from the cowboy's lungs and double him over. Viggo batted away the hand wielding the gun, knocking the weapon free and sending it skidding across the floor.

The big man lifted his arms to bring his meaty fists down on Viggo, but the hitman was still faster, and a whip-fast punch caught the cowboy in his mustachioed face and snapped his back against the wall. Viggo followed that up with a shot to the side, then the kidney, then a kick to the groin. He was a storm, unrelenting in his pressure, giving the other man no time to respond as he forced the cowboy to the ground with blow after blow.

As Viggo laid into the larger man, Marcus turned to his right. Jorge was standing now, his dessert forgotten, yelling a command, and he knew that meant the door to the room was about to swing open and bring a flood of armed men with it.

His eyes drifted to the huge gun on the floor as the gears of his mind ground out a plan. A bad plan, to be sure. But a plan.

It only took him a second to reach the gun and pick it up. As he lifted it toward Jorge, though, his heart stopped.

The look exchanged between them was wordless, but the air was heavy where the conversation hung silent. Jorge had stopped speaking. He didn't raise his hands or offer any opposition. Marcus vaguely registered the door behind him opening before Jorge gave a slight shake of his head to someone Marcus couldn't see.

Fear.

Marcus's mind raced. *Kill him*, he thought one second. Then, *Don't do it; you're not a killer.* And then, *He'll kill the only family you have left.*

He pulled the hammer back.

The whole world seemed to grind to a halt as he approached Jorge, gun raised. The beast was heavy, and sagged in his hand, so he had to hold it up a little higher than seemed comfortable.

Jorge's eyes never moved. They held a constant stare right into Marcus's. As he drew close, he had finally worked up the courage to speak.

"Put your hands–" his voice was shaking, so he swallowed to try and steady it. "Put your hands behind your head."

Jorge cocked his head to one side and didn't move his hands. "What for?"

Marcus frowned. "You're going to walk us out of here. Get us to safety."

And then Jorge *laughed*.

"Why would I do that? Why would I leave my compound, where I have all the power?"

Marcus felt the heat rising in his chest. "What do you mean?" He shook the gun a little. "I'm the one with the gun."

Jorge laughed again and Marcus felt his heart quicken. The cartel leader gestured to the air surrounding him with both hands.

"I have *fifty guns*! If you kill me, you'll be dead in seconds!"

Marcus breathed deep. If he wasn't dead certain Jorge would take the gun, he would've looked over his shoulder to see if his father had any suggestions.

"Do you know what you'll start if you shoot me, kid? Even if you get away, my people will tear this country *apart* to find you. You'll never sleep again, not without a gun under your pillow."

"What happens if I put the gun down?" Marcus asked. He had to know. No point acting like he had a lot of options.

Jorge shrugged. "Who knows? Maybe you walk out of here free men. If you kill me, I can guarantee you won't walk out of here *at all*."

Fuck. Every instinct Marcus had screamed to shoot, but somehow, inexplicably, he lowered the gun.

Jorge smiled that stupid smile as he stepped toward Marcus. "Glad to see you're smarter than your father."

Marcus's chest lit aflame as he steadied the gun around waist level. "What?"

"Come on, I can't give up good merchandise. Nothing in life is free, kid." And he laughed again.

Marcus didn't realize he'd pulled the trigger until the smell of smoke filled his nostrils and his ears went back to ringing. Jorge Lavilla stood in front of him, smile fading as he drew his bloody hand from the gaping wound in his stomach, pouring blood and painting the floor red. He tried to brace himself on the table, but his hand was wet with red death and he slipped to his knees.

Marcus's stomach began to roll and he knew he was going to vomit. But before he could, a bony hand grabbed his shoulder. He spun, bringing the gun to bear before another hand caught his arm.

"Whoa, kid, hold on." Viggo Lassiter stood in front of him, reeking of piss and blood. Marcus registered, barely, that behind him the cowboy sat slumped against the wall, moaning through his shattered teeth. "We gotta go, no time to chuck." He took the gun from Marcus's hand and flipped open the cylinder, counted the bullets and snapped it shut.

Cole was on his feet, too, Katie a teary mess in his arms, her face buried in his shoulder. The look on his face was one of shock, but he nodded as Marcus searched him for an answer to a question he didn't know he was asking.

The door flung open.

As though it was reflex, Viggo lifted the gun with both hands and fired. He caught the first one through the door in the chest. As he fell, he squeezed the trigger of the shotgun in his hands and took a chunk out of the ceiling. The one behind him tried to catch him as he fell, so Viggo took him between the eyes in a single shot. He straightened suddenly, then collapsed in a heap. As he fell, without a second's hesitation, Viggo fired again and caught another man in the stomach. Then he tossed the deep black, gold-embossed gun to the side like a piece of trash and hurriedly retrieved the first man's shotgun before slamming and bolting the door.

"Get back!" He screamed, waving Marcus to the right. He dove to the side just as a torrent of bullets hit the door, pinging it like hail on a tin roof. After dozens of hits, the metal door gave way and let one through, then two, then ten, then fifty. Soon, holes the size of softballs were in the door. Viggo lifted the shotgun and fired through one such hole and Marcus heard a scream.

The storm of gunfire raged on the other side of the door, and Viggo was doing his work masterfully. Jorge was dying quietly against the table, and the cowboy had yet to attempt to move from a sitting position. Marcus's vision swung over to his father and sister. Cole was doing his best to comfort Katie, but she was screaming and panting heavily in place of breathing. If there was any justice, she'd pass out soon.

Marcus and his father exchanged a look, and Marcus searched his father's eyes for strength. But Cole's deep green pools showed only fear.

Come What May

Viggo leaned back against the wall as bullets flew past him and *pinged* against the ornate walls and table, splintered chairs, and chipped and splashed into Jorge Lavilla's body. Blood splattered the floor, leaking from the newfound bullet holes. The cowboy still moaned through his ruined face. Viggo flexed his right hand, cracking his sore knuckles.

Hopefully not done yet, he thought. He cracked his neck and gripped his shotgun, then took in the room again.

Traeger was over to his right, laying on top of Sis – no, *Katie*. He was laying on top of Katie, protecting her from the chaos as best he could. Then there was his son, gone white after killing Lavilla, huddled on the left.

Fucking surprise, I guess. Viggo sighed and rubbed his brow.

Viggo rubbed his brow and gripped the beat up old shotgun in his lap. Bullets still flew past his head and pinged around the room, chipping wood and concrete and sending debris flying. He waited until there was a beat and he heard reloading, then lifted the shotgun and fired out the hole in the door. There was a *boom*, followed by a gory splash and a cry of pain.

Viggo pumped the shotgun and a red shell bounced across the floor. "Hey," he shouted to Traeger's son. No response. Just that wide-eyed look of someone who'd just taken a life for the first time. Shit, when was the last time Viggo had felt that way after killing someone? He blew out air and yelled again. "Hey! None of this is going to mean anything if we fucking die here."

Traeger's son – Marcus? – finally looked up. He swallowed what was probably vomit and nodded. "What do you need?" he shouted back.

Viggo took a deep breath and tossed him the shotgun. "Anyone gets through that door, shoot them."

Marcus picked the weapon off the floor with shaking hands and looked back at Viggo. "What are you going to do?"

Viggo looked at Lavilla's body. "Have a chat with our host." He took off, not giving himself time to reconsider, and sprinted over to the cartel boss's lifeless corpse. Taking it by the arms, he drug the body behind a wall. Once there, he turned out Lavilla's pockets, looking for something, anything to aid their escape. He took the car keys from

Lavilla's pocket, but that was it. Nothing else, not even a cellphone.

Shit, Viggo thought. Just then, a groan came from behind him, where the cowboy leaned against the wall. Viggo stayed low and ran to him, taking the mustachioed face in his hand. "Hey," he said. "Hey, look at me!" The cowboy's eyes were unfocused. *Damn, I really did a number on him.* Viggo slapped him. "Hey!" he screamed.

The cowboy's eyes fluttered open and, upon seeing Viggo's face, widened. Not in fear, but anger. "You fucker!" he spat from the holes between his teeth. He tried to take a swing at Viggo, but Viggo caught the lifeless attempt around the wrist he'd already broken and squeezed. The cowboy gritted his remaining teeth and grunted in pain.

"Listen to me!" Viggo said. "I need a way out of this place."

The cowboy gurgled – or was that a laugh? "Fuck you," he said. "Why would I help you?"

Viggo squeezed the man's broken wrist again and slid his other hand down to his exposed throat. "Because if you don't, a few broken bones and a fucked up smile will be the least of your problems."

After a moment, the cowboy nodded. "Fuck me, fine." He gestured to the ornate wooden table with his chin. "There's a panic button under the table, where Jorge sits.

That'll secure the room for a few minutes. Should be a case with some cash and guns under there, too."

Viggo glanced at the table and would've smacked himself in the forehead if he'd had a free hand. *Panic button,* he thought. So simple, and yet it hadn't even occurred to him. He looked back at the cowboy. "If you're lying to me," Viggo seethed. "I'll kill you."

"Why would I fucking lie? I'm not trying to die here," the cowboy said. "It was always just a job." He laid his head back against the stone wall and continued muttering to himself as Viggo released him and turned back to the cacophony in the room. A glance at the door told him it was moments from fully collapsing. Probably the only thing holding the men on the other side back at this point was that no one wanted to be the first one through. That wouldn't last long.

Marcus Traeger hadn't turned in the door's direction yet, so Viggo half-crawled, half-ran over to him and took the shotgun before the boy could protest, then fired two shots through the door.

"Can't let them forget we're armed," he said when Marcus looked at him quizzically. He handed the gun back to the shaking boy and turned to the table, which was unfortunately directly in the path of the onslaught of bullets. Large chunks of the ornate wooden monstrosity had been ripped apart by the hail of lead, and Viggo wasn't even sure the mechanism to open the compartment would still work. Still, it was their only shot.

He returned to Lavilla's corpse and hefted it up, holding it in front of him as best he could. His weakened physical state made that more difficult than it would normally have been, but he eventually had the cartel boss's lifeless form positioned mostly like a shield. With a deep breath, Viggo took a step out of cover.

One bullet struck the corpse almost immediately, nearly knocking Viggo off-balance. Others whizzed past him. One grazed Viggo's shoulder, which burned like hell and almost caused him to drop his involuntary mobile cover. Still more bullets tore chunks off the table, pockmarked the floor, and generally made Viggo reconsider his life choices that brought him to this position.

After a few steps, though, he'd reached the table. Viggo heaved the corpse off, then dove under the table and began frantically searching for the panic button. Sure enough, right where the cowboy said it would be, his fingers grazed a small plastic circle. He couldn't help but notice the streaks of blood from Lavilla's smeared hand print. He'd been going for the button after Marcus shot him, Viggo assumed.

He pushed the button.

Instantly, the lights in the room went from a bright

yellow to a deep red. Metal shutters dropped in the windows and, mercifully, an enormous metal door slammed shut over the smaller one now shredded by gunfire. Outside of the metal blast door, Viggo could hear shouting. It wouldn't hold forever – there was likely a failsafe somewhere else in the base that would deactivate the panic room.

Viggo laid on the cool tile floor, surrounded by the detritus from the gunfight. Wood chips and shattered tiles lay everywhere, along with more than a little destruction of the human variety. Lavilla's body lay nearby, lifeless and pockmarked by bullet holes, while the cowboy continued to moan through shattered teeth.

"How-how did you know it would do that?" Marcus stammered. Viggo looked to him and saw he'd finally made it to his feet.

"I didn't," said Viggo. He looked at the cowboy, who just shrugged.

A soft whimper broke through the ringing in Viggo's ears. He turned and saw Cole Traeger slowly standing, the small girl in his arms. Reflexively, Viggo made a move toward her, then recoiled as Traeger shot him a look that might as well have been a bullet.

As the father checked on his daughter, then his son in turn, Viggo searched for the cache of supplies the cowboy had mentioned. He found it, not far from the panic button in a compartment built into the table itself. It had been pinged by a few shots, but looked to be in decent condition. He popped it open and found himself looking at a veritable treasure trove; weapons, ammunition, bulletproof vests, and a stash of various currencies and fake passports bearing Lavilla's likeness.

Viggo began arming himself. He slipped on one of the bulletproof vests and took two pistols, then retrieved the shotgun he'd used before. As he was finishing loading the guns and extra magazines, he felt Marcus approaching. Viggo stopped him as he reached for a pistol.

"Nah," he said, shoving a magazine into his waistband.

"What?" Marcus said, a flush rushing to his cheeks.

Viggo regarded him flatly. "You know how to use one of these?" he said, gesturing to the guns in the case.

Marcus gestured to the corpse he still couldn't seem to actually *look at*. "I managed that, didn't I?"

Viggo barked a laugh. "Congratulations, you shot an idiot who let his guard down. It's a little different when they shoot back."

Marcus looked to his father for backup, but Cole was still checking on Katie. "I can help," he said finally.

"You're more likely to shoot me in the back," Viggo said.

"You think I can't find a way to do that anyway?" Marcus's voice was barely above a whisper this time.

Viggo stopped arming himself and turned to the boy. For the first time, he really *looked* at him. Maybe twenty years old, shaggy brown hair and a beard that had gotten too long. Thin, but also soft. His hands were uncalloused, his arms unworked. He'd never been in a place like this, never done the things he was talking about.

Viggo stepped toward him and spoke low, his eyes never leaving Marcus's. "There's nothing stopping me from putting you down right here."

The boy stared back at Viggo for a moment, then faltered. "Fine," he said, stepping back and looking down.

Viggo nodded, then turned to get back to his equipment. As he did, though, he caught Cole Traeger's eyes over Marcus's shoulder. The older man was hugging his daughter, still softly crying against his chest. But his eyes were locked on Viggo.

CHAPTER 23

Fly By Night

Cole broke his stare away from Viggo and hugged Katie to his body. He stood, holding her in his arms and walked to the table.

"Marcus," he said, voice hoarse. "Take her." He handed Katie over to her big brother. "Take her over there and try to get her calmed down." Marcus nodded and walked, still somewhat sullen, to a corner away from the corpse and bloodstains, where he sat down and tried to calm his sister's cries.

Cole turned to Viggo Lassiter and immediately felt his blood pressure rise. That had been happening whenever he looked at the man who'd stolen his family from him. He took a deep breath and tried to get his emotions under control. He'd need to be clearheaded for whatever came next. There would be enough time later to deal with this... man.

"What's the plan?" Cole asked through gritted teeth. Another deep breath. Viggo turned and looked at him, looking...was that sheepish? Was he embarrassed? Cole took another deep breath.

The gaunt man cleared his throat before speaking. "With any luck, there will be an exit from this room, some sort of escape route. Lavilla wouldn't have locked himself in here without a way out."

Cole nodded. "And if there isn't?"

Viggo looked at the guns, then back to Cole. "Then we go out that door." He gestured to the thick metal door that had closed when he'd pressed the button on the table.

Cole whistled. He hadn't meant to, but it seemed appropriate anyway. He looked back to Viggo. "How many of those vests do we have?"

"Three," Viggo replied, fiddling with something – was that a grenade?

Cole looked at Marcus and Katie, huddled together in the corner, then took the two remaining vests and walked toward them, careful not to turn his back on Viggo. *Can't let him see,* he thought. He needed Viggo to believe he was fully in control. *For now.*

Marcus looked up as he approached. Katie had finally stopped crying, but from the looks of the puddle on the floor, she had vomited. Or maybe that was Marcus? In any case, he didn't blame them.

Cole handed his son a vest, then moved to Katie and

started sliding the last vest over her head.

Marcus seemed to realize what he was doing and spoke in a tone just short of panic. "Hey, wait, are those all the vests we have?"

Cole nodded, not looking away from where he was cinching Katie's vest tight.

"Dad–" Marcus stammered, then he looked to where Viggo was finishing loading something into the pockets of his own vest. "*He's* taking one?" he asked, incredulous.

Cole finished adjusting Katie's vest, then kissed her on the forehead before answering. "Yes, Marcus. He's taking one."

Marcus scoffed and rubbed his eyes. "Dad, there's no way he's getting a vest over you."

Cole smiled a little. They really *were* a lot alike. Lillian would've laughed at that look on his face, his furrowed brow, the way he cocked his head to the side when he wanted to be taken seriously.

"Son, unless you've been in a few cartel gunfights I wasn't aware of, he's our best chance to get out of this alive."

Marcus eyed him. "And what about *after* we get out of here?"

The implication was unspoken, but crystal clear. If Viggo Lassiter has a gun, everyone around him is in danger.

Cole nodded, then clasped his son on both shoulders and looked in his eyes. "Your dad has a plan," he whispered. "Trust me." Then, he did something he should've been doing all along.

He gave his son a hug.

It wasn't a long hug, or an exceptionally emotional one. Just a quick squeeze and a pat on the back, but Cole knew instantly he'd been a fool to disregard his relationship with Marcus for so many years. He'd held back a piece of himself from his children, especially Marcus, and they had both paid the price of that choice many times through the years. He wiped away a tear and took a deep breath, then spoke.

"Stay with your sister. I'm gonna go check and see if he's ready." Cole patted Marcus on the back and walked back to Viggo, who seemed to finally be done arming himself.

"Are we ready?" asked Cole.

Viggo nodded. "I think so."

"Did you find our exit?"

Viggo looked to Cole and rolled his eyes before responding in a huff. "No, I thought that was your contribution." He shouldered past Cole and moved to the far side of the room. Cole took another deep breath, calming himself, then turned and followed him. Outside the metal door, he could hear more yelling and shouting. It wouldn't be long before they found a way inside, Cole knew.

We need to get moving. Fast, he thought.

Viggo was feeling the wall, Cole assumed in search of a panel of some sort that would open a door. That side of the room seemed bare except for the fireplace that sat in the center of the wall. Two golden lions were carved out of stone and the fireplace seemed to be configured to look as though they were breathing fire when it was lit. Cole approached the lion statues and examined each in turn.

They looked like typical statues until Cole ran his hand inside the mouth of one and felt one of its fangs shift a bit as he brushed against it. His heart leapt into his throat and, as he pulled the fang up, he heard a click and a grinding sound. The fireplace split down the middle and slid open to reveal a dimly lit passageway leading out of the room.

"Alright, there we go," Viggo said, stepping past Cole and into the passage. "Let's go."

Behind them, a *boom* sounded from the large metal door, followed by a scraping of metal on stone. The door was open.

"Go!" Cole screamed. Marcus, Katie in his arms, ducked into the passage, shouldered past Viggo, and took off in a run. Cole took a step into the passageway as Viggo stepped toward him. Cole eyed him suspiciously as he kicked a lever on the ground. The fireplace door began to slide closed. As it did, Viggo took a grenade out of his pocket, pulled the pin and tossed it through, just as the door slammed shut. From the other side of the thick stone, a loud *boom* sounded, strong enough to shake dust and dirt from the ceiling of the passage.

"Alright, then," Viggo said. "*Now*, let's go." And he turned and headed down the passage.

Cole took a deep breath, feeling the cold metal against his back, then proceeded after him.

CHAPTER 24

The Best-Laid Plans

Viggo leaned against the wall of the passageway and breathed deep. His weeks of captivity were catching up with him as they jogged down the musty tunnel. His muscles – or what was left of them – screamed in protest. His hand ached every time he flexed it. His entire body seemed to be coming apart at the seams.

He exhaled, hefted the shotgun he'd stolen from Jorge Lavilla's armory, and continued on. Cole Traeger jogged along behind him while Marcus and the girl set the pace up ahead. They had no idea how far, or how deep, this tunnel went. They seemed to be heading steadily down into the earth.

Sweat beaded on Viggo's forehead. Something about this place reminded him of that basement. His breath came in ragged gasps as he tried to push the thought from his mind. But if he wasn't thinking of the basement and his captivity, he was thinking of that night when he'd found himself in Cole Traeger's house. Neither thought comforted him.

Cole caught up to him and poked Viggo in the side.

"Let's go," he said. "Gotta keep moving."

Viggo groaned. "If you want to go faster, you're free to go on ahead."

Cole barked a laugh, then gestured down the tunnel. "No, thanks," he said. "Lead on."

Viggo rolled his eyes and resumed walking. Marcus and Katie had gotten far enough ahead now that he couldn't see them.

"Your boy needs to slow down," Viggo said over his shoulder to Cole. "We don't know where this tunnel leads. He doesn't want to get there before we do."

Cole seemed to consider that. For a moment, he said nothing. Viggo was about to speak again when Cole yelled down the tunnel.

"Marcus!" He yelled. "Slow down! "

There was no response, save a slight breeze that wafted from further into the darkness.

So we're close to the exit, Viggo thought. His heart pounded against the inside of his chest. Once they were outside, he could try to lose the Traegers, slip off somewhere and keep moving until he was out of the Scolessas' – and now the cartel's – reach.

He frowned as another thought occurred to him. *Might*

have to kill them. He didn't want to do that. But it seemed a little late to have qualms over it now. He took a breath. If they had to die for him to escape, they had to die.

"Marcus!" Cole yelled, leaning into the darkness ahead. Still no reply. "Let's go, we need to catch them." Viggo sighed, hefted his gun, and took off at a slightly faster jog.

"Do you feel that?" he asked Cole after a moment.

"Feel what?" Cole asked absentmindedly.

"The breeze," Viggo said. "We're almost at the end."

Cole said nothing, but when Viggo glanced at his face, he could see his jaw clenching and unclenching with every step. Sweat had gathered on his forehead and was running down his face now. He had a slight limp.

Was that there before? Viggo thought. *Or did I...is that from me?*

It wasn't often Viggo had to face the families of those he killed when working for the Scolessas. Every kill served a purpose, every life he ended saw the Scolessas gain more territory and money, and saw Viggo's star rise. Always reliable, always efficient, Viggo had made a name for himself. But he knew that was all over now. He would never be a made man, he would never sit around the Cabana with the other big hitters.

He banished the thoughts and continued forward into the darkness, chasing the open air.

Fear gripped Cole's heart.

Marcus, he thought. *No, no, no, not again.* He could scarcely breathe. His chest felt like it was caught in a vice grip. His breath came in ragged gasps and his throat felt like sandpaper as he continued to call out Marcus's name to no response.

"Stop yelling," Viggo said from beside him. Cole had almost forgotten the man was there. But he was right, he needed to be quieter. Cole forced himself to come to a stop. He leaned against the tunnel wall and heaved in breaths. Viggo did the same across from him.

"The breeze is getting stronger," Viggo said when he regained his breath. "We're nearly to the end now."

Cole couldn't help himself. "What do you think happened to Marcus and Katie?" he asked.

Viggo shrugged. "Maybe they're just out of earshot and totally fine. The kid is quicker than you or me."

But there was something sinister left unsaid.

"Or...?" Cole beckoned.

Viggo hesitated. "Or...I'm just saying, there's bound to be *someone* else in the cartel who knows where this tunnel leads."

A shock of cold ran through Cole's chest. *Of course they know about the tunnel,* he thought. And he suddenly felt very stupid and *very* out of control. The weight of all the decisions that had brought him here felt in that moment as heavy as a truckful of cement. The earth was pressing down on him and in from all sides. And when he looked for a friendly face, he saw only his wife and son's murderer. And now Marcus and Katie might die, too.

Marcus and Katie. They were still ahead, and might be in trouble. Cole's focus snapped back to the moment as his breathing slowed.

"We need to keep moving," he said, straightening. "We're nearly there."

They proceeded down the tunnel without speaking and without stopping, keeping a steady pace until they felt the cool air of nighttime breezing down the passageway to them. The air carried a cold, earthy dampness that reminded Cole of the spring rains back home.

As they came close enough to see the exit up ahead, Viggo stopped.

"What's wrong?" Cole asked, slowing beside him.

"Something's off," Viggo said, eyes fixed on the exit from the tunnel. "There's no light up ahead. If they were just ahead of us, they should be right around here. If the cartel had them, we'd be able to see the lights outside. Unless..." Viggo trailed off.

"Unless what?" Cole asked, frustrated.

Viggo turned to him. "They're waiting for us," he said matter-of-factly.

Cole looked at him, confused. "Like an ambush? Why?"

Viggo checked his ammunition and grenades. "Because of me," he eventually said. "But they're not expecting us to have our guard up. So we can still catch them off-guard. But we've gotta make them think they've got us. Get them cocky. Then strike."

Cole watched, equal parts amused and horrified, as Viggo went about double checking his gear. He had to be carrying at least five guns, and Cole saw three grenades in the process.

"So how do we do that?" Cole asked.

Viggo looked up and met his eye. "I'm going to need to kill you."

CHAPTER 25

A Hope and a Dream

Marcus tried, and failed, to control his breathing. He was kneeling on some small rocks, making his knees ache, and the cool night air gave him a chill. Or maybe he was shaking from fear. Either way, his heart was pounding against the inside of his chest, and if he hadn't vomited earlier, he certainly would've now.

Off to his right, he could hear Katie whimpering. Aside from that, the group of at least fifteen cartel members made eerily little noise. An occasional scuffle of a boot on dirt, a stifled cough. Otherwise, silence.

Stupid, Marcus thought. *Stupid, stupid, stupid. Running ahead like I knew what I was doing. Should've let Viggo lead. Safer anyway, not having him behind me.*

Marcus tried to swallow and felt his throat crack like dry desert ground. He coughed, and got a hard smack to the back of the head for it, sending him into the dusty sand. He was hauled back onto his knees and this time, a foul-smelling handkerchief was forced into his mouth as a gag. It tasted of salt and sweat and, had it not been there, Marcus definitely would've coughed again. As it was, he did his best to stay quiet.

He couldn't tell exactly how long he'd been kneeling in this spot, but it had been long enough for the last traces of the sun to vanish behind the horizon, draping them all in darkness. And there, in darkness, they had stayed. Silent. Watching. Waiting.

BOOM

The gunshot cracked the night like thunder and stirred Marcus from his ruminations. His heart leapt as all the men around him readied their weapons, training them on the cave door in front of them. A moment later, as the echoes of the gunshot faded into nothing, a figure strolled from the exit. Marcus realized he'd been holding his breath, but he exhaled as he made out the details of the lone man – tall, gaunt, scraggly beard, muscle like sinew, wearing a bulletproof vest and carrying a shotgun. Marcus screamed into his gag.

Viggo Lassiter stood before him, sweating, looking paler than before, worn out and nearly ready to collapse.

And *alone*.

All at once, light exploded in front of Viggo, blinding him. He shielded his eyes with his hand and tried to make out what he was looking at. Cars, several of them, with floodlights trained on Viggo. A group of cartel goons stood encircled around someone, he assumed Marcus, on their knees. The group was armed well, but there were fewer than he'd expected.

Maybe that grenade dealt more of a blow than I thought?

Either way, he was still significantly outnumbered. He had to hope he could stall them long enough now.

Viggo put his hands in the air, letting the shotgun hang off his arm by the strap. For a long moment, the only sounds were Marcus's muffled screams. Viggo waited. Eventually, the throng parted and a short, stocky figure stepped to the front.

"Hello, Viggo," the shadowy figure spoke in a familiar tone.

Viggo's breath caught and he took a hesitant step back. "Richie?" he said in a whisper. In his mind, Viggo was back in the basement, tied up while Richie ceaselessly pounded on him.

The shorter man smiled broadly. "Well, yes, to you. Ricardo Moncada is what most people call me. Pleased to meet you..." His smile broadened as he trailed off. "...again."

Viggo's heart was racing. The man he knew as Richie was shorter than him, but at that moment he might as well have been ten feet tall. Viggo shrank before him as he advanced, each footfall seeming to shake the earth.

Moncada? Viggo thought. *As in,* Moncada-Lavilla. The pieces fell together in Viggo's mind and presented a picture he'd rather have not seen. Richie, his torturer, was the other half of the Moncada-Lavilla cartel.

"You have caused quite a lot of trouble for me," Richie said, slow steps bringing him ever closer to Viggo, who nearly turned to run back into the cave. Richie snapped his fingers. "Ah-ah-ah, no running."

Viggo stilled, but he hadn't completely abandoned the idea.

"As I was saying, you have made a real mess here, Viggo. My business partner is dead, as are many of my men. My home has been brutalized, and my help," he eyed one of his men, holding a small girl in his arms. "Has been stolen." His gaze turned back to Viggo, who shrank beneath it. "How do you propose we handle this?"

Viggo stammered for a moment, not looking directly at Richie. "I, uh...um, I'm not..." he trailed off, unsure of what to say.

Richie clicked his tongue in what seemed disapproval. "That's what I thought you might say." He stepped right up to Viggo now, and held out his hand. "Your shotgun, Viggo."

Viggo hesitated. Richie sighed, then delivered a swift

punch to the stomach. The impact was like a baseball bat. Viggo felt the air leave his lungs as he collapsed wheezing to his knees. He tried to draw in breath, but couldn't. As he fell to his hands and knees, spittle trailing from his mouth to the dusty earth, Richie gave him a kick to the ribs. Viggo's ribs exploded in pain as he sprawled onto his back. He knew he felt a rib crack. He spat out blood and finally managed to draw in a gasping breath as he blinked away the stars from his vision.

Richie knelt and took the shotgun from where it laid next to Viggo. 'This next part will be bloody, and I hope you know it brings me no pleasure." His voice sounded sincere. "But you've given me no choice, leading your friends here, making a mockery of my hospitality."

"Are you-" Viggo coughed and spat another chunk of bloody mess onto the dirt. "Are you going to kill me?"

Richie chuckled. "No, Viggo. I'm not going to kill you." He stood and pumped the shotgun once, expelling a shell onto the dirt. "I'm going to kill them."

Viggo's heart raced. *Not the girl. No, not the girl.* He looked up at Richie, who was looking between Marcus and Katie, seemingly trying to pick who to kill.

Richie glanced back at Viggo. "Where's the other one? The older one?"

Viggo's mind raced. He had nearly forgotten. "Dead," he

coughed. "I killed him in there." He gestured to the cave he'd come from.

Richie considered that, then shook his head. "Oh, Viggo. Another double-cross, eh? You seem to be fond of those."

Marcus was screaming through his gag, fighting to get free. Viggo could hear Katie whimpering in the dark as Richie took aim, leveling the shotgun at Marcus. Viggo pushed himself to one knee, fighting every instinct that told him to stay down. He drew in a deep breath, then called out.

"NOW!"

As the grenade arced out of the darkness of the cave entrance and rolled to Richie's feet, Viggo stood and took two lunging steps, tackling Katie's captor to the ground. Before the man could react, Viggo took him by the sides and rolled, landing on his back with the man covering both him and Katie. As the ear-splitting *boom* of the grenade rang out, the cartel member acted as a sort of improvised flak jacket, shielding Viggo and the girl from the shrapnel. Viggo couldn't hear his screaming over the ringing in his ears, but he could see his face, twisted into a mask of pain. Viggo pushed him off of them and set to checking Katie for injuries.

"Are you okay?!" he was shouting, but could barely hear the words. She looked to be in shock, barely acknowledging him, but seemed physically okay.

Viggo looked to where the grenade had gone off. A blackened crater marked the spot. At first, he thought Richie must've been vaporized, but no, there he was: crawling away, legs blown away below the knee, stumps dragging blood and bits of tattered flesh and muscle along in a bloody trail.

BOOM

Another grenade went off on the other side of the gathered throng.

BOOM

Another one.

BOOM

Then a beat of silence. Then came the screams. He had given Cole four grenades, so he'd be out now. Viggo checked the still-screaming man he'd used as living cover and found two pistols tucked into his waistband. He verified they were both loaded then moved Katie behind a truck nearby.

"Stay here!" he yelled. "Keep your head down!"

She didn't respond, but did curl up in a ball behind the pickup.

Good enough, I guess, Viggo thought, and he turned to check the carnage.

The flames of overturned cars lit the night all around him. The air smelled of gasoline and gunpowder, and what little of his hearing had returned was filled with screams and random gunfire at nothing. Viggo ducked low and headed for where he'd seen Marcus tied up. He was surprised to find the kid was still alive, laying on his side in virtually the same place he'd been kneeling. Viggo pulled him to a sitting position and tried to make him focus. His eyes were distant, unseeing.

"Marcus," Viggo said, lightly slapping him on the side of the face. "Marcus!" A more forceful slap seemed to shake him. He looked at Viggo, eyes focusing slowly, then coming to recognition. The anger followed.

"You," he seethed. "You killed my dad, too, huh? I guess I'm next?"

Viggo sighed. "Who do you think threw those fucking grenades, genius?"

Marcus looked to the cave, then around at the scene playing out around them, seemingly pulled straight out of a war film. "What do we do?" he asked, turning back to Viggo.

Viggo surveyed the area for a moment, but he already knew the answer.

"Stay down," he said. "Play dead. Whatever. Stay here, and stay down. I'll clean up whatever's left." Marcus started to protest, trying to push himself to his feet, but Viggo shoved him back down. "Stay here," he said, more forcefully. "Your sister is behind that truck over there—" He gestured to Katie's hiding spot. "Get to her if I don't come back." Before Marcus could argue further, Viggo stood in a crouch and skulked away.

The place was in chaos. Only a few of the cartel lackeys were still alive, but they were in various states of disarray. One half-stumbled, half-ran out of the smoke toward Viggo, who lifted his pistol and fired two shots into his torso, sending him tumbling to the ground.

Viggo ducked as a spray of random bullets passed over his head. He turned, and saw the perpetrator and saw immediately why he was firing his gun randomly. Where his eyes had been was now blackened and burned away. Viggo grimaced, then dropped him with three shots to the chest. He gurgled blood, but did not get up.

As Viggo turned to take in the scene, he caught a truck hurling sand as it made a swift retreat. He reckoned there were three cartel members in the vehicle, as best he could make out through the smoky haze. They were already out of range of his pistols, so he let them go. With both bosses out of the picture, he wasn't sure how much bite the *Moncada-Lavilla* cartel really had left.

Still, he thought. *I'd rather not find out.*

Viggo looked around and saw no more movement. No more gunshots went off in the night. The only sound he could hear, aside from the crackling flames, were the groans of dying men. He turned and walked toward the place where the grenade had shorn off Richie's legs.

Viggo hoped Richie would still be alive. In pain, but alive. *That way,* he thought. *I can finish him myself.* A quick check of his pistol's magazine showed it still held two unfired rounds, plus one in the chamber. When he came to the place where he'd left Richie, though, Viggo froze.

Richie was gone, a smeared blood trail left behind. Viggo followed the drag-marks from the place where Richie had gone to the ground. They led away from the worst of the carnage before being swallowed by vehicle tires.

That truck, Viggo thought, eyes widening.

"Son of a bitch," he sighed, rubbing his brow with one hand.

Viggo heard footsteps behind him and whirled around, going to his pistol before realizing Marcus had sidled up. He flinched back, and Viggo gave him a groan before shoving the pistol in his waistband.

"Who was that guy?" Marcus asked after taking a moment to collect himself.

"That," Viggo began. "was the other head of the *Moncada-Lavilla* cartel. Ricardo. I knew him as Richie." He spoke quickly, not wanting to give Marcus time to respond or ask additional questions. "If he survived..." Viggo trailed off, but the unsaid words still hung in the air like the smoke from the burning vehicles.

"He'll try to come kill us," Marcus finished the thought.

Viggo barked a laugh. "No. He *will* come kill us. Unless we get to a border somewhere, and soon."

Marcus nodded, giving Viggo a stab of guilt.

Three shots in the pistol, Viggo thought. *That'll be plenty. Need to wait til the old motherfucker is back, take them both out at once. Get somewhere safe, and raise the girl myself.*

As if summoned, Cole picked that moment to come walking out of the darkness of the cave. Marcus jogged over to him and they embraced.

"Dad," Marcus said, coughing back tears slightly as he spoke. "I thought..."

"I know," Cole said, gripping his eldest on the shoulder. "We had to catch them off-guard for it to work." He looked around him, worry creasing his brow. "Where's Katie?"

Marcus gestured to the truck where Viggo had stashed her, and both father and son went to retrieve the girl. She seemed to still be in a state of shock, but as she buried her expressionless face into her father's shoulder, her body was wracked with sobs. Cole rubbed her back as he consoled her.

"Shhhh," he whispered in her ear. "Shhhh, Daddy's here now. I've got you."

Viggo felt a knot in his chest. Was that jealousy? He choked down outrage he knew was wrong. *I did this to them,* he thought, feeling a little sick.

After a moment, Marcus said what they were all thinking.

"So, what now?" He asked the question with a bit of a huff, his hands on his hips, looking from Cole to Viggo and back.

Viggo took a deep breath as he waited to see what Cole would say. *Pick your moment,* he thought. *Just wait, and pick your moment.*

After what seemed an eternity, Cole spoke. "Let's see if one of these cars will still run. Those guys will be back, and we need to keep moving."

Marcus nodded and took off to look for a working vehicle. That left Cole and Viggo alone, aside from Katie, who'd fallen asleep on her father's shoulder.

"Your plan worked," Cole said. "I saw what you did, covering Katie. I won't thank you, if you're expecting it. But..." He thought for a moment. "...I did appreciate it, either way."

Viggo nodded. "Sure." What else was there to say? Apologies failed in moments like this. And Viggo had never been good at them at the best of times. But, well, there were some questions he needed answers to. "So what's your plan here?"

Cole's eyes flicked sideways to lock with Viggo's. Viggo stared into those deep green pools and saw what lay beneath the surface: hate. A great, vast expanse of hatred. Cole played the part of a doting father, but Viggo could see through him. This man was torn up from the hate he carried. On that point, at least, they shared a common experience.

"You killed my wife and son," Cole said, his voice hauntingly still, barely any inflection. "But you weren't the only one who failed them." He set his jaw and continued. "The police back home won't chase you here. The police here have bigger things to worry about," he gestured in a general sense to the carnage around them. "And the people you worked for, you left them an even bigger pile of bodies than you left me."

Viggo shifted nervously at the mention of the Scolessas. He'd had a sneaking suspicion they were involved in this fateful reunion, but confirmation of it still stung.

"But the biggest failure," Cole continued, not seeming to notice Viggo's discomfort, "is mine." Those green eyes were lined with wet tears now, and his voice trembled. "I couldn't protect them. I couldn't stop you. And then I laid in a hospital bed for weeks, pissing myself with fear that you'd find me, too. And in my dreams, you did. Every night, I fought with you in that bedroom, and every night, I lost. Until I stopped fighting. Until I just laid there, and let you take whatever you'd come for." Tears cut ravines through the grime on his face now, the firelight from the burning cars bouncing off his wetted cheeks.

Cole exhaled a shaking breath. "So," he continued after a moment. "My plan is to bring you home to face justice."

Viggo blew out a whistle. "Why not just kill me? It'd be a lot less trouble."

Cole barked a humorless laugh. "Remember the part where the only way I ever survived that dream was to stop fighting you? Besides, you have all the guns."

Viggo chuckled. "And what's to stop me killing you and your son right now?" *Take the hint,* Viggo thought. *Let me go.*

Cole held his stare and this time he did *not* laugh. "You know what you owe me."

Viggo leaned forward, close enough to be uncomfortable. "And you," he said, trying to seem menacing. "know that I could leave right now and there's nothing you could do to make me come with you."

Cole held his stare without speaking. As the tension in the moment grew, Viggo found his hand drifting ever so slightly to the pistol shoved in his waistband.

Fuck it, he thought. *Do this one now and then get the*

other one.

But he couldn't. Not with Katie sitting in his lap. Thankfully, Marcus returned just then.

"Found a car," he said, breaking the tension as both Viggo and Cole looked at him and nodded. As he led them to the vehicle, Viggo caught himself glancing nervously at Cole and fingering the grip of his gun.

Gotta do it soon, Viggo thought. *Take care of it before you get in the car.*

He knew he'd have to get as far away as he could, as fast as possible. Richie would be sending people after him. *He's probably already putting a plan together.* The thought of it made Viggo's skin crawl. He felt as though the basement might spring up out of the ground right there, even as he watched Cole load Katie into the backseat of the old pickup truck. He could still feel the manacles on his wrists, knew he was on borrowed time as long as he was on the same continent as those cartel fucks.

And Cole and Marcus would be nothing but dead weight to him.

He steeled himself. Marcus had his back turned, checking the truck's tires. Cole had secured Katie and walked toward the truckbed to check something.

Viggo's hand found the pistol stuffed in his waistband. He carefully withdrew it, trying not to move too fast or cause alarm from the Traegers.

Marcus was turning toward him, opening his mouth to speak.

Now's the moment. He gripped the pistol firmly and moved to aim it at the eldest Traeger son.

"Dad, do you have–"

The gunshot split the air like the crack of thunder.

CHAPTER 26

The Smoking Gun

The bullet leapt from the bucking gun in Cole's hand in a burst of flame that was bright enough to make him temporarily see spots. His vision was clear enough to see it crash into the side of Viggo's knee, though. It burst out the other side in a gory mess, bits of cartilage and bone cascading onto the sand beyond him.

A beat passed, Cole's ears ringing from the concussive noise. It reverberated off into the darkening distance, fading to silence.

Viggo screamed. His own gun dropped to the ground as both hands went to his ruined knee. He landed unceremoniously on his side in the dust and sand. Blood bubbled between his fingers and ran over his hands, pooling on the ground. As he kicked and rolled, still screaming, the sticky blood mixed with the dirt to make a sort of muddy paste.

Cole's hand hurt. He hadn't been ready for how hard the cowboy's gun would kick when he'd pulled the trigger.

But he kept his aim trained on Viggo as he walked over.

"Marcus!" Cole said. His son had ducked reflexively when he'd pulled the trigger and hadn't gotten back up yet. "Marcus!" he said again. "Get that gun." Cole gestured generally to Viggo's fallen gun with his foot.

"What–" Marcus started. "What – oh!" And he scrabbled in the dirt, picking up the gun before standing back up.

Viggo continued to scream. "FUCK!" He moaned, holding his destroyed knee and writhing in the dirt. "Fuck, you shot me!" He fixed Cole with his gaze, which Cole returned flatly. Viggo's eyes were bloodshot, filled with tears that then overflowed onto his dirty cheeks and ran into his filthy beard.

"I said I wouldn't kill you," Cole said, trying to control his breathing and steady the tremble beginning to creep into his hand. "I never said anything about shooting you. Besides, I'm not stupid." He inclined his head toward Marcus, who was still holding Viggo's pistol. "I saw you aiming that gun at Marcus."

Viggo said nothing, but closed his eyes tight and screamed again through gritted teeth.

"Marcus, you're driving," Cole said, moving toward Viggo and shoving the enormous gun into the back of his waistband. "Help me get him in the truck bed." After a few moments spent struggling to get Viggo on his feet, and a few more spent half fighting, half carrying him to the back of the truck and lifting him in, they had him secured in the bed of the truck, despite his cursing and fighting them throughout the process. Cole tied his hands to hooks, meant for tying down cargo, which he found to be a little bit funny, considering. When it was done, he watched Viggo straining against his restraints, veins popping from his neck as he pulled and raged. But there was no moving.

Cole took more than a little satisfaction as he watched his family's murderer rage and scream at him, but still fought with him to secure a makeshift tourniquet.

"It's not much, and it'll hurt like a bitch, but I don't think you'll die before we get you back to civilization." Cole found himself wondering how bothered he'd be if the man *did* die. Ultimately, he'd come here to take him back and have him face justice. But he had his daughter now, so was it really worth the trouble?

Cole shook his head to clear it. *Yes,* he thought. *Yes, it's worth it. He needs to suffer for what he did.*

Katie had woken with the gunshot, but Marcus was working to get her calmed back down. Eventually, she curled up against the passenger side window and softly cried to herself.

Cole climbed into the passenger seat and closed the

door, then laid back against the headrest.

"Let's go," he said, suddenly bone-dead tired. The truck shuddered to life, then rolled away into the ever-darkening night.

When Cole opened his eyes, hours had passed and the truck was rolling down a dark desert highway, bumping and shuddering as it went. Its meager headlights did little to illuminate the vast darkness that lay before them.

"Where are we?" he asked, his mouth cracking as he did. Must've been sleeping with it open again. He wiped drool from his face as he waited for Marcus to respond.

"Hard to tell," he said. He rubbed at his eye with his free hand, the other one gripping the steering wheel. "I've been heading north, I think, but mostly I'm just trying to get anywhere that looks like an actual town, with a phone we can use to call Luke."

Cole nodded at that. "He won't be happy we're calling him from a different phone and lost the one he gave us." He looked out the back window and saw Viggo, head down, seemingly asleep. "Anything from him?"

Marcus shook his head. "Nothing. I think he knows if he makes noise or draws someone over..." Marcus didn't finish the thought, but they both knew the words that hung unspoken in that pregnant silence.

Cole shifted uncomfortably. "Right." He looked to Katie, still curled up, asleep in the back seat. "Has she stirred?"

Marcus shook his head again. "No, nothing from her, either. But to be honest, I haven't been watching for them to wake up. It doesn't really matter if they do. What matters is, we need to find some civilization and fast, dump this truck, get his leg patched up, and get to the border as fast as possible."

Cole regarded his oldest son for a moment. He suddenly looked very *old,* as if he'd aged doubly fast since they got to Mexico. *Can't imagine what it's done to me, then.* Absently, he rubbed his jaw, the coarse beard unkempt from days of not managing it.

"It's just," Marcus said. "I didn't think I'd see *you* do that."

Cole looked at him, feeling a little caught off-guard. "What do you mean? Shoot someone?"

Marcus nodded.

"Son, you had to know it was possible things might get violent on this...trip? Mission? Whatever." Cole sighed before continuing. "He was going to kill you. And then he'd kill me, and he'd kill Katie. Or steal her again. Either way, it wasn't an option."

Marcus huffed. "I know, I know. He didn't give you a choice, it's just..." He trailed off momentarily before collecting himself and continuing. "Seeing you, holding a gun while someone laid on the ground screaming was...harder than I expected. I'm glad you did it, don't get me wrong. It just felt...wrong, somehow." He shook his head again. "I'm sorry, I'm exhausted, that probably doesn't make any sense. Forget I said anything."

Marcus refocused on the road, and Cole leaned back against the half-rotted headrest, but he didn't forget. He knew exactly what Marcus meant. Yet another thing Viggo Lassiter had stolen from his family.

A few tense moments passed with only Katie's soft snoring from the back seat as accompaniment before a diminutive shimmer appeared on the horizon. Cole and Marcus both leaned forward reflexively.

"What's that?" Marcus asked.

Cole considered the greasy yellow light for a moment. "Looks like a town, maybe? Or at least a building of some sort?"

Marcus swallowed hard. "Hopefully it's friendly."

"And doesn't know we're coming." Cole sat back as they rolled on toward whatever awaited them under that shimmer.

Some time later, the little truck rumbled up to an old service station. One look made it plain to Cole, this place was no longer a legitimate business. Cars and trucks were parked at odd angles all around the central building, and it was clear at a glance that something of import was happening beyond the boarded-up windows. The light they had seen was from the single security light that stood sentry outside.

"We should keep moving," Cole said. "This place doesn't look like somewhere we want to be, especially with a gunshot victim and a little girl."

Marcus hesitated. "What if we stole one of their cars?"

Cole must've looked like he'd been punched in the face, so Marcus sighed and continued.

"We need gas, and we have to get out of this truck before someone recognizes who it belongs to." He inclined his chin to the cluster of vehicles. "I'm sure Viggo knows how to hotwire a car. We'll snag one, and bee-line for the border."

Cole sighed. As much as he wanted to believe it was the worst idea he'd ever heard, he had to admit there was some sense to it. The truck was low on gas and wouldn't make it the roughly two-hundred miles to the border. But either way, before he had a chance to respond, the boarded-up door to the place swung open, spilling light and sound from within. Music, Cole realized. The moment the door was open, he saw people gathered around something, and music and warm light permeated the place. The people stumbling out, who he'd at first taken as security coming to check on them, were in fact two drunk old men, slapping each other on the back and hooting laughter.

Cole relaxed a bit. "Cut the engine," he said to Marcus, who complied instantly, plunging them into darkness. The two old drunks stumbled around the corner of the building, their laughter sinking away into the pitch-black night that lingered out of reach of the security light.

Marcus spoke first. "I don't think this place is part of the cartel."

Before Cole could respond, Viggo spoke up in a grinding voice through the open slit in the back window. "Look where you are," he said, his voice thick, as if he'd just woken up. "Everything here is part of the cartel."

Cole cleared his throat. "He's probably right." Marcus's eyes turned down for just a moment. "But I think you are, too," Cole continued. "I don't think they're here waiting for us to drive by. The chaos we caused back there must have at least slowed them down." He took a deep breath. "So I think you're right. Let's steal a car."

Marcus crouched low to the ground and hurried from the truck door, which he'd closed as softly as he could. Still, he could've sworn he heard the noise echo back to him as he'd done it. His nerves were cranked to the max, causing him to sweat and his hands to shake. He gripped and loosened his fists in time to try and stop the tremor.

They'd agreed he would be fastest, so he went alone for now. He was just supposed to check the doors and try to find one that's unlocked. Then, they could maneuver Viggo over to hotwire it. Marcus was more than a little surprised Viggo had agreed to that after what Cole had done to him, but he had. So away Marcus went, alone, to try and steal a car.

The first car, a four-door sedan, was locked. *Damn,* Marcus thought. Some part of him had really hoped the first one would've been unlocked, but nothing seemed to come that easily. So he crouched and half-walked, half-ran to the next vehicle – a slightly larger pickup truck with a light bar on top. Also locked. *Damn.*

As Marcus went from car to car, careful to stay out of the security light as much as possible, he couldn't help but reflect on the insanity that had been the last few months. His mother and brother being killed had set off a series of events that he knew had changed them all irrevocably. And now, he and his father had actually done it. They'd rescued Katie and captured Viggo. Killed a bunch of cartel members, too, somehow. He tried not to think about what bill may eventually come due on that front. But they'd actually done what they set out to do.

Or, partly, at least. They still had to get home, which was proving more and more difficult. A beat-up Jeep didn't budge when he pulled the handle and he moved on.

Still, a heinous guilt nagged at Marcus's guts. His mother and brother had died, and he felt he'd barely mourned them. There had been so much happening, even their funerals had felt rushed. Marcus let his mind wheel back to that day as he tried more doors.

As he thought about it, he could feel the cold chill that had settled on the graveside congregants. He'd looked at his mother and felt a rising bile, which he'd staunched with some effort. The suit he'd worn had felt somehow stuffy and too thin at the same time. And while the wind had blown cold across him, his face had felt flush and hot.

He remembered his grandmother, the only one he had left. She'd just sat in her wheelchair and stared at the two caskets-one normal size, one horrifyingly small. She hadn't cried. Marcus had found that odd, but didn't know what to make of it. She'd just looked so...defeated. Like all the life had rushed out of her when her daughter and grandson had died.

Marcus had approached her, unsure of what to say. In the end, he'd said nothing and placed a hand on her shoulder. Her own bony hand had gripped it, vice-tight. Every breath she'd taken seemed to be shuddering, but still no tears. After a moment, his uncle had come and wheeled her away, giving Marcus a good-natured pat on the shoulder and nod.

And then it had just been him. And in the end, Marcus had stood alone as his mother and brother were lowered into the cold dirt. The air had stung his eyes and blown his too-long hair into his face, but he'd found in the moment that he couldn't bring himself to look away, even long enough to brush back his hair or wipe his eyes. The entire world had been lowered into the ground, and he could no longer find purchase or solid ground beneath him.

Marcus was jolted from his memories when the door of a sporty little 4×4 popped open in his hand. He'd tried so many of the vehicles in the lot, he was shocked when one actually opened. He checked inside as much as he could, but found no keys.

A *bang* emanated from the building as the doors flung open and people spilled into the parking lot. Panic rising, Marcus looked back to the truck they'd arrived in, and realized there was no way to get back there. With no other option readily available, he climbed in the open door of the 4×4 and closed it behind him.

Cole could barely make out the silhouette of Marcus slithering into the little shitbox he'd found unlocked. "Goddammit," he said. Viggo chuckled. Cole spun and glared at him. "Not sure what you find so funny. We're going to *him* now."

As quickly as he could, Cole roused Katie, who'd begun whimpering in her sleep, and moved to untie Viggo. But before he did, he thought to pull the massive revolver from his waistband and level it at the killer's head.

"You try anything," Cole said. "I blow your brains out and take my chances with the crowd."

Viggo nodded. "Fair enough."

After helping Viggo off the back of the truck, Cole looped one of his arms over his shoulders and off they limped, like some sort of sick three-legged race. Katie clung to Cole's leg, but he noticed she did not seem to fear Viggo, looking at him with more confusion than concern. Cole found it odd and more than a little disturbing, but kept it to himself for now.

The three of them tried to stay low as they moved through the sea of vehicles, but it was a mostly futile effort. More than anything, Cole just hoped everyone at this... whatever it was, was too drunk to notice them.

A man emerged from the door to the little place, hooting like a maniac with a large black chicken held over his head. *"Este pequeño cabrón es la mejor verga de México!"* the man screamed.

"Ah," Cole breathed. "Cockfight."

Viggo looked at him, incredulous. "Just now figuring that out, world traveler?"

Cole ignored him and hobbled on toward the car Marcus was trapped in. They were only thirty or forty feet away now. As they approached, a man broke off from his two friends nearby and headed straight for the little car.

Viggo dropped from Cole's grip and hit the ground, then shuffled over behind a car. Cole bent and grabbed Katie, then hid behind the car next to Viggo's.

"Daddy?" Katie asked, fear creeping into her voice.

Cole soothed her, rubbing her hair. "Shhh, baby. Daddy's trying to keep us safe," he whispered. He looked toward Viggo and found him glancing over the trunk of the car he hid behind. More people were pouring out of the building, even as the music seemed to grow louder.

Viggo turned to Cole and held up one finger, mouthing, *"Just one."*

Cole nodded, then turned to Katie. "Baby," he said. "I need you to stay right behind me, and when I tell you, you get down, turn around, and cover your ears, alright?" She said nothing, just looked around fearfully. He took her by the shoulders. "Katie, I need you to listen. Do you understand?" She locked eyes with him, and nodded.

"Good girl." Cole rubbed her head and turned toward Viggo, who gestured to his ruined leg, then shrugged.

Not much Cole could say to that. He hooked his arm around Viggo again and they hobbled toward the car. The car's owner was coming toward them from the other direction and Cole noticed immediately the side-eye he gave them. Viggo must've noticed it, too, because he whispered in Cole's ear, "Follow my lead."

Before Cole could respond, Viggo howled with laughter that sounded surprisingly genuine. That surprised Cole. He couldn't imagine the man laughing. But laugh he did, and slapped Cole on the back, and swayed like a drunk, more convincingly than some of the actual drunks stumbling around the parking lot.

The other man laughed at that and nodded to the pair goodnaturedly. That gave Cole a stab of guilt. He knew what was coming, and there wouldn't be anything goodnatured about it.

Sure enough, as they drew closer together, Viggo grabbed Cole by the hand and slurred in fake drunken stupor.

"I love you, man. Here, this is for you. I know you've always loved it." And he pressed a switchblade into Cole's palm. It made his blood run cold. But he accepted it, wordlessly, then dropped his hand to his side. He leaned Viggo against a car, where he dropped into a sitting position. Cole briefly registered him taking hold of Katie and turning her away.

The other man had his back turned now, fumbling for his keys as he cracked open the car door. Somewhere in that car, Marcus was hiding, Cole knew. No time to hesitate. No time for second guessing. He pressed the switch and the blade snapped open.

Cole readied himself. He raised the knife. He was less than a foot away from the man's back. He could smell his cologne. He could see laundry stains on the soccer jersey he wore, see the sweat beading on the back of his neck. As he was about to stab down, something stopped him; the images of his murdered wife and son flashed through his mind. His stomach rolled as his eyes slid back to the knife in his hand. For a moment, he saw it as both his hand and Viggo's. Shuddering, he dropped it. As he watched it fall, he glimpsed Marcus through the window, laying in the back floorboard, looking up horrified.

Marcus's breath caught in his throat when he saw his father, knife raised, about to stab an innocent man in the back.

For me, he thought. *He's going to do it for me.*

When Cole dropped the knife, Marcus almost breathed a sigh of relief. But of course, there was still the issue of his predicament. He needed a distraction, but had no way of telling Cole. Desperate and scared, he did the only thing he could think of, and violently rocked the car to the side.

The driver stumbled back in surprise, and it seemed to jolt Cole awake. He tackled the man as Marcus scrambled out of the car. When he managed to untangle himself from the cramped backseat, Marcus found Cole laying on top of the other man, holding him down with the knife, recovered from the ground, pressed into his throat.

"Give me the fucking keys," Cole seethed. The man was nearly in tears, but shakily held up the car keys.

"Take," he said in a thick accent. "Take, please, leave. Please, *señor*, please." He was crying, fat tears running down his face and mingling with the sheen of sweat already there.

"Roll over, put your face in the dirt, count to five-hundred," Cole said, climbing to his feet. The man was doing as he said, rolling over to his stomach and counting. Marcus suppressed an urge to vomit, then moved to help Viggo and Katie to the car. He was careful to shield Katie from the sight of the man laying on the ground crying, but he thought she caught a glimpse anyway.

A couple of minutes later, they were all crammed into

the little car, backing up and pulling away from the service station. As they left behind the cartel truck, Marcus couldn't help but think about his father, and what he might've done in the name of keeping *him* safe. It made his stomach turn, and he swallowed hard, then pressed the gas, speeding off into the night.

CHAPTER 27

The Highway

Viggo rubbed his aching leg and cursed ever knowing Cole Traeger's name. He knew the knee would never be right again. His days of walking without pain were over, assuming the thing could even be salvaged by the time he found someone to tend it.

Just as likely I lose it altogether, he thought with a groan. He laid his head back against the seat in the back of the cramped little shitbox Marcus and Cole had stolen. The girl leaned against the opposite window, staring out at the passing scenery, illuminated by the fledgling sunrise.

Watching her there, he was reminded of the hours spent making the trip south, convincing himself all the while that he was just doing what he had to do to survive. He closed his eyes and swallowed bile.

What a crock of shit. Viggo had always known he wasn't a good man. It had been obvious the first time he'd robbed a convenience store with his old man.

"You pulled that trigger a little too quick," his dad had said. "Barely even gave him a chance to give us the money."

An image came to mind of his mother washing blood from his shirt.

"Well he's still gotta have something to wear to school," she'd said to his father's eye roll.

"What's he need to be in fuckin' school for? Christ, he just killed a dude, Joni!" His dad had said it with a laugh that bit Viggo deeply now. In spite of himself, he felt a tear welling at the thought of his dad. He blinked it away and pretended to fish out a speck of dust as he wiped the corner of his eye.

"I'm sorry, Vig, but your pops knew the rules," Luke had said, a meaty hand on Viggo's bony shoulder. "He knows how we handle thieves."

And from that moment on, the Scolessas had been Viggo's family. It hurt to think of them now. His old life seemed so far away. He closed his eyes. Sleep didn't come, but the quiet jostling of the Mexican highway was still preferable to his memories.

The little SUV jostled into a sleepy town as morning fully took over the sky, and Marcus started when he saw the sign: *San Juan el Baptiste*. Reflexively, his hands tightened around the steering wheel.

"Dad," Marcus said, grabbing his father by the shoulder

and shaking him. "Dad, wake up."

Cole roused, rubbing his eyes. "What?" he asked blearily.

"We're back in *San Juan el Baptiste*."

Cole immediately stopped and looked at his son, then swallowed.

"Don't stop," he said. "Don't stop until we're clear. They can't know we're here."

Marcus looked down at the fuel gauge and was dismayed to see it sitting at just above a quarter of a tank.

"We're going to need gas soon."

"We have to risk it," Cole said. "I'll walk back to the border before I stop here." He leaned closer and seethed. "You know they're all over this town."

Marcus nodded, then swallowed. "You're right. We risk it."

By the time they were bouncing along the divots of the highway an hour past the little town of *San Juan el Baptiste*, Marcus was already starting to regret the decision. The mood in the car was noticeably tense, in large part, Marcus assumed, because there was no way they would be able to carry Viggo to their destination.

So it was with immense relief that he sighed when they rounded a bend in the road and saw a fuel station bustling with people. This time, Marcus didn't ask Cole's opinion, and swung into the parking lot, then stopped at the pump. He turned to face Viggo, who was still reclining in the back seat and had said basically nothing since they'd stolen the car.

"I need some money," Marcus said flatly.

Viggo chuckled. "Sorry, I'm not very liquid right now." He mimed patting pockets he didn't have.

Marcus regarded him evenly. "I saw the money Lavilla had stored in that case in the panic room. Don't expect me to believe you left it all behind."

Viggo hesitated a moment, then rolled his eyes. "No point," he said, then reached down his pant leg and produced a bundle of American dollars and proffered it to Marcus.

Marcus examined the bundle of money, which looked to be $20 bills, totaling $1,000. "Is it...real?" he asked, feeling stupid even as he did.

Viggo tossed the money to him, apparently tiring of holding it out. "I guess you're going to find out." And with that, he went back to looking out the window.

As Marcus opened the door, Cole grabbed his arm and gestured to the money. "Let me."

Marcus looked at his father questioningly. "You sure?"

Cole rolled his head around his shoulders, his neck cracking as he went. "Yeah. I need to move."

Marcus shrugged and handed the money over. Cole pulled $100 off the top, then stuffed the rest in the glove compartment. Then he opened the car's squeaky door and climbed out with an audible groan.

As he watched Cole head inside the store, limping a little, Marcus let himself hope for a moment. They were almost home. By tomorrow, with any luck, they'd be back across the border and could finally put this behind them.

Cole shook his leg, trying to loosen up his knee as he walked across the small parking lot and into the service station. A chime over the door greeted him cheerily and for a moment, he was teleported back to his own store, thousands of miles and a lifetime away.

He had inherited the store from his father when he and Lillian got married. And for years, he'd hated every square inch of the place. He'd felt pinned down, unable to move for the pressure it placed on him. The pressure of expectations and responsibilities to a man who'd been dead for fifteen years at this point.

Cole couldn't help but chuckle at the thought of his father. The old bastard would've gotten a kick out of this, his pansy-ass son traipsing off to Mexico to fight cartels. But then, he'd never expected much, and hadn't been slow to remind Cole of his various failures whenever the opportunity presented itself.

Cole grabbed a disposable cellphone from one of the service station's aisles. He knew they needed to check in with Luke, and the phone he'd given them had been left behind in the chaos of their escape from the cartel's stronghold. He added a couple bags of chips, some canned energy drinks, and a coffee to the phone, then proceeded to the register.

"Put the rest on pump five," he told the cashier, who gave him a quizzical expression as he handed over the cash. Noticing the look, Cole pointed at their car, then said, "*Gasolina.*"

The cashier chuckled as he nodded, then took the money and gave no change. Cole raised an eyebrow, but ultimately just shrugged and returned to the car with the bag of junk food and burner phone.

They were back on the road in a few minutes, and Cole admitted to himself that he felt much better rumbling along the highway instead of waiting in a parking lot. Every time they slowed down, he could swear he saw cartel cars following behind them. But, unlikely as it seemed to him, they hadn't actually encountered any resistance since leaving the cartel in the desert.

Cole extracted the burner phone from its plastic shell,

popped in the SIM card, and dialed the number he'd memorized for Luke. He picked up on the first ring.

"Who is this?" Luke's voice was haggard, but urgent.

"It's Cole."

"Who?"

Cole sighed. "Cole Traeger. In Mexico."

"Shit, right." Cole thought he heard a lighter snapping closed before Luke exhaled and spoke again. "I hear you guys have been up to some shit we didn't agree to, Cole."

Cole grimaced. He'd thought this was a possibility. From the driver's seat, Marcus cracked his energy drink open with a *pop*. "Yeah, things got a little out of hand."

"No shit," Luke chuckled. "Truth be told, Jorge and Richie had gotten a little overly inflated, for my tastes. I think I've bought you some time before they come after you."

Cole started. "Really?"

Luke blew out as he responded. "Yeah, Richie needs all the business partners he can get with Jorge gone." After a beat, he offered an explanation. "Jorge was the front man. He did the dealmaking. Richie handles...the enforcement."

"Huh," Cole said. "I guess that makes sense."

"Yeah," Luke said, then inhaled deeply before continuing. Cole would've sworn he could smell the smoke through the phone. "Anyway. What's your status? You find

Viggo?"

Cole looked over his shoulder at the shell of a man. "Yeah, we've got him. He's a little worse for wear."

"Well, consider me surprised. I didn't figure you stood a chance, truth be told."

"Thanks for the vote of confidence," Cole huffed. Marcus looked at him quizzically. Cole waved him off.

"So are you headed back?"

Cole noted Luke never asked about Katie. "Yeah. Should be crossing the border tomorrow morning. Any way you can assist with that? Our passports got taken by the cartel and we can't exactly take Viggo to the embassy."

Luke chuckled again. "I hear you. I think I've got someone in the area who can at least give you some cover. But you should know, I think the feds have already pieced together where you are. They're in the area, and they'll probably be watching the border tomorrow."

Cole groaned. "Fuck. How did that happen?"

He thought he could *hear* the shrug from Luke. "A leak somewhere. Shit happens, Cole. Nothing's really a secret in this business. But it's alright. My person can help cover you across the border with Viggo. Even if the cops know, no way they arrest you. And do you really give a shit what happens to Viggo after he's back on our side of the river?"

Cole glanced at Viggo and felt the slightest pinprick of

guilt before looking at Katie's virtually catatonic stare. That was sufficient to snuff it out.

"No, I do not."

"Great. You should send the kids downriver a little ways to cross on their own. No reason for them to get caught up in a standoff or anything."

Cole nodded. "Good idea. So when we cross, should I call–"

"No." Luke cut him off. "Do not call me again. When we hang up, throw this phone out the window. I'll have eyes on you. I'll know when it's done."

"Oh," Cole said. "Got it."

"Loosen up, Cole. You're almost in the clear. You did it."

"Yeah." But Cole felt very far away from the clear. "Just gotta cross the border and we're done."

Luke exhaled again. "You've got this. I'll talk to you when you're back in the city."

And with that, he was gone. Cole threw the phone out the window and watched the landscape roll by, his mind racing.

CHAPTER 28

The Fear of What Comes Next

V iggo watched the doctor examine his leg. Well, "doctor" was a strong word. He was some sort of neighborhood medic, from what he'd gathered. Either way, he had some sutures, tweezers, and bandages, plus he'd given him a bottle of tequila to swig from when the pain got too bad, so as far as he was concerned, the guy was a doctor.

"How's it going?" Viggo asked. The man turned to look at him through thick glasses, but said nothing. Viggo nodded. "Right, forgot."

The doctor had used the tweezers to get all the bullet fragments out of his knee, then debrided the dead skin, washed it with alcohol, and stitched it up. But Viggo knew he'd never move quite the same. He could live with it. He swigged the tequila again.

Of course, if Cole got his way, none of it would matter anyway. He'd be dead in a week if he made it to an

American prison. The Scolessas had plenty of reach in the prisons, Viggo knew. He'd helped organize those sorts of hits before. It would barely take a phone call.

He sighed. *Not like it matters. I can't go anywhere or get away like this. I can barely walk.*

Truthfully, Viggo had started to come to terms with his impending fate. He was physically unable to escape now, and even if he did, from what Cole said about his conversation with Luke, the clock was ticking for him in Mexico. And once Richie decided he'd waited long enough, whatever was left of the *Moncada-Lavilla* would be coming for him, and he'd be totally helpless. He supposed trying to appeal to Luke's mercy might be the better play in that situation anyway. He pulled from the tequila bottle again, a nice warm buzz starting to settle over him.

No sooner had the doctor left, that Cole Traeger came to see him. Well, he'd been waiting outside the door of the little ramshackle motel room, and now he came inside. When he lowered heavily into the chair the doctor had been using, Viggo knew he wanted to talk about what came next. With a groan, Viggo pushed himself more upright and finished off the dregs of the tequila, tossing the bottle to the floor. As he did, he briefly considered that he should've kept it, in case he needed a weapon. He laughed at himself internally, then tried to put on a serious face as he looked at

Cole.

Cole Traeger was the master of serious faces. He glowered at Viggo from underneath his thick eyebrows. His beard had grown haggard from lack of care, and it gave his bright green eyes a wildness that took Viggo aback slightly. Though he knew he was probably a sight himself.

"Tomorrow," Cole began, leaning forward on his knees, looking like the weight of the word would crush him flat. "we're crossing the border."

Viggo nodded. "Yeah, I gathered."

"We're crossing the border *alone*." Cole emphasized the last word, holding Viggo's gaze. "Marcus and Katie are crossing the river further down, away from what is apparently going to be quite the police presence."

Viggo sucked at his teeth. "Alright, then. I didn't figure you'd want a show."

Cole groaned slightly. "It wasn't my preference, but they've caught wind apparently. According to Luke, anyway." He sat back and rubbed his eyes. "I'm sure they'll take you into custody right away."

Viggo's heart raced just a bit at the use of the word "custody," but he tried to keep his face calm. "Probably."

A long moment of pregnant silence followed, neither man wanting to give into the urge to ask the question that had been hanging, unanswered, since that night when this all began.

Finally, Cole relented.

"Why?" He spoke the word quietly, reverently, his voice cracking slightly as if part of him was fighting to keep it inside.

Viggo swallowed, looking at the ceiling, trying to distract himself in the popcorn stucco. "Does it matter?" he finally croaked, not looking at Cole. "It's done. I can't undo it."

"You owe me this," Cole said, venom rising in his voice.

Viggo's chest heaved involuntarily as he choked back tears. *Shit, fucking tequila.*

"I know," he said, his voice shaking. "You're right. But all I can tell you is..." he trailed off, trying to find the words. "...I was scared. I thought Luke and his brother were after me. I thought they set me up for some reason. I just...I just wanted to get away. And I thought I could get some valuables or cash from your house, get away, and you'd never know it was me. And they couldn't track the money I stole."

He stopped as a husky laugh escaped his throat.

"Shit, I'm not even sure if they can do that." Viggo swallowed, then continued, still not looking at Cole. "And it all happened so fast. I know that's what people say, but it's true. After I hit you, your wife started screaming. I just...

reacted. And then your boy–" His voice finally failed him.

He thought of Cole's younger son, slick with blood, his pudgy young face lifeless and pallid. Tears rolled with the release. "I just...I just *fucking panicked.*" Viggo buried his face in his hands and sobbed, deep heaving breaths punctuating his cries.

"I'm so sorry," he wailed, over and over. "I'm so sorry, I'm so sorry, I'm so sorry." Finally, mercifully, he gained his breath and looked at Cole, hoping for something besides unbridled fury.

Bright green eyes, rimmed with tears, stared back. His face, a contorted mask of rage and sadness. His hands, gripped into fists so tight, his nails dug blood from the skin of his palms. When he stood, he did so with such violence, Viggo thought he was going to attack him. But instead, he turned and stalked from the room, slamming the door behind him, leaving Viggo to his echoing confessions.

Cole gulped deep breaths of the warm night air. His face was wet with tears he'd barely managed to hold in while sitting in front of Viggo. And yet, he couldn't seem to catch his breath. His chest hurt, blood pounded in his ears, and the entire world seemed to tilt on its axis.

Viggo Lassiter was *sorry*. Cole barked a humorless laugh at the thought. What did that even mean? Sorry?

Sorry for murdering his wife and child? For kidnapping his daughter and trying to sell her into slavery? For taking a tire iron to his face – no, to his entire life?

How could any words ever capture the depth of what he'd done? There was no capitulation, Cole knew. He wasn't even sure why he'd asked, other than he'd been wondering for months now and knew he'd never forgive himself if he didn't even broach the topic.

Finally, with great effort, he managed to get his body under control and catch his breath. When he unclenched his fist, he found he'd managed to actually draw blood with his nails. He wiped it on the back of his pants and tried to focus on taking deep breaths.

Marcus came up the stairs to the motel's second floor carrying an armload of snacks from a vending machine. He dropped the pile when he saw his father.

"Dad?" He hurried over, turning Cole to look at him. "Are you okay? What happened?" His eyes moved up to Cole's face. "Have you been crying?" His face was quizzical.

Cole pulled him into a tight hug. For a long moment, neither of them spoke. Finally, Marcus pulled away and took his father by the shoulders.

"Dad," he said, his voice even. "What happened?"

Cole smiled, tears brimming in his eyes again. "I asked him why."

Marcus groaned. "I thought we agreed we wouldn't ask."

Cole looked back out over the motel's parking lot. "I know," he said quietly. "Couldn't stop myself."

Marcus turned and leaned over the metal railing. He offered Cole a snack-sized bag of chips. That prompted a chuckle as Cole took the bag, but didn't open it. They stood there silently for a long moment before Cole had calmed enough to speak again.

"He said he was sorry,"

Marcus turned to look at him. "What?"

"He said he was sorry," Cole said again.

"Hmm," Marcus hummed thoughtfully. "I guess he is. If he hadn't done it, he wouldn't be here now."

Cole nodded. "It just seems so...insufficient." He sighed. "Your mother and brother, gone. Your sister...who knows if she'll ever recover. And all this–" he gestured broadly around, "–for him to just say he's sorry?"

Marcus nodded. Then, after a moment, said, "What else is he supposed to say?"

Cole looked at his son, and for a brief moment, he could've sworn he saw him twenty years older than he was. "What do you mean?"

Marcus shrugged. "I don't know. *Anything* he could say would be insufficient. Nothing brings them back. Maybe

'I'm sorry' is the best thing he could say. Or the only thing. I don't know." He crumpled the empty chip bag. "It doesn't really matter, though. We won, Dad. Tomorrow, this will be over."

Cole hesitated, then nodded. "You're right." He clasped Marcus on the shoulder. "We should get some sleep. You go first. I'll stay up and keep watch for now. I'll wake you before sunrise."

Marcus nodded, then embraced his father in a tight hug before moving wordlessly off to the other room to go to bed, snacks piled in his arms. Cole knew Katie was sleeping in there already. And in the room behind him, Viggo Lassiter awaited his comeuppance. Cole only hoped he had the energy left to bring him to it.

Luke watched tendrils of lazy smoke winding around his office as he swirled his glass of whiskey before taking a sip. A deep, boneshaking sigh escaped his lips as he put a hand to his temple. He knew he was playing a dangerous game, intervening with Richie on the Traegers' behalf, but he couldn't bear the thought of what that maniac would do to those two if he caught them.

Truth be told, Luke was more than a little impressed by the father and son. He had never really expected them to find Viggo, and they'd done it in just a few days. Albeit, that had involved the incredibly risky gamble of intentionally being captured by one of the most ruthless cartels in southern Mexico, then breaking out of their compound. But still, it had worked and they were very nearly home-free. Just one more step, with Luke's assistance, and they'd be safely back across the border in the Land of the Free.

Luke downed the rest of his whiskey and grabbed one of his many burner phones from the desk drawer. After a quick flip through the little address book he kept in the breast pocket of his jacket, he dialed the number he found there. After three rings, a woman answered on the other end.

"Yeah?" Her voice was deep, with a husk that set Luke's nerves tingling.

"Got a job. Tomorrow. A guy is crossing the border with a runaway murderer."

"Yeah," she said. "I'm hearing some talk about it on my end, too. They yours?"

Luke chuckled. "In a manner of speaking. I need to make sure they make it across that bridge alive. Both of them."

A moment of silence passed as she thought. "I can do that. Long distance or up close?"

"Long distance," Luke said. "Deniability is important on this one for me."

Now it was her turn to chuckle. "Pretty much always the case for me. Yeah, I can be there."

"Usual rate work for you?"

"I think this one is gonna cost you a little more." Luke swore he could *hear* her smiling.

"One-point-five," he said.

"Double."

"One-point-seven."

A beat. "Deal."

"One more thing," Luke said. "If anything goes sideways, kill him."

"Which one?"

Luke snuffed out his cigarette in the glass ashtray atop his desk. "The mangy son of a bitch who killed my brother."

Marcus was woken from a dreamless sleep by his father's rough shaking. The room was still pitch black.

"Time to get up," he said simply. "Meet me outside in twenty minutes.

Marcus rose and dressed, then roused Katie and put on her shoes before they headed outside, where he found his father and Viggo standing by the metal balcony railing. Marcus gave Viggo a cursory look, noting the heavy bags under his eyes. But he seemed to be moving around on his leg a little better, and someone had dug up a rusty old crutch to prop under one of his arms.

Cole didn't look much better, all things considered. He clearly hadn't slept, as evidenced by his own set of dark circles under his eyes. Their conversation from the night before still hung heavy over Marcus.

"Alright," Cole said as they approached. "Here's the plan. Marcus, you and Katie will head downriver and cross where it's shallow, away from the bridge where we're crossing. Once you're on the American side, circle back to us and we'll meet you there."

Marcus sighed. He knew Cole wanted them to cross separately, but he still felt uncomfortable with the idea. "I still don't see why we can't cross together."

"Because," Cole said, slight exasperation leaking into his voice. "I don't want there to be any chance of you two getting caught in any crossfire if things go poorly."

"What could go poorly, Dad?" Marcus asked.

Cole sighed. "Is that really a question you want to ask at this point?" He looked at Viggo, who still said nothing. "There are probably going to be a lot of guns and some itchy trigger fingers on that bridge. I won't have you or Katie anywhere near it, if I can help it."

Marcus looked into his father's eyes, and saw resolution. He was decided on this, and that was it. So, Marcus nodded. A beat of silence passed where they all looked at each other. And the weight of the moment settled on the little group.

Cole bent down to Katie and took her into his arms. "Katie girl, Daddy loves you. Never forget it. Go with your brother, and I'll see you in a little while, okay?"

She hugged him back and spoke in a quiet voice, "Okay, Daddy." And then, even quieter, "I love you, too."

When Cole straightened and looked at Marcus, his eyes were wet with tears. With little warning, his father folded him into a tight hug.

"Keep her safe. I love you, son. I'll see you when this is over." Then he broke away and gave Marcus a look that made him think he was sizing him up. Without another word, Cole turned, took Viggo by the arm, and started down the steps.

As they went, Viggo never looked at Marcus. Marcus figured that was for the best. There was nothing there to say. He did glance at Katie and give her a nod.

Katie nodded in return.

CHAPTER 29

What He Lost

C ole stood at the precipice of his journey's conclusion. Next to him, Viggo leaned on his crutch with one arm, the other held firmly in his captor's hand. At the other end of the bridge, Kirkpatrick and Faraday stood, clad in SWAT bullet-proof vests and surrounded by FBI vehicles. Faraday, positioned behind an SUV that was parked sideways in their path, lifted a megaphone and spoke.

"Cole," he boomed. "Come on over. Everything's been worked out on our end. You get him across the border. We'll take it from there."

Cole looked toward Viggo. He expected a comment, snide remark, open threat, *something*. But Viggo Lassiter was impassable. He said nothing, and his face betrayed no emotion. Cole swallowed, somehow more unnerved by his silence than if he'd been screaming and laughing.

"Let's go," Cole said, and tugged on Viggo's arm. There was no resistance. The other man simply started half-walking, half-hobbling on his crutch toward the other end of the bridge.

After fifteen wobbly steps, Viggo finally spoke. Soft, calm, and sad.

"Are you happy now?"

It wasn't a joke, or a threat, or anything so sinister. Cole looked at him and tried to plumb the depths of his face, to find something more in those hard eyes that looked somehow even sadder now than usual. He found nothing, just as he did every other time he'd tried this.

Cole stopped, eliciting an audible groan from the contingent of law enforcement on the other side of the bridge. He turned to face Viggo.

"Look at me." Slowly, Viggo turned to Cole and fixed him with that same sad, empty stare he always had. "What are you getting at?" Cole tried to project confidence, but he felt it came out wheedling, whining, begging. The part of him that had been traipsing across Mexico for a week, running from a cartel, suddenly faded away, and he found himself very much the father and husband who'd lost his family. Images of his wife and son flashed through his mind, and his failure stung all anew. He'd found Katie, and he hoped he could salvage things with Marcus, but what he'd lost still rang so loudly as to deafen him.

Viggo shook his head slowly and looked back to the ground.

"Cole..." His voice was weak. When he looked back at Cole, he forced a swallow as tears gathered at the edges of his eyes, then fell down his scraggly cheeks to settle in the unkempt and uneven beard. "I can never replace what I took from you." He looked to the law enforcement. "But please...please don't give me to them."

Cole was shocked. Begging? *This* is how he was choosing to end this journey? Anger boiled in Cole's belly. After all this man had done, he couldn't even do him the justice of taking his punishment? Cole hadn't killed him when he'd had the chance because some part of him, in spite of his own desires, still felt there was a true justice he'd have to face.

But to beg and whine to Cole, of all people? After all he'd seen? After all he'd *done?*

"What," Cole said through teeth gritted so tightly they threatened to shatter, "are you asking?"

Viggo coughed out a wet laugh. "I know," he said. "I have no right to ask you, I just..." He looked at that gathered cohort of police, all angry flashing lights and guns drawn. He sighed. "I can't go back. I'll never see the light of day again. Assuming I even make it to prison, the Scolessas will kill me in there. I'll be dead in a week." His eyes were frantic when he looked back to Cole. "Please." The last word was quiet, almost childlike.

Cole hesitated. He couldn't let him go, could he? After all he'd done? After all Cole had been through? But still, he knew the cartel, or whatever was left of it, would find him eventually. Even if he stayed in Mexico, he'd live the rest of his life looking over his shoulder, never feeling truly safe. The consideration made his stomach feel cold and fuzzy. He looked Viggo over and saw so much fear in his face.

Fear.

Fear like what Bryce had felt when he was gunned down. Fear like Lillian had felt when she'd woken to find this man standing over her bloodied husband. Fear like Katie had felt when he'd stolen her from her home and driven her to a strange place and *sold her to fund his escape*.

The anger returned from its brief respite hotter than ever. Cole pulled the cowboy's revolver from his waistband and leveled it at Viggo's chest.

"You," he seethed, "would beg forgiveness? From *me?!*" He roared the last words as the fury in his chest reached a flaming crescendo. "*YOU STOLE THEM FROM ME!*" he screamed, shaking the revolver. "*YOU KILLED THEM AND YOU STOLE HER AND YOU RAN!*" He shoved the gun into Viggo's chest, dug the barrel in, hoped it hurt. He looked into Viggo's eyes, the rage so hot now it blinded him, red fuzzing at the edges of his vision. Somewhere in the distance, the police were shouting at him to step back, but he couldn't hear them. He could only hear the blood thundering in his ears as he started to squeeze the trigger.

A thunderous punch connected with Cole's throat as Viggo dropped his crutch, somehow balancing on his one good leg. A grip like a vice ratcheted down on his wrist, wrenching his hand away as the shot went off and the bullet careened into the road surface of the bridge itself. Cole felt a sickening *pop* as his wrist broke and the gun was gone. He snapped his head around to Viggo just in time to see his face.

Blank.

BANG

The gunshot erupted.

Viggo squeezed the trigger before he'd even had time to think. He'd moved on instinct, without even realizing. The muzzle flash blinded him temporarily as the gun bucked in his hand. The sound was a deafening *CRACK*. Cole's face flashed shock and horror before landing on stunned silence as he began to fall. Viggo turned to look at the cops gathered on the other side of the bridge. They were screaming now. One had his hands up, trying to stop the others from shooting at him for some reason. He couldn't figure out why. They *should* shoot him, he knew. He deserved that.

All at once, he remembered his shattered leg as he nearly placed his weight on it. He awkwardly hopped to maintain his balance. He thought he might've screamed something at the cops, but he couldn't even hear himself. He'd killed Cole Traeger. He knew he'd killed him, the shot was too close. No chance of surviving that. He almost tossed the gun away in disgust, but that same instinct that had shot Cole kept him from going that far. He needed to find a way off this bridge, find a way to–

Another gunshot pierced the air and all went dark.

The bullet ripped through Cole's chest, and exploded out his back. The hollow-point round did its job, blasting through his spine and muscles. He fell to the ground in what seemed like slow motion. When he landed, there was no pain. Only cold.

He tried to speak, but couldn't force words past the blood filling his throat. A metallic sensation overwhelmed his mouth as his own blood threatened to choke him to death.

"M-M-M..." His lips were numb and distant, but he tried to form them into words. The cold crept to his fingers, and his legs were long since gone to numbness. "M-M-M..." The sky was vanishing as his eyes failed him. Another gunshot rang out, but he couldn't see from where or toward whom. Someone was shouting. Everything was cold now. The smell of smoke and blood filled his nostrils.

"M-M-M..." More blood gurgled into his throat. He coughed, and for a brief moment, the sky returned to his view. The sun was bright and burning, he smelled of death and blood was seeping from his soul.

"M-"

Dead.

"M-"

Dead.

"M-"

Dead.

"M-"

Dead.

"MARCUS!"

But the word would not come.

CHAPTER 30

Unbroken and Unafraid

Marcus held tight to Katie's hand as they emerged from the water. He pulled her up and pushed her ahead of him onto the bank. Together, they clawed their way up the sand and rocks to scraggly grass. Then both of them flopped onto their backs and breathed hard.

Safely on American soil, Marcus allowed himself to smile. He even laughed a bit. When he sat up, Katie tackled him with a hug that sent him back to the ground.

"We made it!" she yelled.

"I know!" he responded.

He scrambled to his feet and pulled her up with him. "Come on, we have to go find Dad." He took off jogging in the direction of the border bridge, mostly dragging Katie behind him. The bridge came into view in less than an hour. They stopped about a half-mile away.

"What are we waiting for?" Katie asked. "Let's go!"

Marcus rubbed her arm. "We need to wait here for a

minute."

"No!" she yelled. "I want to see Daddy!" Tears were welling in her eyes.

Marcus softly shushed her and took her in his arms. "I know," he whispered. "But he has something important to do first. We'll wait here for a bit, then walk on over."

She nodded, and the tears flowed. "I missed you," she whispered.

Marcus clenched his eyes shut to keep them from wetting his cheeks. "I missed you, too. But it's over now. You're coming home."

She heaved as she softly sobbed into his chest. No more than ten minutes passed before she fell asleep against him.

They sat huddled in the dirt for another half-hour before the shot rang out. Katie woke with a start and Marcus reached for the gun he'd given his father.

"We have to go," he said as he hurriedly stood. "Let's go! Come on!" He took off running before realizing she couldn't keep up. He turned and scooped her in his arms before taking off at a sprint for the bridge. As they drew close, he heard the yelling. Faraday had his hands up.

"Don't shoot!" he yelled. "We can't kill him on Mexican soil!"

Marcus's stomach dropped as he drew close.

No, no, no, no. Please, no. He hid Katie's face in his chest. "Don't look."

As Marcus looked to the bridge, he nearly collapsed. Viggo stood over his father, the cowboy's enormous black revolver in his hand.

Viggo was screaming, seeming manic. "I didn't want to do that!" he screamed. "He made me! He would've made me go back! I didn't have a choice! I didn't-" His last words were cut off by a piercing gunshot that rang in from somewhere in the distance. The shot took Viggo through the jaw. Marcus saw the bottom half of his face explode in blood and bone as he collapsed. What would have been a scream was muffled by gurgling blood as he went down.

Katie screamed and wrenched herself free from Marcus's grip and dropped to the ground.

"Katie, no! Don't!"

"DADDY!" her scream was piercing as she took off for the bridge. Detective Faraday caught her quickly. She beat on his arms as he pulled her back to the roadblock and handed her over to another officer. "Get her out of here!"

Marcus stood in dumbfounded wonderment as he watched the police officers rush to cover.

"Sniper!" Faraday was yelling as he drew his pistol and ducked behind an SUV. "Marcus! Get down!"

Marcus barely registered the command. The world

around him spun in a blur of noise and pain, but he felt nothing.

Faraday grabbed him by the shoulder, shaking him free of whatever restraints he imagined held him.

"We have to get to cover, Marcus! Now!"

Marcus turned to look at the detective, then back at his father, bleeding out on the bridge. "No."

"We don't have time for this!"

"No!" Marcus screamed. Faraday caught him around the midsection and tried to haul him back to cover.

"We have to get to cover, Marcus! There's a sniper!" Marcus wrenched out of the older man's grip and turned to run to Cole. Faraday spun him around with a hand on the shoulder, but Marcus's fist connected solidly on the detective's jaw, causing him to let go. Faraday stumbled back for a moment, rubbing his jaw. Marcus seized the opportunity and made a run for the border.

"Stop!" Faraday yelled behind him. "Goddammit, stop!"

When Marcus passed the halfway point on the bridge, he glanced over his shoulder. Faraday stopped and put his hands on his hips.

"What the fuck are you doing?" he yelled.

"I have to know if he's alive!" Marcus came to a stop where his father fell. He glanced at Viggo and was shocked to see he was still breathing. His lower jaw was gone, completely shattered and ripped away. The bottom half of his face was nothing but gore, and his breathing was shallow, labored, and brought gurgling to his throat.

Suffer and die, then. However you want it.

He turned his attention to Cole. His father's chest was opened by the bullet, and blood was pouring from the wound, pooling next to him on the street. He was breathing, but it was barely noticeable, and his skin was pale to the point of being nearly translucent. His lips were turning purple, and his arms and legs lay unmoving in the pooling blood.

"Dad," Marcus took his father's hand and held it in his. Cole gripped his hand weakly in return. "Dad, can you hear me?"

Cole gurgled a response. His eyes stared up at the sky, darting from side to side, seeming to search for something. He spoke, so softly Marcus could not hear him. He leaned down to his father's face and listened again.

"I'm...sorry. Love...her. Love...you."

And Cole Traeger's hand went limp.

Marcus screamed. He hugged his father and cried heaving sobs into his destroyed chest. For a while, he just sat there, wrapped in the cold wind cutting across the bridge as the world descended into chaos around him; a slice of eternity carved from a moment he hated, but couldn't leave.

The Last First Step

Katie smoothed the front of the black dress and looked in the mirror. Her dark hair pulled back in a tight bun with little makeup on, she felt she looked appropriately dour. She sighed and turned away from the mirror. She didn't like how much of her parents she saw in it. Her mother's dark hair and sad smile, her father's stern brow and bright green eyes always seemed to look back at her. She barely saw herself. Just pieces of other people.

And of course, she thought. *There's a piece of him, too. Buried. But there.*

She shuddered and banished the thought. Dr. Rollins had told her to face her past, but right now, it was all too much.

Besides, I'll be doing a lot of facing the past in a couple hours.

She retrieved the small black clutch - one of her mother's - she planned to carry tonight and moved out of her room, closing the door behind her. Out the window in the living room, she could see the dark sky, and the city spread out like a carpet of stars, the streets far beneath the condo. She paused for a moment and took in the sight, then moved on through the living room and down the hall to the unit's other bedroom, where she knocked lightly on the door.

"Come in," came the man's voice on the other side.

He sounds like him, she thought, then chastised herself. *I don't even know what he sounded like. Just someone else's idea of him.* She pushed the door open and saw him, standing in front of a mirror, much like she had been only a moment ago.

Marcus Traeger had grown older, his hair and beard tinged with gray. He was constantly complaining about how his hair was getting too long, or his beard was getting too messy, but he never took the jump of cutting them off. She was glad. She could already see so much of their father in him, she didn't want to know how much resemblance he'd bear to their father if he cut his hair like a grown-up. Katie moved into the room and sat down on his bed, still unmade.

Marcus glanced at her over his shoulder as he straightened his tie.

"Are you nervous about today?" he asked.

A bark of a laugh escaped before she could stymie it. "No, not at all," she said, injecting as much sarcasm as she could manage. "Why would I be?"

Marcus scowled at her with a look she thought was supposed to be reproachful. She smiled back at him, then let her face drop.

"You know I am, Marcus." She rubbed her brow. "I've thought about this day so much, I just can't believe it's actually here."

Marcus unspooled his tie and started over, speaking as he measured it out around his neck. "Are you happy?"

She sighed. "I don't know. Are you?"

He paused, seeming to consider the question. "On some level," he said after a moment. "I know it's what Dad wanted." He pulled the necktie tight. "But I honestly don't know if it's what I want." He gestured toward his suit jacket, laying on the bed. Katie threw it to him and he slid it over his shoulders.

"What time is it?" she asked.

Marcus checked his watch and blew a sigh through his lips. "10:30. Let's get going."

The drive through the country was mostly uneventful. Trees flew past the car windows as the city gradually evolved into rolling hills and countryside. Katie's breath caught in her throat when the car turned into the prison. News vans filled much of the parking lot, and the frenzy descended on his car in moments, a committee of vultures to a fresh corpse. Katie slid down in her seat, hiding her face with her hand as Marcus edged the car through the crowd.

The gate guard let them through after seeing their identification. They parked in a reserved spot and walked from the car to the door, where the warden met them.

"Mr. Traeger. Ms. Traeger. Nice to see you." The warden was a tall man, thin and lanky. Still, he was an intimidating presence. His voice was deep and full, simultaneously warm and cold, like a stern father.

Marcus and Katie shook his hand in turn.

"Thank you, Warden," Marcus said.

"We'll begin at midnight. We have a room for you to wait in." The warden led them through the facility, to a waiting room. There were two tables and a couch in the room, with a small television and a snack and drink machine. He left them with a small nod and said he'd be back later to get them.

Time passed slowly in the room. Marcus and Katie sat, mostly in silence, waiting for the call.

Katie fidgeted endlessly as she watched the room's singular clock, situated over the door, tick away. She'd spent so much time waiting for this day. Now it was here, and she felt...numb? That was the only word she could put to it.

Her eyes drifted to her brother, staring a hole through

the opposite wall, his thumb mindlessly flicking the popped top of a soda can, growing warm as he turned it round and round in his hands. But she knew where he was, really. He was on the bridge.

The Bridge.

It was never far from her mind, either. But her memories of it were so fragmented, it was like looking at a faded picture through broken glass. It was there, when she squinted, just never fully realized. But it was different for Marcus. Those memories haunted his every dream, slid through his mind every time he closed his eyes. She knew when he thought of their father, he could see him as nothing other than the man whose stomach was blown open, bleeding out on the hot pavement.

"I saw him," he said, voice distant. "A few times, after the bridge. He was...broken. So weak." His eyes flicked down and met hers, just for a second, then back to staring at the wall. "I tortured him, Kate." He swallowed hard before continuing. "I shoved a mirror in his face, day after day, made him look himself in the face." He buried his face in his hands.

"He cried all the time," he said, his voice muffled by his hands. "And it made me so angry." He gritted his teeth, fighting to hold back tears. "I lost part of myself in that room with him." Now he turned to Katie, eyes ringed with angry red circles.

"I'm sorry I'm all you've got left."

Katie watched for a moment, too stunned to move. Why had he never told her this? She moved to put a hand on his arm, but the moment was broken by the creaking of a door.

"It's time." The warden signaled with his hand for them to follow him. Marcus wiped his eyes and stood, clearing his throat. Katie stood, too, slower, her eyes never leaving her brother. The warden led them out the door and through the prison again, down a dark hallway. Marcus walked in front of Katie, eyes fixed straight ahead. He'd barely spoken since they'd come here, and she worried for him. But even still, her mind was heavy with the suppressive silence hanging over the prison. Outside, she knew the media circus was raging. But inside the cold, concrete walls of the prison, the whole world seemed to be bowing their heads in reverence.

All but two.

Katie slid her hand into Marcus's as they approached the door. He looked down at her, then nodded and squeezed her hand. The nondescript, green, metal door stood before them, a sentry to her nightmares. She tried to take a deep breath, but it caught in her chest and she felt tears rising to her eyes.

No, she thought, defiant. *No tears.* She blinked them away, wiped the corners of her eyes, and stared at the door.

It obeyed in time, opening with a heaviness Katie thought she was imagining. Prison guards in special black uniforms held it open for her and Marcus to walk through. The Warden ushered the siblings through before leaving them.

"I have to be a part of this," he said. He placed his hand on Marcus's shoulder and gave him a small nod before leaving.

Katie and Marcus entered the room. It was simple. Mellow green paint covered the walls, and a gray carpet adorned the floor. Two rows of blue plastic chairs provided seats for the viewers. Across from them was the viewing window.

A whitewashed room, an empty bed with restraints, and a doctor in a black hood were all that sat there now. Katie knew, though, what would soon stare back at them from that room.

Aside from Marcus and Katie, there was only one other person in the viewing room. An older man, broad through the shoulders and chest, sat leaning on his knees and staring at the proverbial hangman's noose beyond the window.

"Luke," Marcus said, a tone of disbelief in his voice. Katie's eyes snapped up, taking the larger man in for the first time. As far as Katie knew, Luke Scolessa had forgiven Marcus's debt and functionally retired. If Marcus knew more, he'd never told her.

Luke looked at Marcus with weary eyes, bloodshot from lack of sleep. "Hey, kid." His voice was rough, like shaking a can full of gravel.

"I didn't expect to see you...here."

Luke coughed out a laugh. "I could say the same for you." His eyes turned to Katie. "And you must be her. I've heard a lot about you. You were the reason for their little crusade, right?"

Katie blinked as she registered the words. He wasn't wrong, she knew. She was the reason her father and brother had come to Mexico and saved her. She was the reason her father died on that bridge. She was the reason her brother was still plagued by nightmares of what happened. Of what they did.

For me.

"My name," she forced out, seeing Luke Scolessa was still looking at her, "is Katie." Then she turned, moving to the other side of the room to find her seat. She made sure she wasn't far enough away to be out of ear shot of Marcus's conversation with the gangster, though.

"Don't mind her," Marcus was saying. "She just tries not to think about what happened. She doesn't remember much of it, and she blames herself if she dwells on it too long." Katie suppressed a sigh at that. After a beat, he continued.

"So, why are you here, exactly?"

Luke sighed. "Got some regrets. This is one of 'em. I never should've sent you and your dad to Mexico to clean up my mess." Tears gathered at the corners of his eyes. "I never told you, but...I'm sorry for what happened to you, Marcus." He paused before continuing, his voice thick with emotion Katie hadn't expected. "I'm sorry for your old man, too."

Marcus took a breath before continuing. "It's alright, Luke. My dad was hellbent on going after Viggo. You just gave us a way to justify it." He added, quieter, "And thank you for keeping our deal."

"Don't mention it." Luke said. "I made certain he'd get here. No easy death in prison for that piece of shit." He cleared his throat. "I've done a lot of bad shit, kid. I fully own up to that. But I never wanted to hurt innocent people. With what I did for a living...well, there weren't a lot of innocent folks to begin with. It wasn't ever much of a concern. But I put you and your dad in a position to get hurt, for my own sake. Because I couldn't let my guys go. They could've handled it well enough. But I was scared. After what happened to Marc... I just couldn't be without them. So, I'm sorry. My cowardice got your dad killed. That's on me." Luke spoke without allowing Marcus time to interject, then took a shuddering breath that seemed much softer than Katie had expected from the man.

Marcus sighed. "Viggo Lassiter killed my dad. And my mom. And my brother. That wasn't your fault. That's just what happened." Katie saw him out of the corner of her eye, placing a hand on the big man's shoulder before moving toward her.

Marcus took his place beside Katie. Again, silence fell while they waited for the macabre main attraction. They didn't have to wait long. Soon enough, the door in the back of the room swung open, and the warden stepped through. Katie felt Marcus's hand tighten around hers as the warden stood to the side, and two prison guards edged through the door, a prisoner in a white jumpsuit between them.

Katie gasped. She had never been to see Viggo, had never laid eyes on his face since that day on the bridge. She had once remarked to Marcus that he must've been the luckiest man alive, to have survived the sniper's bullet. Marcus responded by telling her she wouldn't think that if she had seen his face.

The killer's hair had been shaved. His face was gaunt, mostly from the loss of his lower jaw, an injury he had elected to not have surgically repaired. It left him looking much like a walking corpse, with massive amounts of scar tissue adorning the lower half of his head, and gave his face a lopsided, twisted look.

The guards strapped his legs to the chair, his throne for

the dead. As the doctor was hooking Viggo up to the machines that would monitor his heart, the murderer never looked away from Marcus and Katie.

When the preparations were complete, the warden spoke from Viggo's side.

"Viggo Lassiter, you have been sentenced to death for your involvement in the murders of Bryce Traeger, Lillian Traeger, and Cole Traeger. Do you have any last words?"

Viggo had lost the ability to speak, so he was allowed to give his final words in sign language before his hands were secured. An interpreter stepped into the room from the back. Viggo's last words were short, barely a few motions. They all looked to the interpreter, who swallowed before he spoke.

"You've grown so big, little sister. I'm proud of you."

Katie's grip tightened reflexively as the breath caught in her throat. She could feel tears welling in the corners of her eyes again and willed herself to blink them away, to not cry.

You can't have anymore of my tears, she thought as she wiped the gathering moisture away with her free hand. She glanced at her brother, but she didn't think Marcus even felt her presence. His jaw was set hard, the muscles on the side of his head jumping as he ground his teeth. His eyes were fixed on Viggo, a brutal scowl written across his brow. Katie wanted to ease his pain, take it from him, but she knew he needed to feel this, to reside in this moment. She turned back to the viewing window.

The guards strapped Viggo's hands to the chair as the doctor made his final checks on the equipment. A nod from the warden was all it took, as the doctor began pressing the buttons that injected Viggo with life-ending drugs. As they took effect, the twisted creature that had taken nearly all of Katie's family closed his eyes. Behind his eyelids, she could see his eyes flitting one direction, then another.

Katie hoped he was afraid. Aside from his fists clenching and bulging veins in his neck and head, though, it was hard to see any difference in Viggo being asleep or dying.

As the moments dragged on, the prisoner's arms and legs began to shake, then his whole body. Then, all at once, he stopped. His hands unclenched and went limp, and his head rolled to the side. And it was done.

Katie released Marcus's hand. They were ushered from the room by prison guards, then escorted back to their car. The media was still there, and no sooner had the pair stepped out of the prison than they descended on them. Katie felt Marcus's arm snake around her shoulders, and they walked together to the car. Once inside, they both sat there for a moment before he started the engine and began to edge through the throng.

The drive home was silent. Neither Katie nor Marcus felt the need to fill the silence. So much had been said, and would still be said, but in this moment, they were both content to retreat into their minds. Katie felt the nausea for the first time in the elevator back up to the apartment. By the time Marcus pushed the door open, she had to shove past him and sprint to the bathroom, where she barely bent over the toilet before retching everything in her stomach.

"Katie?" Marcus called. He was coming down the hallway. "Are you alright?"

She reached out a foot and kicked the door shut before he could come in and do his typical big brother routine of trying to make everything better. She wanted to sit in the sick and live with this for a moment. She wanted to rot in the stench of the mounting deaths on her conscience and hate herself. There would be time for rationality later.

The moments dragged on. Marcus eventually moved away from the door, and after a beat, she heard the television. But all she could see was Viggos' stony final look, and his final words, spoken through the interpreter, filled her ears.

"I'm proud of you."

What right did he have to say that? She knew he had none. Her therapist had told her a thousand times, Viggo

Lassiter had no right to anything of hers. It did little to lessen the hold his memory had on her.

More tears welled in her eyes, and this time she did not fight them. The heartwrenching, crushing weight of years crashed down on her, and Katie let go of a breath she thought she must've been holding since the night Viggo Lassiter had stolen her life and killed her family. She wanted to slide into the floor, wrap her arms around herself, and think of what she'd lost. But in that darkness, she instead thought of what she still had.

Katie climbed to her feet and washed the sickness from her face, then opened the bathroom door. She moved down the hall, to the living room. As she approached, she thought she heard someone crying. Turning the corner, her eyes came to rest on what remained of her family. Marcus Traeger laid in the floor in front of the television, his body wracked with sobs, palms of his hands pressed into his eyes as if to staunch the flow of tears.

Katie felt her own tears welling again as she crossed the room and came to rest on her knees beside her brother. There was a heat in her throat as she choked back bile. Gently, she wrapped her arms around Marcus and held him, burying her face in his shoulder.

"Shhhh," she said, trying to sound soothing. "Shhhh."

"They're all gone," he heaved between sobs.

Katie coughed out a sob of her own. She said the only thing that came to mind. "I'm here. It'll be okay."

And there they remained, holding tight to what was left, knowing one day, they would be okay. Because they had each other.

And that was enough.

Afterword

What you just read took me 14 years to write. To look at it now, clocking in at less than 80,000 words, that might surprise you. But in those intervening years, I grew, becoming the man I needed to be to finish this story.

I was surprised at how difficult it was to bring this story to life. The drafting was, of course, one piece of that puzzle. But the editing, re-writing, formatting, and marketing have been a significantly larger hurdle. However, with the unending support of the people around me, it's now done.

I understand, this book is not perfect. No story is. However, it is the story I needed to tell. Cole, Marcus, Viggo, Luke, and everyone else within these pages deserved an end, as did I.

I hope I gave them a good one.

Acknowledgment

First off, I would be remiss to begin this section by mentioning anyone other than my wife. Tana has stood by me and listened to me rant about this book for the entirety of our marriage. I'm sure she's very happy for it to be put to bed.

My children, for making me the man who could finish this story.

My parents, for always supporting me, even if I wouldn't let you read the book until now (sorry, Mom).

My sister, for finishing her book first and giving me the motivation to never let you win.

Jenna, for being a beta reader and comprehensive editor, all wrapped in one.

My beta readers: Audrie, Reid, Scott, and Austin, for giving me unflinching feedback when I needed it most.

My writing group: Trevor and Thomas, for keeping me up when I got down.

My cover artist: Josh, for bringing my vision to life.

My Booksta friends: Noah, Parker, Mary Kate, Julia, Z.B. Steele, and A.C. Hobbs, and I'm sure many others I'm forgetting, for helping spread the word about this book with your platforms.

I wrote this book, but I was not alone in bringing it to you. If I sat down and thought of everyone who could be acknowledged in this book's creation, I would have another 80,000 words, I'm sure. To anyone I have not mentioned by name: know you have my undying thanks. A million small steps comprised this journey, and every single one of them was taken with the aid of someone.

About The Author

C. William Phillips has been telling stories as long as he can remember. He lives in Kentucky with his wife and their ever-growing brood of children.